Conversations
at
Warp Speed

Published in the USA by:
BearManor Media
PO Box 1129
Duncan, Oklahoma 73534-1129
www.bearmanormedia.com

ISBN 978-1-59393-289-3

Printed in the United States of America.
Cover Art by Ken Scott.
Book design by Brian Pearce | Red Jacket Press.

Conversations at Warp Speed

By Anthony Wynn

Table of Contents

Dedicated to:
Paul Carr, Bibi Besch, James Doohan,
Gene Roddenberry, and Barry Morse

Acknowledgements

Several of the conversations in this volume were taped for television broadcast in Oregon at the facilities of MetroEast Community Media (formerly Multnomah Community Television), while others were one-on-one talks expressly pursued for this book. There are a number of studio staff members and volunteers who deserve specific recognition for their help and assistance (although there's far too many to list individually). They include: Loren Coulter, Carolyn Neufeld, Emily Vidal, Bea Coulter, and Alison Hardin.

Special thanks go to my good friend and production partner Daril Anthes, who directed more than a dozen of our joint programs and without whose hard work and dedication the television interviews just wouldn't have happened. Primary crew members who brought their technical expertise to bear on those shows were: Denise Stone, Noah Larsen, Don Fitzgerald, Tracy Orr, Tom Kelly, Sandra Askelson, Maris Strautmanis, and Cindy Matson.

My appreciation is also extended to George Takei. The television broadcast of my interview with George was honored by the *Best of the Northwest* Video and Film Festival through the presentation of their prestigious "Award of Excellence." The interview competed for, and won that honor, out of some 240 entries from public cable outlets throughout the Western United States, British Columbia and Alberta, Canada.

I would also like to express my utmost posthumous gratitude to Paul Carr, Bibi Besch, James Doohan, Gene Roddenberry, and Barry Morse — the dedicatees of this volume. Their words continue to inspire and their work on television, stage, radio, and film will continue to live on.

My gratitude is given to Eric A. Stillwell for the use of several important photographs in the book. In addition, I am thankful to Eric for not only for sitting down with me for two separate conversations — but also for allowing me to use his interview with Gene Roddenberry conducted in 1983 at Oregon State University in Corvallis, Oregon. His interview originally appeared in the *Starfleet Communique* fan publication. I know I speak for both Eric — and myself — in thanking Gene posthumously for his willingness to converse forthrightly with writers from fan publications about his creation. His words seem just as prescient now as when he spoke them.

I had the pleasure of interviewing Grace Lee Whitney for my afore-mentioned television program, and followed up with two additional conversations with the actress. I appreciate her hospitality and for welcoming me into her home near Yosemite National Park in California. Taking a tour of that famed national monument with Grace in her convertible is memory I'll always treasure. Special thanks also go to Corinne Orr, a longtime friend, who kindly hosted my visit to New York City. She also accompanied me to the theatre and on a memorable walk through Central Park.

The amazing book front and back book covers were designed by graphic artist Ken Scott. My special thanks to him for a job well done. May the "USS Microphone" fly with grace and beauty through space on its mission for many years!

Other special contributors to this volume include Charlene Scott, Dr. Susan Doyle, Dan and Camilla Sundholm, Paul Bennett, Carol Jennings, Marlene Daab, and Scott Mills. This book wouldn't have been possible without their support and assistance. I also give my appreciation to Robert E. Wood for allowing several of his images to be reproduced herein, and for his advice and assistance with Chapter Fourteen.

Lastly, my heartfelt gratitude is given to my publisher, Ben Ohmart of BearManor Media.

His patience is infinite and for that I am truly grateful.

Foreword BY BARRY MORSE

I've had the great, good pleasure to have known many "character" actors during my career — and indeed proudly consider myself to be included in their number. The men and women who have spent their lives playing passers-by or cabmen or "the other girl" or the hero's uncle, never really expecting great riches or fame; are the heart's core of our trade — the real flesh and blood of it. All of us who have been in this lunatic trade of pulling faces and making noises for a living know what a good old lot they are.

This volume is mostly devoted to the doings and careers of a number of "rank and file" actors who have appeared, at one time or another, in one or other variants of the *Star Trek* series and films. I'm not a member of that rather select group of performers, but I do know and have appeared with a number of them over the years.

I worked with James Doohan in many dozens of radio and television productions in our native Canada, and in fact, Jimmy and I played together in one of the very first science fiction series ever shown on television — a show called *Space Command*. I also had the opportunity to work with Grace Lee Whitney in *The Outer Limits*; and Jimmy, Grace and I also appeared together in an episode of Quinn Martin's series *The New Breed*. Both Paul Carr and Jimmy Doohan guest starred in varied episodes of our highly regarded series, *The Fugitive*. My old friend Nick Tate and I worked together for more than eighteen months in England on the first series of our old show, *Space: 1999*. And while we've not worked together professionally, I had a highly memorable meeting and dinner with George Takei and his partner, Brad Altman, along with Eric Stillwell, and other friends on a visit to Hollywood.

Interestingly, I've worked with Captain Kirk himself, William Shatner, on a number of occasions, including the series *Naked City* and, later, in *TekWar*. I also hold the distinction of being the one who gave him his first job in the theatre! That all came about in Montreal, when my wife, Sydney Sturgess, and I opened in a play called *The Man Who Came to Dinner*, which was a popular pot-boiling comedy of the time. I played the leading role in it of an irascible, crusty old man. This character is a critic who comes to a small town to give a talk and is supposed to be going to have dinner with some family in this town, but falls on the

A memorable dinner in Hollywood at Café des Artistes. From left to right: Anthony Wynn, Eric A. Stillwell, Barry Morse, George Takei, and Robert E. Wood. PHOTO COURTESY OF ROBERT E. WOOD.

path leading up to their front door. The result is that instead of just spending an evening having a dinner, he has to spend two or three weeks in these people's home, in a wheelchair. It's a rather farcical relationship that grows between the critic and the family in whose house he happens to fetch up.

Playing the son of the house, in a relatively small part, was the young Bill Shatner. He was just trying to get his foot in the door in the performing field (and wasn't troubled by having to wear a toupee in those days). Now, Bill at that time — and he reminds me of this whenever we meet — was very much under the influence, as many young actors were, of The Method. In particular, someone who was reckoned to be the greatest practitioner of The Method: Marlon Brando. Well, Brando's characteristic acting style really consisted mostly of him mumbling into the carpet.

Influenced by him, many young actors of the day adopted this mumbling method. In this case, William Shatner was called upon to provide many of the feed lines for my character's witticisms. Of course, it was very important that his dialogue be absolutely clearly heard. But poor Bill, under the influence of Marlon Brando, would persist in mumbling his lines. So I would very often make him say the same line *twice* by saying things like, "What's that you say, son? I can't hear you, boy!" and so he would have to say it again!

Not long afterward, I began to work quite a lot in both Hollywood and New York. When I first started to work in California, people would say to me, "Where are you from?" and I'd say, "All kinds of different places." Then they would ask, "Are you one of those *television* actors?" and I would answer, "I'm an *everything* actor."

There was almost a sense that there were two armies of people in the dramatic entertainment world: One represented by New York and the theatre, and the second represented by the movie trade, which at first was very resistant to the encroachment of television. The rank and file actor, though, was present in both of those worlds and indeed in every facet of show business: radio, stage, television and film. And most of the performers featured in this volume have worked in each of those mediums.

In my own varied career I've been what you might call "famous" one or two times. It comes and goes, like some sort of rash. But sometimes we all receive a reminder that obscurity is never very far away and that this week's *Top of the Pops* can so readily become next year's *Whatever Happened To?* It happened to me not so very long ago — I was riding on a bus in London and sitting just across the aisle from me there was a dear old chap who was looking at me in a very quizzical, puzzled sort of way. After two or three minutes half a penny dropped in the back of his head and he leaned over and prodded me in the ribs and said, "'Ere, half a minute; didn't you used to be somebody?"

We mustn't forget those whose names rarely go up in the lights or become household names or pass into history (and that means most actors). The rank and file often spend their lives hoping that some miracle or good fortune will bring them their hour of glory, and it scarcely ever does; until now. This book highlights and gives a good insight into the establishment and beginnings of the working lives of performers, and chronicles their experiences in the world of entertainment. It's a confirmation that despite all the clichés and the fallacies written and spoken about our trade, there really is no business like show business.

For all those performers — famous and obscure — there's the saddening thought that the work they love is fleeting. It can last only as long as you, the audience, remember.

Barry Morse
London, England

Preface

As a child, one of my first memories in the early 1970s was of watching reruns of the original *Star Trek* series on Sunday afternoons. Over the years, the characters seemed like old friends and my enjoyment of that show led me as a young teenager to other programs, such as *Space: 1999*. In succeeding years, I had the pleasure of attending, working on, and ultimately organizing a number of varied events, conventions, and personal appearances featuring many of the *Star Trek* and *Space: 1999* actors and actresses. Hearing these men and women speak about their lives, experiences, and their craft has always been fascinating to me. It led eventually, in fact, to my work with Barry Morse, co-star of *Space: 1999* and *The Fugitive,* on the actor's theatrical memoir *Remember with Advantages* and this book.

For a time, I also hosted an interview program on a local cable television outlet which gave me the opportunity to sit down with a number of the performers who brought my favorite shows to the screen. I found those talks to be immensely interesting and informative, because we were often able to cover many areas in their lives and careers.

A number of the individuals featured in the book have overcome substantial odds and a fair amount of adversity to arrive at the places they've made it to today. It was a pleasure to learn about their experiences and hardships for the lessons that they impart to younger performers and the rest of us when facing similar situations or going through periods of misfortune and trouble. There may be a few names here that you don't immediately recognize, but chances are good that you have seen their faces on the screen or the stage; or perhaps you know of the results of their work from behind the scenes.

I found it fascinating to learn about projects that may not have been spotlighted in the past. For instance, Grace Lee Whitney is probably best known for her role in *Star Trek* as "Yeoman Janice Rand," but it's a pleasure to bring to light her experience working on the classic film *Some Like It Hot* with Marilyn Monroe and Billy Wilder; and it was quite moving to hear about her battle with addiction.

George Takei is well-known for his portrayal of "Sulu" in *Star Trek*, but his interview stands in my mind as possibly one of the most in-depth and profound of the conversations. It provided an opportunity to talk to the actor in a detailed and thorough manner about a part of U.S. history that is often forgotten or not known by many Americans — the internment of Japanese-Americans during World War II. George was interned as a child, along with his family, and he passionately, elegantly, and intelligently explains and interprets that experience for the reader.

Then there are the people behind the scenes; the ones that labor virtually invisibly to produce *Star Trek*. It was great to speak with my old friend, Eric Stillwell (we first met each other in the eighth grade!) and talk to him about his dream-come-true of working and writing for *Star Trek*. He also had made another important contribution to this volume by allowing his own rare interview with Gene Roddenberry be published here in book form for this first time.

When speaking about the legacy of *Star Trek*, I think it's important to remember that this show was the first science fiction vehicle that appealed to about as many women as it did men. *Star Trek*, from the beginning, promulgated the idea that women alongside men would help to shape the future. So, along with the actresses included in this collection, I had the pleasure to interview *Star Trek* fans Marlene Daab and Carol Jennings, a couple of the best-known enthusiasts and supporters on the West Coast. They bring a different and unique perspective to the talk about *Star Trek* in this volume.

Several of the notables featured here in *Conversations at Warp Speed* are, unfortunately, no longer with us. Gene Roddenberry and Bibi Besch died in 1991 and 1996, respectively, while James Doohan departed in 2005. This book includes the final conversation with actor Paul Carr, who passed away not long after completing our inter-view, in 2006. Barry Morse, who contributed the Foreword and again appears in Chapter Fourteen, left us in 2008. The words and work of each one are a lasting tribute and testimony to their individual and collective legacies.

The participation of Barry Morse and actor Nick Tate serve as a bridge to bring two of my favorite science fiction series together in this volume. Nick has had a wonderfully varied career, and in addition to his work in *Space: 1999,* he also made notable guest appearances in popular episodes of *Star Trek: The Next Generation* and *Star Trek: Voyager.* It's also a great joy to also include "bonus" conversations with actresses Gretchen Corbett and Corinne Orr (also a talented voice artist), as well as the concluding chapter with Barry Morse. When I conceived the idea for this book, Barry and I had worked together on a number of projects, and he was very supportive of a collection of conversations with actors. He immediately contributed the lovely Foreword that opens this volume and I'm happy that he was able to do so before his passing.

Even though the interviews in *Conversations at Warp Speed* span some twenty-five years, the information they convey is timeless. It's my hope that you will laugh and learn — perhaps even shed a tear or two — as you take the journey with these widely varied men and women, leading us through the course of events that shaped and formed their careers.

Anthony Wynn
Portland, Oregon

Conversations at Warp Speed

Grace Lee Whitney is a versatile actress, vocalist, and all-around entertainer who began her career literally as a "girl singer," opening in clubs for the likes of Billie Holiday and Buddy Rich, and touring with such luminaries as the Spike Jones and Fred Waring Bands.

Aside from her musical experience, she has appeared in numerous films and on a multitude of television series, filming three true entertainment classics: The Outer Limits *episode "Controlled Experiment" with Barry Morse and Carroll O'Connor; the classic film* Some Like It Hot *with Marilyn Monroe, Jack Lemmon, and Tony Curtis; and the widely popular* Star Trek *television and film series.*

Of all of her work, she is probably best known worldwide for her portrayal of Yeoman Rand, then eventually, Commander Janice Rand in the Star Trek *franchise.*

Initially hired as one of the principal characters, her starry dream became a nightmare when she was prematurely written out of the series only days after being sexually assaulted on the Star Trek *lot by an executive of the production company. Grace attributes this event with triggering a decades-long addiction to drugs, alcohol, and sex.*

Grace was brought back to the Star Trek *family for appearances in four of the six films featuring the original, classic cast. She was also invited to return, along with fellow actor George Takei (Captain Sulu), as Commander Janice Rand, USS* Excelsior *Communications Officer in the* Star Trek Voyager *episode "Flashback," penned to celebrate the 30th anniversary of the classic series.*

I want to talk to you a little bit about your childhood. I understand that you were adopted, but you didn't know that at first.

Grace Lee Whitney

"Keep on Trekkin'"

No, I didn't know it for a very long time. I was adopted into a beautiful family and everyone in the neighborhood knew that I was adopted; the only person who didn't know was me. My mother went away one day and then brought a baby home — of course, she had never been pregnant. So the kids were kind of snickering behind my back, called me "the bad seed" and a lot of parents were not too kind to me and didn't want their kids to play with me. I could feel the rejection. I think because I *could* feel it, and I told my mother I didn't feel good about it, she sat me down one day when I was about seven years old and told me that I was an adopted child — and that she was not my mother. She said she was my mother, but she wasn't my *real* mother. At seven years old I couldn't digest that.

It had to have been painful.

Well, it was like finding out there was no Santa Claus. When kids find out there's no Santa Claus and then find out that the person they've been living with is not their mother — or their father, or their grandmother, or their grandfather, or their cousin — who are they? In other words, who am I then? They didn't know who I was; they didn't know where I came from. They told me this story and I just "stuffed it." I buried it. I didn't want to hurt my parents, I didn't want to complain, and I didn't want to seem confused; but I was. When I would go to bed at night I had such bad migraine headaches that I couldn't go to school for three and four days. They were awful. I didn't handle the truth very well.

Did you cry yourself to sleep a lot?

Oh, gosh yes! And pain, I had so much pain. I would get nauseous from the sickening headaches. They took me to a psychiatrist when I was nine years old, and nobody went to the psychiatrist in those days; that's a long time ago. The psychiatrist told my mother that I was "a volcano waiting to happen" and that I "needed help." Of course, she ran with me out of there, she just couldn't digest that there was something wrong with me. And I never did get any help.

It wasn't too much later in your childhood that you discovered alcohol, right?

Yes, I was with a group of kids that was experimenting and we would go bowling every weekend and then we would go out and party. I remember drinking Southern Comfort; it was my first drink. I knew it was wrong because my mom and dad were teetotalers. They were very devout Christians and there was no drinking in the house at all. There was no dancing, drinking, gambling — nothing! They were very, very straight. I knew I was doing wrong. What I'm saying is that I knew I was wrong and I had a tremendous conflict. The conflict was between wanting to please my friends and be loved, be liked; and wanting to obey the moral code of my parents. So I had this tremendous angst. It was pain, a lot of pain and it's called a "*dis*-ease" by the American Medical Association. Not a "disease," a "*dis*-ease" right here. [Grace touches a fist to her stomach]

When a lot of people have that *dis*-ease they overeat, they drink; they try to take some kind of Prozac or some kind of valium; or something to get out of the *dis*-ease. And whatever they take they become addicted to. It's because whatever fixes you — you become addicted to. That's what happened to me.

You've described it, in interviews, as "a hole in your gut, with the wind blowing through."

It's like there's a wind blowing through and it's OH-OH, its pain; it's just pain and its floating anxiety, and it's being overly sensitive. I would jump when hearing loud sounds. The only time I was ever completely comfortable in my skin was when I had a "fix." Alcoholics are never comfortable in their own skin until we get a fix: we're food-aholics, we're sex-aholics, or gamblers. I know friends who are addicted to sleeping. When they get into problems they can't do anything but go to sleep! I was like that as a child, also. I would escape through sleeping. You just will try everything to get away from the pain and, of course, mine manifested in weekend drinking with my friends. That was fun; that was acceptable; that's what they were doing. We would drink! It was not anything more than that. Of course, I became alcoholic. Ten out of a hundred people become alcoholics and the rest of the ninety can drink fine without any problem. I just happen to have the "bug" and I know now, after finally doing a search for my family, that it came from my family. My grandfather died from an overdose of his bootleg gin when he was forty. Now that's young to die. He died from an overdose of his own gin. But for the grace of God, I should have died too. How I made it out, to me, is a miracle.

Even though you had problems growing up, you also had some talent.

A tremendous amount of talent; I was gifted.

You started singing and you were on the radio.

Yes! But before I started singing I won tremendous awards in the decathlon. I was a wonderful athlete.

I didn't know that.

Oh, yes. I won the fifty-yard dash! It's still a record at my grade school, after all these years! I hold the record! I *had* to win. I *had* to be the best. And I drove myself because of my inferiority complex. I'd been thrown out by my birth mother, yet my mother saved my life, I later found out. After I could get on the other side, instead of pointing a finger at her — when I crossed over and got on the other side after I got sober, I could see that my mother actually saved me life. She could have aborted me very easily, and she didn't. Because she didn't, she saved my life and I'm eternally grateful to her.

It was quite early when you started appearing on radio.

Yes. I went right to radio from winning, getting all the applause and the accolades. I was in band in grade school. I played a lot of instruments, played the bass drum; I had great rhythm! (Laughs) I was just *good* at everything I tried. I learned to read music, played piano for eight years; so when I auditioned for the WGR spot for the chorus, they grabbed me right away. I could read music, I could sing different parts, I had a wide range, and I fit right in. I was right in the spotlight at thirteen years old.

Not long after that you were opening in nightclubs.

I went to Chicago to do the Miss Chicago contest, as a model and as a singer in clubs, and I won second place in the Miss Chicago Contest. I told everybody for a long time that I was "First," but of course if my lips are moving I'm lying! That's what they tell the alcoholic when they get sober. "You can't tell the truth, honey, so get honest!" So when I got honest I had to come down and realize that I didn't place first; another girl placed first, I was second — and I never liked to be second. I always wanted to be Number One.

You went on to open for one of the biggest legends in show business: Billie Holiday.

Fabulous! It was a padded "toilet," it was in Chicago on Randolph and State Street. The Brass Rail was upstairs and the Band Box was downstairs and it was a padded toilet. It was a *bar*, is what it was. They had B-Girls shaking the dice, lots of cleavage, lots of sex, and all that stuff. The sleaze was *fabulous* and I loved it. And Billie Holiday was in there and she was shooting up in the john; she was on heroin.

She had a lot of demons, didn't she?

She had so many demons and yet she was a very spiritual lady. She had God in her life; she used to talk about Christ all the time and talk about her love for God and her love for spiritual life. And yet she was hooked on heroin. It was tragic, totally tragic. To this day it's hard for me to speak about it because I've lost so many wonderful legends to this dis-ease; either drugs or alcohol. Even my friend, the one I did *Batman* with, Victor Buono — ate himself to death. He was a beautiful man, a beautiful man. He died young also; a wonderful actor. He couldn't get off the sweets and the carbs.

You went on — you went to New York.

I went to New York after Chicago, had my own group, and auditioned for *Top Banana* and *The Pajama Game*. I auditioned a couple of times and was turned down. They said, "Please go home and have children, get out of here; you have no talent!"

That's awful!

That's what George Abbott told me! He said, "You're terrible!"

George Abbott? One of the top Broadway producers?

The top Broadway producer! He said, "Please, young lady…" I got out there for the audition and sang something with a pair of guns and a cowboy hat, I'll never forget that. And he said, "I don't know about you, please go home and have children, you're not meant for the stage." Of course, that's again a put-down. I cannot, I *will not* be put down. It's that tenacious perseverance that all actors have to have. If an actor doesn't have it, they won't make it! You have to have it because you're put down all the time. So I went home, but I showed him when I came back and auditioned a year later and got a couple of parts. For Hal Prince! Hal Prince was the reining king after George Abbott died. He fell in love with me and I fell in love with him. I did a lot of his touring shows that were very successful; one of them was *The Pajama Game*.

You also did a little naughty burlesque part in *Top Banana*.

I was Miss Holland; I had propellers on my boobs! I had the Dutch hat and the braids, the high heels, and the propellers. *THE* propellers. And they would spin! I would walk up to Phil Silvers and then stand and look at the audience and he would go, "PLOOOM" and around they would go, really fast. Then he would reach out and stop them; the audience would get *hysterical*! It was a great bit, classic vaudeville. We did a movie too; first the Broadway show and then the movie.

Then you auditioned for what I think you described as one of your favorite roles; the part of Lucy Brown in *Three Penny Opera*.

It was *THE* favorite role of mine, yes. I was doing a show called *Vintage '60* in L.A. and I was very thin, blonde — platinum blonde — short hair, very pixyish and I got a call to go and audition for *Three Penny Opera*; the part was Lucy Brown. Now let me tell you whose role I was taking: Bea Arthur was playing it in New York. Now Bea Arthur is LARGE! And here comes this little skinny broad in there. So they gave me birth control pills so that I'd gain weight. I didn't even know what they were; I didn't find out till a year later what they were. The doctor gave them to me, for me to get buxom. I had to get buxom and gain weight for the part of Lucy Brown. I dyed my hair henna and when I came out onto the stage my mother did not know who I was! She looked at the cast, we'd come out and parade on stage — she looked and she was saying, "Where's Grace? Where's Grace?" Of course, I was there with henna hair and big boobs, buxom and gorgeous.

We opened in L.A. and I got great reviews, *great* reviews. While I was doing *Three Penny Opera* I auditioned for a television show, a screen test for a show called *Peter Gunn*. The test was done at Screen Gems and I auditioned for the Lola Albright part. She was a singer from New York, blonde, and used to sit on the piano with her legs crossed and sing. It was perfect for me because I was coming right out of the musical. But they thought I was too young, too innocent to play across from the star, Craig Stevens. I was very disappointed that I didn't get it. There was a grip or one of the crew members — I always got along very well with people in the crew — and one of the guys tipped me off and said, "You know, they're casting a new film, a Billy Wilder film with Marilyn Monroe. Why don't you go over there and see if you can get an audition?" So I drove over to Goldwyn Studios and told the guard at the front gate that I was auditioning for the Marilyn Monroe film. And he let me in! It was a lie, of course, but they *were* casting it so they let me in.

I parked and I started walking and asked someone for directions. He pointed, "They're casting right over there in that building." So I walked in the sound stage and the man who was casting was Matty Malneck, who was in charge of all the band singers in Los Angeles, and I had worked with him many times. He looked at me and said, "What are you doing here?" I replied, "Well, someone told me that you were auditioning." He took me right over to introduce me to Billy, Billy Wilder. Billy said, "Put her up there with the girls." They had all the girls sitting in bleachers to see how we looked together. So they took another girl out and put me in there! He looked at me and said, "Yeah, you fit. But I can't give you the job because there's another girl there. If there's a dropout, I'll call you." He called the next day. There *was* a dropout and I got the show.

Was that your first meeting with Billy Wilder?

Yes.

You got the part of the trumpet player, right?

Her name was "Rosella." I had a speaking part because I was an actress. Most of those girls were just musicians, they didn't speak; they were extras who played instruments. Matty hired all the girls who played instruments. There were four of us who were actors and we had the roles. There was Beverly Wills, Marian Collier, Laurie Mitchell, and Grace Lee Whitney. Only I wasn't "Grace Lee Whitney" at the time. I was "Lee Whitney." I had dropped Grace, I couldn't stand the name.

That's why a lot of people that you knew in those days still call you "Lee" today...

They never called me Grace. My husbands called me Lee!

So, wow — *Some Like It Hot!* Let me ask about the alcohol; it certainly was a big part of this movie, I mean its prohibition and everybody is trying to drink, right?

Everybody is drinking and everybody is trying to stop you from drinking! It was just a madhouse; and then Marilyn's character almost getting fired, the flask falling off her.

Was there partying going on in real life?

We used to bring in martinis right on the set, Billy Wilder did, when we did a lot of these shots. I don't know how we every got the movie done; it was just amazing. There were several Academy Awards for the film, by the way.

How long was the shoot?

It lasted about four months. For two weeks we were down at the Del, the Del Coronado in San Diego, shooting at the big hotel there. Amaaaaaazing!

It's a beautiful hotel.

And Arthur Miller was there all the time with her [Marilyn]. She was great to be with, be around. Just to see; she was just amazing. You know, I practically audited the whole film. I was there all the time, behind the camera watching everything, because I really wanted to soak up every bit that I could of what it was like to make a film. This was my first attempt at being in the movies. I'd done a lot of live TV work, but I'd never been really in the movies. So I watched Billy, because Billy is a genius.

A master.

He has six Academy Awards. He's huge! So, I was watching and it was wonderful.

What kind of director was Billy Wilder?

He was the best. There was nobody better that him. He acted out all the parts; he did Monroe, everybody. Now he didn't act them out on camera. He would give you the attitude of what was behind the words if you didn't get it. If you got it, he didn't say anything. But if you didn't get the inflection of what it really meant, he would give it to you and all of a sudden you'd go, "Oh! Ok." And you could do it.

He would then stand back and let you do your job, right?

Yes. He would pace all the time; smoke and pace. You could smoke on the sound stage at the time, you could sit and smoke! Can you imagine?

Did he smoke cigarettes or stogies?

Mostly cigarettes; occasionally stogies. I.A.L. Diamond, the other writer who wrote with Billy, eventually died because of his chain smoking. You would never see "Izzy" without a cigarette. Now I have to tell you, the final scene of the movie — well, that's just the greatest line, one of the greatest lines ever written for a movie. I was *there* in the room with Billy and Izzy when they wrote that last line. It's when Jack Lemmon's character Daphne pulls off his wig and looks at Osgood; they're riding backward out to the yacht in the boat. He pulls that wig off and looks at him, "I can't marry you Osgood — I'm a boy!" And Osgood calmly replies, "Nobody's perfect!" Joe E. Brown gave the most perfect delivery of that line. And the movie ends! The advance screenings of the movie were just incredible. There was so much laughter and noise in the theater that you could hardly hear the dialogue.

Do you remember the very first scene you shot for the movie? What was it?

It was the musical number "Runnin' Wild" in the train car where Marilyn fronts the band with her ukulele. We were all sitting and standing around the compartment with our instruments while Marilyn danced in the center aisle.

The movie was filmed in black and white, which I thought was interesting. Was there a reason why?

Yes. Billy Wilder loved it. Ernst Lubitsch was his idol and Ernst Lubitsch said that all great films are in black and white, even photos. The greatest photos are in black and white. Because you really, I don't know, there's just something about black and white. Now let me tell you what the other reason was: The guys were in drag, you know, and they thought that if it was in *color* the guys would look so garish that it would never sell. So they did it in black and white because then everybody was the same color. They dressed as women because they were trying to get away from the mafia and the only way they could do it was to dress as women and join an all-girl band, because they really played instruments. It was hilarious.

It's one of the best comedies ever.

It is one of the best comedies ever filmed, you're absolutely right.

What was it like to work with Marilyn Monroe? What was she like?

She was amazing, totally amazing, but she was loaded. She had to drink on the set. Arthur Miller was with her all the time, on her arm, and sitting right out there on the other side of the camera. Now when she did the number "Runnin' Wild," she was actually looking out at Jack Cole, the choreographer. He was dancing, "doing" her. He was doing what he wanted her to do and she was mimicking him.

Tell me about your sleeper car scene with Marilyn and Jack Lemmon.

I remember it vividly, even though it was 1958. It took four days to shoot the one scene. *Four days!* Just to shoot the scene in the upper berth. We were so cramped up there, but that's what's so funny. Then the train stops and we all fall out. There were mattresses all over the floor for us to fall on.

You've described yourself as having a lot of similarities to Marilyn Monroe. You're both beautiful women, both blonde...

And we both used, both wanted to win, and both were ready to sell our souls for a good part. I was ready to sell my soul for a good part — and for love! I did it as a kid and I did it all along. I tried to be good and then I wanted this so bad that I knew what I had to do to get it, and I would do it. I paid the price and part of my remorse was that I was going against my own moral code. In a lot of the AMA [American Medical Association] books on alcoholism there's a sentence that really jumps out at me, it says that "a person cannot become an alcoholic unless they go against their moral code. You really have to go against it; it's a moral *dis*-ease.

Interesting.

Yes, it's very interesting. Believe me, there's volumes to be read, that I could read. I just would never have a full lifetime enough to read them all.

After this film you sort of had a little bit of a change, your life took a little bit of a different turn...

I did *Irma La Douce* after this film, yes, right, with Billy Wilder. The second film that we did was *Irma La Douce*. That was also written for

Marilyn, but Marilyn had overdosed and was gone, so they had to recast her with Shirley MacLaine.

You played Kiki the Kossack.

People used to say I bought my hair at Wil Wright's every morning; Wil Wright's is an ice cream shop. Because it was piled up so high it looked like cotton candy. You know, they back-combed it *waaaay* up on top of my head, it was amazing.

During this time you converted to Judaism.

Oh, way before this. I converted to Judaism when I was 17! Way back. By the time I was 22 I got married and I married a Sephardic Jew who was a Syrian Jew; he never would have married me if I hadn't been Jewish at the time. If you're Jewish and you're going to marry a Shiksa, as they called me, a gentile, the gentile has to convert to Judaism or supposedly they can't get married. It's kind of like the Catholic-Protestant thing. There's a lot of angst there. I had already converted by the time I met him and that's what impressed him so much. That's why he actually married me, because I'd already done the conversion. He could not *believe* it! Then I had to go through all of the Jewish rituals. Of course, basically in my heart I became Jewish, I still am. Of course, I love Christ now; I'm a Messianic Jew. Oh, it's wonderful!

You also had two lovely sons.

Two beautiful boys, both Jewish, one of them is also a born-again Jew. My older one is a secular Jew, kind of atheistic like I used to be. I ended up being atheistic. After I became Jewish, I became atheist. That is really crazy, how you can do that? That was alcoholism. It was alcoholism: I was just nuts.

When your boys were quite small you wanted to send them to a Hebrew school.

I did! Yeshiva. When I was doing *Irma La Douce* and I was a member of the PTA, I went over to Emek Hebrew Academy where the kids were. They wanted to buy a school bus, they didn't have any way to get kids to school in the morning; they didn't know how. They were picking up kids, they had carpools, they didn't know how to do it and the PTA said, "We'll buy a small bus and we'll put 'Emek Hebrew Academy' on it and we'll come and pick the kids up." I said to them, "You know, by the time you get enough money to do this, my kids will be in high school; not grade school, but high school already!" So I said, "I'm going to give you the money, I'm going to take it out of my savings account and give you the money." And they said, "But how can you do that?" I said, "Well, I'll make it back with residuals. I'll make it back. I'll just give you the money so you can buy the bus." They were thrilled! I came home that day and told my husband, "Guess what I did today, honey. Guess what I bought!"

"What did you buy today?"

"I bought a *bus!*"

Actress Grace Lee Whitney, circa 1965. PHOTO COURTESY OF GRACE LEE WHITNEY.

"You did WHAT?"

Anyway, I practically had a divorce over that. About a week later I was down at the studio and went in there and told Billy Wilder what I'd done. I said, "I've got to tell you guys…" There were three of them sitting in Billy's office; there was Billy, Walter Mirisch, and Izzy Diamond. Izzy's the writer, Walter's the producer; all big, big Jewish guys; sitting in the office, smoking their cigars, and drinking their martinis. I walked in and I said, "Guess what I bought…I'm going to be divorced by my husband! It's terrible, but I had to do it." They were just so impressed! Billy pulled out his wad of money and gave me $500 dollars. He said, "Come on, Walter, cough up." Walter gave me $500 dollars and Izzy said, "I'll cough up too!" And they all gave me $1500 dollars to pay for the bus! That's what the bus cost. So I went and told my husband, "Guess what I got? I got $1500 dollars for the bus!" It was amazing.

What you give comes back to you.

Exactly! Exactly. A little while later the bus came by the house to pick up the kids and I just stood there and cried. It was a wonderful experience.

You've done really so many classic projects, everybody remembers you for *Star Trek,* but you've done so many other things. *The Outer Limits* is something special that you were involved with.

Yes, it was with Barry Morse and Carroll O'Connor. I used to sit on the set between takes and watch them play chess. That show was a classic. It was called "Controlled Experiment" and was about two Martians who came down to observe Earth. I did *Gunsmoke*, I did *The Rifleman*, I did *Batman…*

You met Gene Roddenberry and he invited you to do a pilot for a new series he was doing called *Police Story*, along with DeForest Kelley. You played a wonderfully sexy Police Sergeant, Lily Monroe. Why did they give her that name?

(Laughs) It was for Lili St. Cyr, the stripper and, of course, Marilyn Monroe. We had a great time! But this pilot didn't sell. It was with DeForest Kelley and Steve Ihnat. So when *Star Trek* sold, they took this character; they took myself, Grace Lee Whitney and DeForest Kelley and put us in *Star Trek*. That's how we got *Star Trek!*

When *Star Trek* was conceived and you were hired, you were really hired as one of the three main stars of the show. It was more or less patterned after *Gunsmoke*, wasn't it?

Actually, "*Wagon Train* to the Stars." That's what Gene Roddenberry called it. But I was more or less Miss Kitty to Matt Dillon who was, of course, William Shatner. I was to be his right-hand girl and part of his team on board ship that took care of things. I had the tricorder, I logged in all of the happenings, I logged in all of his commands, I took care of his clothes, took care of his meals; I really watched over him. I think I did *more* than Miss Kitty did for Matt Dillon! Miss Kitty was there when Matt came back to the bar, but I was there *all* the time for the Captain.

You have some fun stories about your boys during the filming of the series.

Both of my sons were in the episode "Miri," in the group of little kids. Leonard Nimoy's son was also in that group! I had to be at work at five-thirty or six o'clock in the morning and the production office wanted the kids to come in too. So I said, "Ok, I'll bring them in." They replied, "No! We can't have you bring them in." I asked, "Why not?" and they replied, "Safety regulations." I was told that I would have to come in my car and they would send a car out to pick up the kids. Both of them were quite young, only about seven and nine years old, and the studio sent the big limousine for these two little boys! So there we were on the freeway; the limousine with my two boys and I followed in back in my own car. The kids sat in the back of the limousine and waved at me!

The set for "Miri" was beautifully done and it really looked like the old city. The show was fun for the boys. My youngest, Jonathan, was the one who stole the communicators! "Miri" was a lot of fun for them; after I had made them take a bath that first morning and get them all ready, they were driven to the studio and made all dirty! They put powered stuff all over them, dirtied their clothes all up — the boys loved it. Later on, when we filmed *Star Trek: The Motion Picture*, my older son Scott came in and was an extra in the rec-deck scene. They made him up to look like Spock and they put the ears on him and everything!

Did you keep any souvenirs from *Star Trek*? What about the boots or that fantastic basket weave wig you wore?

No I didn't. But I guess I should have! They'd really be worth something now. That wig they had me wear was something else. It was actually *two* different wigs, woven together. I'd come into the studio every morning into makeup and I swear, they'd nail that wig right onto my head! It must have weighed forty pounds. Who knows where *it* ended up — probably some drag queen found it and put it to use after I was gone!

You were only in about the first half of the first season when something happened.

Yes, something tragic happened. One of the reasons why there's now called "sexual harassment" in the workplace, it's now a law: you cannot sexually harass any woman on the job or she can take you to court and sue you. But, this was *before* that law. And I was probably one of the ones that should have had courage enough to carry on.

But you were worried about your career, weren't you?

It was awful. I was sexually harassed in an office by one of the executives from Desilu. I was fired; I was written out. I have something very interesting that I'd like to talk about. About two months ago I got a call from Bob Justman [Robert Justman, co-producer of *Star Trek*]. He said, "I've been looking through the archives of my communications with Gene Roddenberry and I have a letter I'm going to send to you. It's the original letter — I've made a copy for myself; but I'm sending the original letter to you." The letter says something to the effect of:

Dear Gene,

I think this episode would be a great time to bring back Janice Rand and put her back into the show. We've missed her, people have missed her, people have asked for her; I think now is the right time to have Grace Lee Whitney come back.

Bob

I don't remember what episode that would have been, but I have that letter at home so I know that people were trying to get me back.

Well, this was one of the biggest disappointments of your life, wasn't it?

It was terrible; terrible because I lost my job. They took my name off the parking space, they took my name off the door, they took the star down, they cancelled Jack Parr and other interviews, centerfolds (not *Playboy*), but I mean centerfolds with pictures of Rand in the uniform with that hair. They cancelled plans for big posters, all kinds of stuff. They cancelled it all and I was *out*. I was praying — well, I didn't pray because I didn't have God in my life — but what I was doing was hoping that *Star Trek* would go right down the tubes. And you know, eventually it did. At the end of the third year they cancelled the show, and I was clapping and cheering. Then, of course, it came back in reruns and we all became stars and I had to say, "Oh, darn!" I'm glad now, I'm glad that that it turned out the way it did. At least I was in that first year of *Star Trek*, which I think was phenomenal.

The first year is really great. The stories, the acting; everything was just perfect. So from there, we move into the 1970s

I kept drinking and using and trying to work, and going in on interviews reeking of alcohol. I was sick to my stomach, I couldn't function. Talk about a "hole in the gut." I was so upset. I was bottoming out from alcohol, I was crazy, self-willed, self-centered, couldn't get any peace anywhere. Finally, I bottomed out and got sober in 1981. The whole of the 1970s is a blur. I got into gambling. I kept switching addictions, going to different addictions. I was anorexic for a long time, I had an eating disorder. I went to the opposite of my overeating and went down to anorexia. I kept swinging back and forth. Finally, I did *Star Trek: The Motion Picture* and I looked like my own grandmother. I'll never forget it. I saw myself on the screen and I couldn't believe it was me. There were *gasps* in the theater when I came on. I weighed 113 pounds and I was anorexic. I was skin and bones and I looked old. And they didn't put any makeup on me to help me! We were just kind of blended all out. *Bleeeccch.* It wasn't just me; everyone looked awful. The only one who looked good was "Ilia" [Persis Khambatta]. It was like doing a picture with Marilyn Monroe where they made everybody else look terrible and just Monroe beautiful.

I remember [director] Robert Wise saying to me, "Yeoman Rand is not Yeoman Rand anymore and I don't want any glamour; I don't want any of that Hollywood glamour." Robert Wise also said that he didn't like the way Yeoman Rand looked in the series. "I want you to play her as a mature woman," he told me. I think that took some of the wind right out of my sails. I just felt strange and restricted.

There were lots of things we all disliked about the movie; I did not like the uniforms which were uncomfortable and not very flattering, nor the hairstyles imposed on the females. Marcy Lafferty, who was Bill Shatner's wife at the time, was given part of my role when the character of Lieutenant DiFalco was brought it. Rand was supposed to do all the things that DiFalco did. But that's Hollywood; Bill wanted a role for his wife and Bill was the star of the picture. You know, I had a feeling of doom from the beginning, that something wasn't right. Then when I fell asleep during *The Motion Picture* three times I knew the feeling was on the ball. I felt it was too slow. I just wanted to yell, "Crank it up, crank it up; get going!" It just seemed to kind of fizzle, which was really too bad.

So it was around this time you came to the realization that you had a personal problem?

Yes. I was sick and tired of being sick and tired! I did an episode of *Hart to Hart* and a friend of mine was also in the show. We went out to lunch and I had a couple drinks and started talking to her. By the time we were through with lunch she said to me, "You know you're an alcoholic. You should go to 12-step — you could be the main speaker." She played to my ego as an actress. But she took me to my first meeting.

Had the thought of alcoholism ever crossed your mind before?

Never. I didn't know anything about 12-step programs. She introduced me to her husband, who was an alcoholic but had stopped drinking, and was now attending 12-step meetings himself. This was Hollywood and there were a number of people there from the industry, from show business, so I felt comfortable. It was jokingly called the "Gucci meeting." It made a positive impression on me because they were my peers. To get sober I had to go to 12-step meetings, twice a week, for five years. I got a sponsor and I did the steps.

How long have you been sober?

Since 1981! It's a long time — between drinks. No drugs either. No antidepressants, no marijuana; nothing that changes you from the neck up. No mind-altering chemicals of any kind for all of those years! That's why I'm so hard to get along with. I don't take anything to dull my thoughts or emotions. I don't have any screen from my character defects. So my anger, my envy, my pride — all that stuff — gets in the way of my relationships with people. I agitate people. I know that if I took antidepressants I wouldn't be as aggravating.

But you're afraid they could be addicting if you did that.

Well, number one, they *are* addicting; and number two, you're not really sober. You'd be dry, but if you're taking antidepressants you're not sober. So in my head, I would ruin my sobriety if I did it. Other people justify it, "Well, it's given to me by a doctor." We become sheltered from life on life's terms.

One of the great loves throughout your life has been music. It was in the 1970s that you released your record, *Disco Trekkin'*, right?

Yes. I wrote the lyrics while my former husband and manager Jack Dale composed the music. I performed at clubs and conventions around the world, while Dale handled the bookings, set-up the sound equipment and took care of the details so I could go onstage and do my thing. My first live performance singing the *Star Trek*-oriented songs was at 'Equicon '76' in Los Angeles where I sang "Disco Trekkin' " and "Star Child" to a wildly enthusiastic audience of several thousand people. "Star Child" was the "B" side of the record, back when records had "B" sides. Well, in the days when they still had records! Anyway, that Equicon audience gave me the loudest, longest ovation I had ever received in my life! I'll never forget it.

But those weren't the only songs you wrote.

No. We followed up those first two songs with a number of others based on the episodes I had been in. First, I re-read the scripts to get inspiration, then sat down and started to write the lyrics. One of my favorite of the songs is "How Will He Love Me," which is the story of the repressed love of Yeoman Rand for Captain Kirk. In it, Janice Rand

pours out her heart into a song. In "Miri," Rand confesses to Captain
Kirk that she has always tried to get him to notice her and "Charlie X"
is the story of a teenage boy with strange powers who falls in love with
Rand. Those two were just plain fun to write, produce and perform!
One of our other songs is called "Enemy Within" and talks about the
dark side of *Trek*.

Grace Lee Whitney in the disco years, circa 1976. PHOTO COURTESY
OF GRACE LEE WHITNEY.

Those pieces were ones associated with the original series. You also wrote about the movies too, didn't you?

That was during the production of *Star Trek: The Motion Picture*. I was so happy to be back working on *Trek* again! It resulted in "USS Enterprise," which has a strong melody set against a throbbing bass line, kind of hinting at power of the ship's engines. We also did a song called "Ilia's Theme," which tells the story of Decker and Ilia and their eternal love for each other. I think the lyrics tell such a beautiful story. After the film wrapped production, we held a cast party at my house. Everybody was there, even Robert Walker, Jr. who played "Charlie X" in the original series! We all gathered around our pool in the big back yard and Dale played the backup tracks for the songs over big speakers we had set-up and I sang "Ilia's Theme" to Stephen Collins and Persis Khambatta, and "Charlie X" to Robert Walker, Jr. It was a truly magical and once-in-a-lifetime event.

Artwork of Grace Lee Whitney as "Commander Janice Rand" in *Star Trek*, by Robert E. Wood. PHOTO COURTESY OF ANTHONY WYNN.

You were invited back for *Star Trek III*, *Star Trek IV*, and then *Star Trek VI: The Undiscovered Country*.

Star Trek VI was great. On the USS *Excelsior* with George Takei!

With George Takei as "Captain Sulu" and you came back as "Commander Janice Rand."

Star Trek VI was 1992 and then in 1996 we did the *Star Trek Voyager* episode "Flashback." So I went from a Yeoman to a Commander, even after getting written out! I came back; that's pretty amazing.

You were in the internet miniseries *Star Trek: Of Gods and Men*, along with Nichelle Nichols [Uhura] and Walter Koenig [Chekov]. How did you get involved in that project?

I met the producer Sky Conway through another fan-film project that I appeared in called *New Voyages*. Of course, I already knew Tim

Russ — he was "Tuvok" in *Voyager* — and was thrilled when I found out he was directing it. So I said, "yes," just as long as it didn't conflict with what we'd done in *New Voyages*.

What part did you play in *New Voyages?*

It was just a small part, but I played the mother of the new Janice Rand.

What character did you play in *Of Gods and Men?*

I played my original character, but in the beginning I was a little bit different. I don't want to say too much for those who haven't seen it, but I'm kind of different, and then I am "me" again in a nice scene with Chekov at the end. I also have a scene with Uhura.

I can't wait to see it! Well, our time has come to an end, but I'd like to thank you for taking the time to talk with me about your life and your work. Anything you'd like to say in closing?

Just "Keep on Trekkin'!" It's been my pleasure to talk to you, too.

Grace is a woman of many seemingly conflicting views and attitudes; one moment she can be quite bawdy and the next, pious. But above all, she is always sincere. She is Jewish and she is Christian. She can tell a risqué joke in one breath and in the next will tell you of her relationship with a higher power and her struggle with addiction. In any other person except Grace Lee Whitney these may be considered contradictions; but coming from Grace — nothing but absolute honesty and sincerity.

I first saw Grace in person when I was young teenager. She burst onto the stage in my hometown of Eugene, Oregon and sang her now-classic songs "Disco Trekkin' " and "Star Child" to a wildly appreciative and enthusiastic full house. Her beautiful features and long blonde hair were striking, and her svelte figure and ample bosom fed many an adolescent fantasy.

Many years later I had the opportunity to work with Grace at a series of *Star Trek* conventions and film screening events. She consistently gave her all to fans, signing autographs and answering questions until the last person was satisfied. Grace appeared at the first *Star Trek* convention held in Southern Oregon, where she created a sensation from the first moment she walked onto the stage in Ashland. An audience member complimented her looks and figure, asking if she had ever thought about plastic surgery. "Oh, Honey," she exclaimed, "thought about it? I always say that my face is 10, my boobs are 20, and my ass is 30!" The end of her reply was punctuated by a sly turn and a knowing look: "Charlie X, eat your heart out!"

When Grace attended the Portland, Oregon premiere of *Star Trek: Generations*, the seventh film in the series and the one in which James T. Kirk meets his end, I introduced her to the sold out theatre as she stood out of sight of the audience, "Ladies and gentlemen, Grace Lee

Grace Lee Whitney patrolling her property near Yosemite National Park in California: "No Trespassing — Violators Will Be Shot."
PHOTO COURTESY OF ANTHONY WYNN.

Whitney!" She bounded into the theatre, the audience rising to its feet, exploding in applause and cheers. Grace raised her arms in fists of triumph, crying out, "Are you ready? Tonight Kirk dies!"

There's really no other way to speak of Grace Lee Whitney than with the use of multiple exclamation points. She talks with excitement, moves with excitement; the woman is the embodiment of that special breed of woman — the blonde bombshell borne of the 1950s and 1960s. Grace is both a reminder and a survivor of the age of Marilyn Monroe, Jayne Mansfield, Mamie Van Doren, and other buxom blondes — a little bit larger than life, but her heart is bigger than most.

I went to visit Grace on the set of *Star Trek Voyager*, where she guest-starred in a special episode with Kate Mulgrew (Captain Janeway), Tim Russ (Tuvok) and George Takei (Sulu). I watched as she filmed a scene on the bridge of the ship. The director called, "Cut!," ending the scene and the cast drifted off the set in various directions, while sound and lighting technicians moved in to make their adjustments and set-ups for what was to come next. Suddenly, Grace spotted me from across the soundstage and quickly bounded the distance. As she neared, she thrust her breasts forward and her bosoms bounced against my chest.

"Whaddya think of *this?!,* she screamed, pushing at her chest. "Can you believe they gave *me* fake boobs? *Me,* of all people!," she laughed enthusiastically. It was true. Her burgundy red tunic was completely and fully filled by a combination of real flesh and rubber. Amazingly, however, on film the massive size of her augmented mammaries were cinematically reduced to more normal proportions. But, I'll never forget her final words on the subject:

"These are my *Star Trek* boobs; my intergalactic boobs! They enter the room five minutes before I do!"

Nick Tate comes from a long line of performers and began his career as a child actor, in theatre. His first important role was in 1956 when he played "Amahl" in the Sydney Opera Company's production of Gian Carlo Minotti's Amahl and the Night Visitors. *His success in that demanding singing/acting role led to early roles on Australian radio, where his parents had established themselves to considerable success.*

His career as an actor took off in the television production of The Purple Jacaranda *and then as one of the leads in the highly-awarded series,* My Brother Jack. *However, it was Nick's two seasons on the popular syndicated British television series* Space: 1999 *that gave him a worldwide following. He appeared as "Captain Alan Carter," and was one of the most popular characters on the series.*

His film work includes the film The Devil's Playground *in the part of "Brother Victor," a movie that won a number of awards,* Summerfield, The Gold and the Glory, Cry Freedom, *and Stephen Spielberg's* Hook. *He has worked consistently in England and Australia; his work in the USA includes the FOX television series* Open House, *a situation comedy. He followed that up with appearances in* Star Trek: The Next Generation, Star Trek: Deep Space Nine, JAG, Lost, *and many others.*

Nick is one of the top voiceover artists in the business and has worked on theatrical trailers for such films as Jurassic Park, Mission: Impossible, The Day After Tomorrow, Troy, *and dozens more. His work in commercials includes spots for Guinness beer, Lexus, Acura, and Ping. Recent work includes appearances in the award-winning HBO series* The Pacific *and the film* The Killer Elite *with Robert DeNiro, Jason Statham, and Clive Owen.*

The breadth and scope of Nick Tate's career is so vast that it is not possible to cover all of his work in an interview of this type. I very much look forward to the day when he is able to write a comprehensive theatrical memoir covering his extraordinary experiences.

Nick Tate

"A Large Appetite for Life"

It's great to talk to you on the phone from Australia! I'd like to start off by asking you about your background. I understand your family has a long theatrical history.

That's true. My grandfather on my mother's side, my mother's father, was a man called Adolphus Carr Glyn and he was a vaudevillian actor who was born in County Derry in Ireland. He married my grandmother, Marie Carr Glyn, who was a singer and a young actress at the time. They lived in England then moved to Australia. My grandfather died at a very young age, my mother Neva Carr Glyn was just eight years old at the time. She was born into this theatrical family and was always traveling with them in theatres, and by the time my grandfather died she was already showing signs of wanting to be in show biz. She started out as a young dancer in musical theatre then started taking on comedic roles.

By the time she was a teenager she was a full working actress here in Australia and Sydney, working mostly in the light entertainment area of musicals. She went to South Africa with a theatre touring company, finished up in England, and at the age of twenty-one began work with the famous actor/entrepreneur Leslie Henson. My mother returned from England to Australia just before the war where she met my father, John Tate, who was a young aspiring actor. They formed a wonderful husband-wife theatrical partnership and became very well-known in this country. So I was born into a theatrical family in the middle of the war in 1942.

My parents tried to dissuade me from becoming an actor because it was, and still is, a fairly risky proposition. But, you know, with that kind of heritage I guess it was pretty hard to stop me from becoming a performer. I was very much a show-off at school, I was in every school production; and my son Tom has followed my footsteps. He's now working in America as an actor in Los Angeles.

I understand that very early on you were interested in television and television production; how did that come about?

I like the process of building a production, I'm interested in the script and what makes a good story; more than anything else, it's important. You don't have anything if you're doing a play or a film and you don't have the story; you have to have a story that has a beginning, a middle, and an end. Without it you might as well not start. It's great to have some fun characters, but if they don't have purpose and there isn't an arc for them to follow, then you might as well give up. Now that's not necessarily true when you're working in sit-com; *Seinfeld* is great example of how you can make something out of absolutely nothing. But you're dealing with a whole team of writers and actors who put productions together like that. It's very different from the central way that a William Shakespeare or a George Bernard Shaw would have gone, where they just sit down and they write for days, weeks, months on any given idea or story until they get it right.

It's been said, and I think it's absolutely true, that the most expensive single item in a film is the script. The script, obviously, makes you or breaks you. It can also be the cheapest item in a film because you should never start filming until your script is right. You can be lucky, somebody can walk in and hand you a script they might have spent years writing — and you don't know that — but day one they walk in and give it to you and it's brilliant, you want to film it straight away. But if you've just come up with a concept and you give it to a writer and say, "Will you write that film script for me?" it could take six days, six weeks, six months, or six years. You just don't know.

Did you get your start in Australian television?

We didn't have television in Australia until the late 1950s, in fact it first came in 1956 when the Olympic Games were here, but very few people had access to it — only rich people had television. It took another four or five years for every Joe Blow to have a television set in their house. That meant that television wasn't a local production thing until the early 1960s in Australia. So I didn't have the natural forum of being able to go into a whole host of television work in my teens; it just didn't exist. I did a little bit of theatre and some radio, but there wasn't a lot of work in that either. So I decided that if I couldn't work as an actor, what I'd like to do is to start out work training to become a director and work on productions, and maybe somewhere down the line I could be an actor-director. That pretty much was my plan. I wrote to all three of the local television channels that had started up asking them for interviews. I went in and met with the production people and was eventually accepted on ABC television — the Australian Broadcasting Corporation — as a studio hand. That meant I swept the floors, helped erect the sets, did the queuing, made tea for the actors, did the graphics — and generally worked as an assistant on productions. They were very few and far between, about one a month. In the meantime I worked on news, religious broadcasts, and sporting programs; just everything that was being made. It was a very interesting and productive time and I did that for about four years.

My first show was working for *The Purple Jacaranda* which was a series for ABC. They were casting, amongst the other roles, for a young surfer in the show. The part was for the nephew of the lead actress in the thing and he gets embroiled in some of the drama. There weren't too many young actors around who could fulfill the role and I was a floor manager on the production, involved in the auditioning process with them. The lead actress, Margo Lee, said to me, "Nick, why don't you take those headphones off and audition." I said, "No, I can't do that, I'm working on the show." So she went and had a quiet word with the director and said, "I think Nick Tate should audition for this role." And he replied, "But he's my floor manager!" She said, "Yes, but he's so right for the role — look at him!" He left the control room and came down onto the floor and said, "Nick, I think that Margo is right. You should audition for this role." I told him, "How can I if I'm working on the series?" He replied, "Don't worry about that. You audition for it and see what happens." I had been there all day long auditioning other actors so I had picked up the words; I knew the character by this point. So I took the headphones off and just did it. I guess I had a great advantage, really, because I had seen it done about ten times. They thought I nailed it and I was given the role. That was pretty much the beginning of my adult career. By then I was twenty-one.

I followed up with another television series after that for ABC in which I played the second lead, called *My Brother Jack*. It was a big award-winning series here in Australia. Then in 1965 I went to England where my father was now working as an actor. He had divorced my mother and was living over there. He introduced me to his agent and to various elements like Rediffusion, BBC television, Grenada, and so on; and I started working there as a young actor. It was a wonderfully productive time for me. I traveled all over England with various theatre companies doing repertory theatre, and then I did a lot of British television, as well. I spent about four years in England, doing all kinds work, before heading back to Australia.

Had you developed the ability for accents and doing different voices by this time?

I always had a facility for doing that. I don't know; some actors do more than others. My hero in my early days was Peter Sellers and other clever mimics like him. I love doing, particularly, comedy voices, and I learned to mimic all of the same voices that Peter Sellers did, and many more. So when I went to England it was natural for me

because there are so many different dialects. It was fun to go looking for those characters he had portrayed: the North Country voices,
the public school, the Cockney. So in my four years in England from
1965 to 1969, I developed a great love of the regional dialects and
worked very hard at learning them. Similarly, when I went to America;
it was the same thing there, too. I've just been lucky that I have quite
a facility for accents.

Therefore, that led me to working on microphone a lot which in the
end, I guess, is how I started working on doing movie trailers. It was
natural for me to be able to copy the movie trailer voice that a couple
of big guys in the States were doing. I was lucky; there was a period
of several years where I got a lot of movie trailer work. I was involved
in some of the most successful productions in the world: *Apollo 13,
Independence Day, Jurassic Park: The Lost World,* and the James Bond
movies. I was involved with some of the most exciting film productions in the history of Hollywood and it was my voice, singularly, that
was promoting those films. So I felt a tremendous responsibility and a
tremendous pride in having been the chosen one to vanguard those
films; it was an honor, quite frankly. I remember one time I was working on *Jurassic Park* and Universal Studios took my voice off the trailers
because they had somebody else in mind that they wanted to use,
somebody they'd used for years. Steven Spielberg was in Romania
shooting *Schindler's List* and he called up Universal Studios and pulled
them over the coals and said, "I want Nick Tate back on my movie
trailer!" It wasn't that they didn't like me; they just didn't think at the
time that I was well-known enough or that my voice carried what they
wanted. But Spielberg really liked what I was doing and he insisted
that they put me back.

**That has to be pretty gratifying to have Spielberg going to bat
for you.**

Yeah! (Laughs) It was wonderful. I don't think Spielberg particularly
knew who I was as an actor; he just knew that he liked that voice. It
was later on that I worked for him on *Hook.* I didn't point out to him
that I'd been involved with doing voiceover work for him.

**I don't think we can escape talking a little bit about *Space:
1999* — it's what brought you to the public eye in the USA. How did
you get involved in it?**

Well, when I returned to Australia after having been in England,
I did a production of the musical *The Canterbury Tales* playing the
part of "Nicholas the Gallant" for about eighteen months on stage

and on tour throughout the country. I absolutely loved that. I also shot a television series called **Dynasty** — and this was not related in any way to the later American series of the same name. It was on this series that I worked with my father, John Tate, for the first time; we played father and son. Another Australian series that I worked on was called *The Chaser* in which I played a private investigator. There was

Nick Tate with his daughter Jessica. He is holding an image of "Captain Alan Carter" from *Space: 1999*. PHOTO COURTESY OF ROBERT E. WOOD.

a man involved with that show who suggested to Gerry and Sylvia Anderson, the producers of *Space: 1999*, that I was the right kind of person to play an astronaut in their show. I went through the general screening process and eventually got the part, but it wasn't the part of Alan Carter; it was his co-pilot. Alan Carter was supposed to have been played by an Italian actor and they had planned to name the character "Alphonse Catani." It so happened that just before shooting started, the Italian couldn't get out of a movie that he was filming so last minute juggling took place.

They interviewed several people to replace him, but the director of our pilot, Lee Katzin, liked me and felt that my sort of Australian aggression was what they wanted in the series. They hadn't been successful in trying to replace him and I was in the right place at the right time. Sylvia Anderson, though, jumped in and said, "No, he won't do. Australians sound too much like Cockneys!" When I heard that, I saw absolute red and, for the first time, I really spoke up for myself. It worked! At first, I was only supposed to be in the premiere episode, but then they offered me another five shows because things were looking interesting. At the end of the sixth episode they said, "We'd like to sign you up for the series." The character of Carter was one I didn't have to dig into too deeply; he was just about all the things I was as a young man. Alan was friendly, happy go-lucky, someone who would be up for a challenge, and someone who loved adventure.

Generally speaking, we had a happy time on the series. Martin Landau and I became close while working on the show; I liked Barbara Bain, too. I had a great rapport with the rest of the cast — Prentis Hancock, Barry Morse, and Zienia Merton. The original concept had been a joint conception of both Sylvia and Gerry Anderson, so when they divorced it really destroyed a lot of what had been established during the first series. It seemed as if Gerry was prepared to allow somebody else to come in and totally change the humanity Sylvia had brought to the program. I must say that I greatly missed Sylvia because she seemed to intrinsically understand what was at the heart of the show, the human element.

With Sylvia gone, Fred Freiberger was brought over from America to produce the second series. It quickly became clear to me that Freddy had no love for the original show whatsoever. He invited me over to meet his family at his house, and while we were there he told me how much his kids were great fans of my character, Alan Carter. I guess that's why he brought me back! I feel that one of the reasons

Space: 1999 didn't last was because the second series didn't have the same sense of truth and honesty; it seemed to be more about the action than about the characters or story. I think we did have some good episodes of the second series, but it's clear that our best shows were the first twenty-four.

So after *Space: 1999* you went back to Australia?

Not immediately. It was around 1981 that I was offered a television series called *Holiday Island*. So I came out to Australia to shoot it and it was supposed to be about a warm tropical island, but in the end we shot most of it down in Victoria which is very cold. My wife Hazel and young son, Tom and I (Hazel and I were married in 1977 and Tom was born in 1979) settled in Melbourne. But *Holiday Island* finished after its first year, and it became clear there wasn't enough work down in Melbourne and really, if we were going to stay in Australia, we should come back to Sydney. So we moved to Sydney and I started working there, which was much more productive. There were a lot of nice things happening here at that time. I worked a lot in theatre, places like the Sydney Opera House and local theatre companies; I was really enjoying my young married life and my young son. My daughter Jessica was born in 1986 in Sydney. Things were good and we were doing very well here and loving Australia.

I spent quite a lot of time flying up to Queensland where they have Queensland Film Studios doing a television series called *Dolphin Cove*, which was about a crazy millionaire who owned a big ranch-style station that bordered a beach. So he decided to open a dolphin area there and had to get American marine biologists to come and work with him. That was the genesis of the television series. Frank Converse and Trey Ames, both of them American actors, came out and I played the head of the ranch. It was a great idea for a show but it was very hard to do logistically. We actually shot it at Seaworld in Surfer's Paradise which meant you couldn't pan the camera left or right because you'd see all the Ferris wheels and so forth! (Laughs) Again, this was supposed to be a tropical island but at least we were shooting it in the tropics. We got nearly a year out of that.

The show was owned by Paramount and CBS and I had been getting very good reports back from Paramount about what I was doing in the show, so I decided to come to America and meet those people. I wanted to try and encourage them to do some different things with the series as I felt that just working with the dolphins was too limiting. I had some good ideas to go into the outback of Australia and work much more with the Aborigines because we had a very good Aboriginal actor working in the show called Ernie Dingo. I wanted to expand on some of the storylines that we had with him. The producers in Los Angeles at Paramount Studios liked that idea a great deal. They said, "How long are you going to stay in town?" I told them, "Well, I'm here for a couple of weeks then I've got to go back and continue with *Dolphin Cove.*" They said they wanted me to come back in and see them the following week, but I didn't know what they were on about. So I went back in the next week and they told me, "We have some good news and some bad news; the bad news is that *Dolphin Cove* is not going ahead so there's not much point in you going back to Australia." That was very depressing. So I said, "What's the good news?" They replied, "We like you a lot and want you to stay here and we'll try to find you something."

Good to their word, they had me audition for various shows. I auditioned for a replacement in *Star Trek*; I auditioned for a replacement in *Cheers*; I auditioned for several shows, one of which was a thing called *Open House* for FOX television and I got that, surprisingly. So within eighteen days of arriving in L.A. to talk to them about the series I was doing in Australia, that was cancelled and I was now in a new series. I had to ring Hazel and say, "Well, do you want the good news or the bad news first?" She was absolutely stunned — and mortified, actually. She loved Australia, and still does. That's why we're back here now because she always wanted to come back. We have a beautiful home here and she didn't want to be in Los Angeles. But we did make the move to L.A. and I did *Open House* for one season. It was just an eye-opener enough for me to recognize that all the struggling I'd done in Australia and England financially was finally being rewarded with this television series in America where you earn so much more money. The kind of work you do in England and Australia, no matter how hard you work, doesn't make you wealthy. You can come to the States and just as a working actor you can make a living, but there's the opportunity to make a bonanza of a living if you can get into a big series on network television or in film; it's just not the same in Australia or England.

You worked with Sam Neill and Meryl Streep in the film *A Cry in the Dark*. What do you remember about that experience?

The director of that film, Fred Schepisi, is a good friend of mine. I met Fred back in the 1970s when he was a director of commercials in Australia and he took me to New Zealand to do a cigarette commercial.

We became firm friends. He then told me that he wanted to write a feature film called *The Devil's Playground*. When I was shooting *Space: 1999* at the end of the first series in 1975 I got a message saying the script was finished and he wanted to shoot it in Australia. They sent me the script and I loved it. There was a long gap between the first and second series, so I was able to fly to Australia to make the film. I

Nick Tate with a poster for the play *Woman in Mind* in which he appeared with Helen Mirren. PHOTO COURTESY OF ROBERT E. WOOD.

stayed with Fred and his wife at their house, as did a lot of the actors in the movie, and we rehearsed at his home on videotape for about a week. Then we went to shoot the film at a Catholic seminary. It's the most beautiful film and it won all kinds of awards in Australia and I'm fiercely proud of *The Devil's Playground*, it's a magnificent picture. It launched Fred as an international film director and he's made many movies since then, including *Barbarosa, Six Degrees of Separation, Iceman*, and *Roxanne*.

A Cry in the Dark is the true story about a family who was camping in the outback of Australia and lost their baby. The woman claimed that while they were camping near the famous Ayers Rock — which we now call Uluru, the original Aboriginal name of the rock — claimed that an Australian wild dog called a dingo stole her baby. Nobody believed her; the police came and it was a huge scandal. There were several court cases and she was thrown into prison for more than three years. Sadly, Australia and the rest of the world just didn't believe this woman because it hadn't ever been reported that a dingo had taken a child; not even stories from Aboriginals that this had ever happened. After two court cases, documentaries made about her, and the ensuing international publicity, Fred decided that he would make a film about the case. The woman was still in prison when he started work on the film and many people advised him not to make the film because it wasn't a story that seemed to have a nice ending to it at all. But Meryl Streep wanted to play the role and Fred was very clever in having found a woman of her great acting prowess and international standing. Meryl was convinced, based on the literature that Fred had been able to garner and based on an underground swelling of people that believed she wasn't guilty; that it was possible and indeed might have happened. There was also another reason for this — speculation that perhaps it hadn't been a dingo, but a cross-breed dog that had joined up with a dingo.

In the midst of all this while Fred was putting the film together, an American tourist on Uluru fell to his death and when the police went down into the craggy area to recover his body, where no one had ever been before, they discovered a piece of cloth which turned out to be part of the jacket that the child was wearing at the time, exactly as the mother described it. It was at a dingo's lair. The woman was then released from prison immediately and vindicated. The film is really about the way that idle tongues can build a story of hate and mistrust. Fred asked me to play the part of Charlwood and it's a wonderful film;

Meryl is an extraordinary talent and I worked in very close proximity with her. She has quite an aura about her when she's working on a film.

I was told by Fred and his wife that I should not try to interact with Meryl in any way when we were off-set, that her principal way of acting is that she takes on a lot of the elements of the character that she is portraying in a film. If her character in a film doesn't like your character, then she doesn't want to form any kind of relationship with you off-camera because that would be destructive to her process while working as an actress. I'd never worked with anybody before who behaved like that and it was disconcerting. Most of the actors on the set were upset with Meryl for doing it because they wanted to have social time with her, or at the very least they just wanted to be able to feel comfortable and be natural with her. But when the cameras weren't rolling — and we were together for over twelve weeks on and off — you'd think that she could spend some time with her cast mates, at least at night when the show was finished. The thing about it is that Meryl does befriend quite a few of her cast members, but they are always cast members that her character is friendly with. So some of the actors would say, "Oh, we're going out to the movies with Meryl tonight...and you can't come — ha ha." It's a strange way of working and I know that she's upset a lot of other actors that she has worked with by using that process.

Is that a result of Method acting, or some other technique?

Method acting comes from the famous Russian expert Stanislavski. I've read something of Method acting, but I've never studied it fully, so I can't tell you. Other people have said to me that, yes, it is part of Method acting. It's certainly a method because we all — I employ various kinds of methods when I work as an actor and I use various elements from my past to conjure up certain feelings and understandings and interpretations of what I'm doing with my character. I did hear a story about a director who was trying to tell a young actor how to respond to a very sad moment in a film. This young girl had to cry about the loss of her mother in the film and he was getting nowhere with her because she just couldn't bring the real tears. So he went to her and said, "You have to dig back into your past and find a parallel moment in your life; surely you've lost somebody." She told him, "No, no; I haven't lost anybody." Apparently nobody had ever died that she knew or cared about. Then the director discovered that the girl had a dog that she loved and the dog had died, so he worked on that with her and helped return her memory back to that time when the dog that she loved greatly was dead and managed to help her produce the tears in that way. I don't like that. For me, that is so pseudo; it might fool somebody, but for me, actors are people who are able to have vivid imaginations and if you cannot imagine what it might be like to lose your mother — even if you *haven't* lost your mother — and how devastated you may be, perhaps you're in the wrong trade. You've got to get out of the role of yourself because you're not playing you, you're playing somebody else. You have to take on the mantle of that character and how *that* character may respond to those things.

As an example, I am not Alan Carter, the character on *Space: 1999*. My personality and style was rather like him since the character was written for me. The character wasn't an original concept on their part so they decided to build him very much around my own personality. They even asked me to devise his character and his history, so I wrote a history about him which I gave to the Andersons and that became something that the writers worked with. I urge all young actors, when working on a production, if the writers and producers have not given you a biography of your character, to sit down and try to work one out. If you're just playing a waiter that comes in and says, "The soup is ready" then obviously you don't need a biography. But if you're playing a fairly complex character in a play or a television series or a film, you really do need to know the history of the character that you're playing. It's really important to go back and understand what drives that character, as long as you're not doing something silly like upsetting the intentions of the writer or the producer by making him an Irish left-wing assassin or something which has nothing to do with the story. It's probably a good idea to converse with the writer or director if you can. It helps you respond in the ways the character should respond, which are different to the ways you as a person may have responded.

To that end, I've always loved studying people and their reactions. If I'm on a public transport or something and there are people having an argument or there are people talking rather loudly about something, I'll sit and listen; I'll sit and watch them quite unashamedly. I remember my father once saying to me, even though he was an actor himself, saying, "You're just being silly, it's the way you listen to people or the way you look at them." I said, "But I'm studying them, Dad; it's really interesting! Look, this guy's nutty as a fruitcake." It's interesting to me to observe those situations because I know that I'm going to use that sometime in the future. Even when there are really sad things happening, it's important to understand what drives pain and sadness in people. It's fairly morbid, but I've always had this fairly huge curiosity about people's emotions. I think I just have a large appetite for life.

You once said in an interview that "musicals are my one true love." Can you talk a little more about your experience with musicals?

When I did the musical *The Canterbury Tales* I played the young love interest in the piece and I had two beautiful solos, three duets, and several other ensemble numbers. It was the most joyous time of my life. It was a wonderful musical and I played 418 performances over a period of eighteen months. But I didn't make another musical for many years. Cameron Macintosh auditioned me for *Cats* and over a period of three months short-listed me for the role and brought me back several times, but in the end I didn't play the part because they changed the character. I was to play "Gus the theatre cat" and originally that character was an old English theatre cat that sang pub songs. When I did the original audition for the role, that's what I played. But when they took *Cats* to America they changed Gus into an opera cat and he sang bad opera songs. It's a true story! When they came back to me three months later and said now I would have to change and sing in an operatic style. That was hard for me, much more than I could manage. To cut a long story short — I didn't play Gus the theatre cat.

Years later when they came to do *Les Miserables*, Cameron Macintosh remembered me from *Cats* so again asked me to come and audition for the part of "Thénardier" the innkeeper and I really enjoyed the experience that transpired. Again, after several months of training for the role I didn't get to play it because the opera singer I was training with, John Crawford, expressed to me that he would not play a role like this for eight performances a week. A lot of opera singers don't sing every night; they change over with other people. But that isn't true with actors — eight performances a week and if your part is a large and taxing role, well, that's just your misfortune. I was offered a film at the same time *Les Miserables* was to go into production and I had to make the decision if I really wanted to give up what I thought was becoming a film career for me. I was offered *Coolangatta Gold*, later released under the title of *The Gold and the Glory*, which I decided to accept, so I didn't go into *Les Miserables*. So again another missed opportunity for being in a musical theatre production. With Cameron Macintosh you don't just sign for six weeks. His productions go on for two, three, four, five years and you sign for the run of the play. They may let you out at some point but the option is their way. I did not want to sign for the run of the play, I wanted to do that role for maybe six months; but they wouldn't hear of that. In 2006 I finally did make it back on the stage in a musical theatre role; I played "Captain Smith" in the Australian premiere of *Titanic: The Musical* in Sydney. It was a great challenge for me as I had several ensemble numbers in the show; we opened to great reviews.

You've appeared in both *Star Trek: The Next Generation* and *Deep Space Nine*. What do you remember about those experiences?

My first *Star Trek* was with Wil Wheaton on the episode where his character leaves the show, the last mission that he had, so hence the title of it: "Final Mission." I've done two episodes of *Star Trek*, the other was on *Deep Space Nine* and was an episode called "Honor Among Thieves." It was loosely based on the story of Donnie Brasco; *Star Trek* will often make tributes to famous films. I loved doing that one and I loved doing "Final Mission" which was on *The Next Generation* also with Patrick Stewart. I did that one first and I did "Honor Among Thieves" several years later.

I hadn't been a great fan of the original series of *Star Trek*, which had been on before *Space: 1999*, of course. *Star Trek* started nearly seven years before *Space: 1999* did. Although I had seen some of the episodes I guess I had seen ones in which there was a lot of fancy dress and very kind of tongue-in-cheek response to some of the situations that didn't really appeal to me. I like the concept of science fiction when it is closer to fact and I haven't read a great deal of science fiction, but I've read some Issac Asimov and Arthur C. Clarke. It appeals to me when it had a lot of truth in it and *probability*, as against *possibility*. When *Space: 1999* came along and I looked at the storylines and the facts and so forth, I was thrilled to be involved with it. I always thought that the original concept of *Space: 1999* was more about "science faction" than it was about science fiction. So there was this difference with what we were doing with *Space: 1999* and what had been done with the original *Star Trek* series. I thought *The Next Generation* years later with Patrick Stewart was an altogether better idea. They also had access to all the modern special effects that could be used and it was indeed a wonderful series. Amongst the fans in the 1970s there was this dedication: you were either a *Star Trek* fan or a *Space: 1999* fan, and never the twain shall meet. It was very rare for *Star Trek* people ever to invite, at that time when *Space: 1999* was made, anybody from any other show to their conventions. But in 1975 I *was* invited to a *Star Trek* convention and there were quite a lot of people there who had decided they quite liked *Space: 1999*.

So it was interesting, many years later, that when I was cast to play "Captain Dirqo" in *The Next Generation* he was a real crossover. "Alan Carter" — or Nick Tate — was now playing a true astronaut in *Star Trek!* I got a real kick out of doing it, for that reason and I knew that a lot of the *Star Trek* fans who liked *Space: 1999* would be happy that I was the one who had come in and bridged the gap. I don't think that

A recent photo of actor Nick Tate. PHOTO COURTESY OF NICK TATE.

Martin Landau, Barbara Bain, or Barry Morse have ever been in an episode of *Star Trek*.

That's right — you're the only cast member from *Space: 1999* to have done that.

The Next Generation was a joy to work on; it was an extraordinarily well-made series. We did a lot of exterior work. If you've seen the episode, you know it. A lot of it was shot on a desert planet and we actually went to the Mohave Desert and shot there, all those sequences walking across the salt plains. It was very eerie and very hot, but wonderful to work with Patrick Stewart and Wil Wheaton; two very nice people. Here is an example of an actor who was incredibly friendly to me. His character was very wary of me. My character was a bit of a rogue — he drank the rocket fuel! Patrick's "Picard" was never quite sure that my character was really on their side. But unlike Meryl Streep, Patrick was very friendly and we spent quite some time together when we weren't filming.

There's a lot of down time for actors, we have to sit and wait while the crew gets prepared, gets the lights right, and so on. So we had time to talk and we talked a lot about our past experiences working in British theatre and how much he loved the theatre and would prefer to be doing it. I said to him, "Well, just about every theatre actor I ever worked with in my life would give their right arm to be doing exactly what you're doing right now!" (Laughs) He's been very fortunate and very lucky. I think he understands that and respects it. His success is probably the most extraordinary success story of an actor, when you consider his career was fully shaped and rounded within the British theatre, and in particular the classical theatre. He hadn't had any real success in films. I don't think he had even thought of a career in the film world. Patrick was doing a Shakespeare anthology in a university tour of America with two other English actors. One of the producers of *The Next Generation* [Robert Justman] who was looking for a lead actor came to see this Shakespearian production and immediately recognized the power and strength and great acting ability of Patrick Stewart. But, as I said, Patrick is a very friendly and easy-going man and I enjoyed my time working with him immensely.

Our time is at a close, but I'd like to end with a mention of the Nick Tate Fan Club. I know that you're proud of it.

You know, it's really quite extraordinary. Phyllis Proctor and Eileen Skidmore took over my club in 1975. It's now one of the longest-running fan clubs in the history of movie fan clubs. They've been wonderfully supportive and have made a lifelong project out of this — purely out of love. They are two wonderful women and they know more about me than *I* know about me! There are quite a few members in the Nick Tate Fan Club and numbers go up and down, generally depending if *Space: 1999* is being played somewhere in some part of the world. Anyone who is interested can reach the fan club through my website at *www.nicktate.com.*

Nick, thank you for taking the time to talk about your career today; it's been a lot of fun and very interesting.

You're welcome — it's been my pleasure.

Bibi Besch was born on February 1, 1940, in Vienna, Austria, the daughter of theater and film actress Gusti Huber (The Diary of Anne Frank). Mother and daughter fled the Nazi regime shortly after Bibi's birth. Beginning in the mid-1960s as a teenager, Bibi followed in her mother's footsteps and landed roles on television. Her first work was in a variety of daytime serials, including The Secret Storm, The Edge of Night, Love is a Many Splendored Thing, *and* Somerset.

Bibi also worked on Broadway, Off-Broadway and in regional theatres, concentrating her talents in classics like MacBeth, The Cherry Orchard, Private Lives, *and "Eliza" in George Bernard Shaw's* Pygmalion. *By the 1970s she began appearing in numerous primetime television and film roles, including the miniseries* Backstairs at the White House, Meteor, Who's That Girl, *and* Date With An Angel.

Her most famous role is probably that of "Dr. Carol Marcus," the former lover of "Captain James T. Kirk" and mother of his son in Star Trek II: The Wrath of Khan. *She delivered what critic Pauline Kael called "the best line ever to adorn a sci-fi movie." The following short interview, mostly focused on* Star Trek, *was conducted in 1983, following the release of* Star Trek II: The Wrath of Khan, *and originally appeared in a* Star Trek *fan periodical.*

Do you live in Southern California?

Yes, in Los Angeles.

Where were you born — and do you have siblings?

I was born in Austria, and yes, I have two sisters and a brother. My older sister lives in Paris and my younger brother and sister, who are twins incidentally, both live in New York.

How was it to audition for *Star Trek II: The Wrath of Khan*?

It was through the casting woman, for whom I had worked before at Paramount television. I'd never done any Paramount pictures before and this was all handled through the television department. She

Bibi Besch

"True to Myself"

submitted my name and it went on from there. I knew the producer, Harve Bennett, from a previous job. I was very, very lucky. I never even auditioned for this part. So, it was quite easy. I came in and met with the producers and I knew I had the part just a couple of days later.

But let me tell you, I've had auditions that would curl your hair! Probably the worst ever was for a television show not long after I came to Hollywood from New York. I was so new to it all and every audition was a big deal to me. I didn't really know the ropes. I walked into this rather expansive office where a man was sitting behind a very large desk. I had hardly even gotten into the room when he looked up at me and his voice boomed out, "Now I remember why I don't like you!" There were at least a dozen other people in the room too. What do you do in that sort of situation? I was so astonished and more than a little bit overwhelmed at that moment. I just pretended he hadn't said anything, although my heart was beating a mile a minute and my face felt flushed, as I tried to go on with the session. You can imagine, as it turned out, that I didn't get the job. And I never did find out what he meant!

So you had the role of Carol Marcus — in *Star Trek*, a science fiction film. How did this job compare with some of your past work in drama?

You can't really approach it as doing a science fiction movie. You have to approach it as an acting assignment and try to make it believable to the audience. With doing *Star Trek*, it is a bit like a cartoon, but you can't play it like a cartoon.

Had you met William Shatner prior to this time?

No. It often happens that you're cast in parts where you are supposed to have a relationship with someone — you're married or a mother or whatever — to this other person, and you've never met until you arrive on the set. That was the case in *Star Trek*. It's a challenge to establish a relationship almost instantly, one that comes across on film as a relationship. So it helps to spend some time together, to get to know the other actor and be with each other, and look at each other from the heart as opposed to when one actor is trying to figure out just who this other actor is.

How much of your own personality do you put into the character of "Carol Marcus"?

The words were there on the page, but the interpretation of those words was mine. I wanted to make her a strong character; however you can play the words a lot of different ways. But I wanted to make her an equal of Kirk's. When they meet they're as equals.

During the filming of the movie were you ever on the set just to observe?

Yes, I did watch some of the stuff. I watched the sand planet, some of the sand planet stuff, because for one thing it was an incredible set. I don't know if you've ever been on the soundstage in a movie studio — they're huge, and the sand planet was an entire stage with maybe that much walk space (gesturing, about two feet) around the outside of it and they took truckloads of sand into it to make the sand planet and then they had to take the same truckloads of sand back out again!

What was it like playing to an ensemble of actors who had known each other for so many years?

It was strange, like walking into a club. You have to carve out your own way and your own place in a club like that.

Did you have any trouble fitting your character into the established group?

I didn't do it as a counterpoint or contrast to how everybody else was. I brought it down to a very simple human level. Carol is a scientist, a young scientist, when this guy was a young cadet. I tried to make her as human as possible, rather than trying to fit into something that already was, because this character hadn't existed before and I didn't really feel that I had to do that.

Was there anything left on the cutting room floor about Carol and Kirk that we don't know about?

There was a little bit more about that relationship that didn't end up on the screen; but not much, really. It was sketchy to begin with. Sometimes, I think of my character as just a lot of exposition — a means of getting to the plot line. I would love to do a future *Star Trek* with a little more exploration.

Have you tried to imagine what Carol's relationship with Kirk was like?

Yes, of course! I imagined myself twenty years ago, relationships I've had, where those people have ended up and where I've ended up. The night of the screening was interesting. Bill Shatner's manager said to me, "You know, when I first read this script, I didn't know who I would believe as having had a relationship with Kirk all those years ago. But, when you came on the screen, I had no difficulties. I absolutely believed that you had known each other and that you were up to his level."

It's difficult to play a woman who has had a relationship with someone that everybody knows. So I tried to make it believable for myself.

I fantasized about an early affair and why it turned out the way it did. What kind of people we both became, how I got to be where I was, not just as a scientist, but as a woman who wouldn't have told Kirk for all these years that he had a son.

Were you pleased with the way the theme of aging was handled in the film?

Actress Bibi Besch at her first *Star Trek* convention in San Antonio, Texas in 1983. PHOTO COURTESY OF ERIC A. STILLWELL.

I thought it was sweet. There was a sense of humor about it, a slightly melancholy point of view. I thought it was handled wonderfully. I didn't think there was anything jarring about the fact that they were that much older, because of the way it was handled.

Having grown up with *Star Trek* like the rest of us, how did it feel to be a part of it all?

I liked it! It was very exciting — the very first day I went up and sat in Kirk's chair, you know, I just couldn't resist.

You beautifully conveyed Carol Marcus' awe at the creation of the planet and your delivery of the line at that moment has been praised...

Well, "Can I cook, or can't I?" (Laughs)

How difficult was it for you to act, to convincingly say a line like that, while dealing with the special effects? Did you have to perform differently?

It's not easy, because you never see the effects. You have to pretend because they're all put in later. When we're looking at the blue screen, at that wonderful planet being created out there, we didn't see anything. They had a light stand with a dot on it for us to look at. We could pretend, and hope that what we were supposed to be seeing was as magnificent as how we reacted. But we had no idea at the time!

How do you feel about special effects being such a big part of today's films?

I think it makes the actor's job harder, because for the effects to work properly there has to be a lot of time to set them up. They have to be lit and shot effectively. Usually, that means the actors hang around a lot waiting for the special effects to be perfect. If they don't work, then you don't have a picture.

Did you find that to be frustrating?

Sure it is. You go to work in the morning, you get all revved up, and then you wait for four hours for the effects to be right. Then, when they're ready — you'd better be ready, too!

Before *Star Trek*, you starred in *The Beast Within*, a well-received suspense film. Did you have to wait around on that set?

Not as much, but definitely more than in other types of films. For *The Beast*, it took hours to get the makeup ready. There was a transformation, and you had to wait for them to get it right, and sometimes it didn't work. It's fascinating to watch, to see how they do that — but over and over and over again is another thing!

What is most important to you as a person — most important in life?

You mean what is the most important thing *to me* in life? My...

In addition to your daughter, Samantha.

I was going to say my daughter! Honesty is very important to me. What's the most important thing to me in my life? God's very important to me in my life. I try to live my life in such a way that I don't hurt anybody else and I try to be true to myself; and that's a neat trick to combine those two things. It's very important for me to be honest with people. If I'm going to communicate with someone — to have communication, you know, that's very important to me.

What would you like to be best remembered for?

That I contributed to somebody's life. My life meant something to someone else — contributed to somebody's life.

Bibi Besch with her daughter Samantha Mathis in San Antonio, Texas. PHOTO COURTESY OF ERIC A. STILLWELL.

It was a pleasure for me to co-produce a *Star Trek* convention in 1983 in San Antonio, Texas, where Bibi Besch was guest of honor. It was her first appearance at a convention following her role in *Star Trek II: The Wrath of Khan*, and she attended with her young teenage daughter, Samantha. This short interview took place several months later at her second public appearance in Dallas, Texas.

Following *Star Trek II*, Bibi Besch continued to appear in films and on television. Her television work included guest appearances on the hit shows *ER* and *Melrose Place*. She also starred in such films as *The Day After*, the acclaimed made-for-television film directed by Nicholas Meyer; *Mrs. Delafield Wants to Marry* with Katharine Hepburn; *Steel Magnolias*, and *Tremors*. She received an Emmy Award nomination for the landmark TV-movie *Doing Time on Maple Drive* and received another a year later for her performance as Janine Turner's neurotic mother "Jane O'Connell" on *Northern Exposure*.

Bibi maintained a busy work schedule right up until her death in 1996 at the age of 56, following a long battle with breast cancer. Ironically, she died just a day before the 30th anniversary of the premiere of *Star Trek*. She was herself a single mother, a piece of biography that was echoed in her role of "Carol Marcus" in *Star Trek II* and, as alluded to in the interview, helped her to mold and define that landmark character in the film. Bibi is survived by her daughter, actress Samantha Mathis.

In addition to acting, George Takei is the author of two books, including his autobiography To The Stars. *He has starred in over thirty motion pictures and hundreds of television series, however, he is probably best known as "Mr. Sulu" — now "Captain Sulu" in the classic* Star Trek *television series and films.*

He received a star on Hollywood Boulevard's Walk of Fame in 1986 and he placed his signature and hand print in the forecourt of the landmark Grauman's Chinese Theatre in Hollywood in 1991. Among his credits is a music industry accolade, a 1987 Grammy nomination in the "Best Spoken Word or Non-Musical Recording" category.

George's distinctive voice is featured in Disney full-length animated feature, Mulan, Star Trek *audio novel recordings, FOX Television's* The Simpsons, Futurama, *and in numerous voice-overs and narrations. He is also a member of the Academy of Motion Picture Arts and Sciences (presenter of the Academy Awards), and the Academy of Television Arts and Sciences (the Emmy Awards).*

I'd like to start by asking you about a time that maybe wasn't particularly pleasant, maybe even a little painful; the imprisonment of you and your family during World War II.

The internment of Japanese-Americans was the reason I wrote my autobiography, I wanted to share that historic event with the American public. So many people, particularly east of the Rockies, are totally ignorant of that chapter of American history, because our history books are rather mute on it and it's not something that's taught as "the most egregious violation of our Constitution."

Is there a reason you think it's not well-covered in history books? Is it embarrassment?

George Takei

"Born With These Instincts"

Well, it is a time when we failed the Constitution, the ideals of this country. It was a time of hysteria and my father used to say that, "The ideas of this country are glorious. They're the best things in the world. But, it's dependent on people and people are fallible." And so, fallible people fail these shining ideals that we have. That's why we need good people to be participants in this process to make those ideals real, to make them what they're supposed to be.

I talk about my boyhood in those two internment camps because I think it's important for Americans to know how glorious our system is, but also how fallible it is, because we are fallible people. I wanted to personalize that story so that people can connect with it as human beings. When it's mentioned it's always "those Japanese-Americans." It's kind of dehumanized. But thanks to *Star Trek*, I think people can connect with me and when they discover that I was a part of that experience of American history, they are able to more directly personalize it. Fortunately for me, I was young enough so that I was able to get a different kind of perspective of that experience. And I'm grateful that I was young enough, because I don't know how I would have reacted if I were older and understood what was happening.

For my parents it was a devastating, traumatizing experience. You can just imagine: To be overnight stripped of your property, home, forcibly moved — and in jeopardy. For my parents to have three young children and sent out first to the swamps of Arkansas and later to this desolate, dry lakebed in Northern California. It was an absolutely devastating experience for them.

Did it change your parents for the rest of their lives, after release?

It did change their lives, completely. But it didn't change what they were made up of. They're resilient people, I'm proud to say. Yes, it did affect them terribly. It certainly affected their marriage for awhile after we came out. I think that the incarceration experience tends to bring us together, but then when you're out and you're struggling to get that foothold that you lost, there are a lot stresses and strains which make it very difficult on a marriage. I think the camp experience was the definitive experience for all of us. But those that were challenged the most — if they had the resilience in them — were able to overcome and re-establish themselves. There were others that could not and it did contribute to a different standard of living for many Japanese-Americans.

There were two different camps that your family was in. What was the background behind that and why were you transferred to a different camp in the middle of the internment?

To begin at the beginning: when Pearl Harbor was bombed, young Japanese-American men rushed out to the recruitment offices like all Americans to volunteer for the services. Because of racial hysteria against Japanese-Americans at that time, they were denied with the classification "4-C," which means "Enemy, Non-Alien." What is a non-alien? It's a citizen. But they didn't want to say that, because it had the adjective "Enemy" in front of it. So young Japanese-American men were rejected as they volunteered. Those that already happened to be in the military had their weapons taken from them, which is the gravest insult to a soldier, and when they protested, they were thrown into the stockade. With that rejection, we were all transported to these ten internment camps in some of the most God-forsaken places in this country. After a year in internment, the Government realized they had a manpower shortage and here are all these young men behind these barbed-wire fences — let's tap that. But how do we do that when we've accused them all of being potential traitors and saboteurs? So they came down with what they called the "loyalty questionnaire" a year into internment. This loyalty questionnaire caused a great upheaval in all the camps. This was a series of about fifty questions, but the two key questions in that loyalty questionnaire were questions 27 and 28. Question 27 asked:

Will you bear arms to defend this country?

A simple enough question for any citizen, but this to people who were first of all accused of being potential spies, traitors, and then forcibly moved and then put behind barbed-wire and guarded with machine guns pointed at them. And then, they're asking you to carry arms to defend this country; it was an outrageous question! The remarkable thing is that so many still answered "yes" to that. The second question, Question 28, was one sentence but with two ideas. It in essence asked:

Will you swear your loyalty to this country and forswear your loyalty to the Emperor of Japan?

Now, two ideas — but in the second idea they used the word "forswear" which means they assumed that there already was a pre-existing loyalty to the Emperor. You can't forswear something that you don't have! So they were just assuming, up front, that all Japanese-Americans had a loyalty to the Emperor that they were willing to forswear.

Catch-22!

Yes, Catch-22! So if you answered, "No, I don't have a loyalty to the Emperor to forswear" to begin with, then you were saying no to first part as well, "Will you swear your loyalty to the United States." So if you answered "Yes," meaning you are loyal to the United States, then you were "fessing-up" that *ah-ha*, you were loyal to the Emperor but now you are ready to set that aside. It caused great consternation. My parents answered "No" to both. My Father said, "The Government's done all this to me, but they're not going to take my dignity. I'm not going to grovel in front this Government that's already done *this* to me." And my Mother echoed his position. So they were both "No-Nos" — that's a term you'll hear in the Japanese-American community. Because of that, we were taken out of the camp in Arkansas and moved to another camp in Northern California, Tule Lake, which was considered high security because they answered "No" to those two questions.

My Mother was born here, and my Father was brought here as a child by my immigrant Grandfather when he was ten years old. He was educated here, he spoke English fluently, and he went to college in San Francisco. He was, for all rights and purposes, American in education and values and attitudes. But because he was born in Japan he was denied naturalized citizenship. For those reasons, we were taken to the second camp, this high security camp Tule Lake, in Northern California. What made this high security was they had three layers of barbed-wire fences, half a dozen tanks patrolling the perimeter, and machine guns aimed at us from the guard towers. The other irony of that is more than half of the people in those camps were children, like me. I was about five and a half years old at the time. My brother and my sister, even younger. So the majority of the people in the Tule Lake camp were youngsters.

As far as the questionnaires were concerned, did they have everybody fill those out or just from a certain age on — or both men and women, then?

It was everybody; everybody over the age of seventeen. Men or women, whatever age, citizen or immigrant. An 88 year old immigrant lady had to respond to those questions as did a seventeen year old girl! "Will you bear arms to defend this country?" being asked of a seventy year old immigrant lady, or asking a seventy year old immigrant lady "Will you swear your loyalty to the United States and forswear…" Now, she may have had a loyalty to the Emperor because that's where she was born and raised, and immigrated to this country and this country denied her naturalized citizenship, just because of who she was; a Japanese. She may have had some fond feelings and they're asking her to *forswear* that loyalty, eight-eight years old or seventy years old or whatever? And they won't accept her as a naturalized citizen? It was a preposterous position that these people were put in.

Has our Government — and maybe this is a naïve question — has our Government ever apologized for this action, for this behavior?

That's the other part of this story and that's the more shining, glorious part of this story. The war ended, we all came back and my parent's generation struggled to re-establish ourselves. But because they were so profoundly affected by that internment experience; and I must say I felt that same kind of impact that they felt initially; I was eight years old when we came out. I was able to understand by that time that we were in something like a prison. And we were in that prison because we were Japanese-Americans. And bad people go to prison. So there must be something bad about us. I felt ashamed, first and foremost for being Japanese and certainly I didn't want to talk about the fact that I was in internment camps. So when my friends in school would ask me where was I before I came back to Los Angeles, I would tell them, "I was far away." And they would say, "Where were you?" "I was at a place called Arkansas." I would try to slough it off.

For my parents, it was a very difficult thing to talk about. So that generation didn't talk about it. But as I grew up and others of my generation started to understand what that whole experience was, we became outraged — that initial outrage that is the arrogant, teenage thing of blaming your parents — but we matured and we realized that there is a system to this Government, where we can get redress and an apology for a mistake that was made by the Government. It began with my generation in 1970s, this movement to campaign for redress for the internment of Japanese-Americans. We did the fundraising, we did the organizing, and we did the building of coalitions with other groups. I think that came about because of our involvement in the civil rights movement in the 1960s. That made us aware of the importance of asserting the ideals of the system, particularly when they've been violated in terms of our own personal involvement. And so the redress campaign began with the generations that were children at the time of the internment and those that were born after the internment. But by the late 1970s there was this other extraordinary phenomenon of Japanese-Americans now in the Halls of Congress as Representatives and in the Senate. In the Senate there was Senator Daniel Inouye from Hawaii, a veteran of the 442nd, he lost his arm in Italy; he has an empty sleeve. He was a recipient of the Congressional Medal of Honor.

He was a true hero.

A true hero! There was another, Senator Spark Matsunaga. In the House of Representatives from San Jose there was Norman Mineta, who was Secretary of Commerce and the first Asian-American in the Cabinet of the United States. These people were in Congress at that time — that's remarkable. But it was even more unbelievable that thirty years after we were placed behind barbed-wire fences we had Japanese-Americans in the Halls of Congress. So the movement for redress began out of the community and from my generation. We were able to get that political leadership, from those elected officials that were already in Congress and it was spearheaded by these Japanese-American legislators. In 1988 President Ronald Reagan signed officially the Redress Bill. It took a long time, but that Bill said that there would be an official apology from the Government of the United States and a token redress payment of $20,000 dollars. That doesn't come close to what was lost in terms of dollars and cents in 1988 dollars, but it was a symbol of the Government's recompense for the damage that they had done.

Unfortunately, in our family the one that felt the pain and the sting of the internment the most was my father. He had passed on in 1979 and you had to be a survivor, you had to be alive at the time of the signing of that Bill. My Mother, as his Widow, could not get his portion of that $20,000 dollars. But this Government *did* make that apology. And it's a great commentary, an extraordinary commentary. No Government had apologized for a mistake that it'd made. So this is a very affirmative statement about this system: That through the system, via the process, by participating in the democratic process we can rectify a mistake that was committed by this Government. It's a shining commentary about our system and that's why we need good people to be participants. When some of my friends say, "Oh, my vote doesn't count, I'm not going to be a part of this system," it's *they* who are really the ones that sap away at what this system of Government should be. We have to take the responsibility for our own Government; by default they're giving it over to the exploiters and the corrupters.

You're the Chairman of the Board of the Japanese-American National Museum located in Los Angeles. I want to find out a little bit about the Museum and what your involvement is and what you're doing.

It's a relatively young museum, as museums go; there are museums that have been around for hundreds of years. Our museum has not only garnered attention, but — I pop my buttons a little bit — we've been praised and we've gotten some major recognition from throughout not only the country, but throughout the museum world. We opened our first building 1992 and because we are a history museum, we wanted to have our building make that statement. We were fortunate enough to find a building, a historic building in little Tokyo; the Japanese-American section of downtown Los Angeles in a former Buddhist temple that was built in 1925, but had been abandoned in 1970. We went in there and restored it and that became the first building. But we didn't stop there. We knew that we were going to grow, so we began the fundraising to build an expansion building and we set ourselves a goal of $45 million dollars to build an 85,000 thousand square foot expansion building. In January 1999 we opened that building and since then, our exhibits have traveled throughout the country. We did one titled "America's Concentration Camp" about the internment camp experience. That originated in Los Angeles and traveled to the Ellis Island Museum in New York and from there went to Atlanta, George to the Freeman Jewish Heritage Museum. The Jewish people are very much interested in this American experience as well. From there it went to the California Historical Society Museum in San Francisco, then to Little Rock, Arkansas. The mission of the Museum is to tell the story of the cultural and ethnic diversity of the United States from the perspective of the Japanese-American experience. Certainly that's a broad mission statement, because the Japanese-American community and the Japanese-American people are indeed changing. Now, a good number of Japanese-Americans are not "pure" Japanese-Americans so we want to tell that story as well. We are a future-oriented museum: Our first building is an historic building, but our second building is starkly modern and we want those two building to symbolize our pride in our heritage and our history. But the modern building symbolizes our view of the future, learning from our history, but looking to the future as a great challenge.

As a representative of the Museum you traveled to Washington, D.C. and you were at the White House for a special presentation, which you alluded to a little bit earlier. Can you tell a little bit more about this?

It was a profoundly moving experience. I didn't really talk about it, but despite all of the outrages of the internment experience, some extraordinary young men and women volunteered to fight for this country. They said, "I grew up pledging allegiance to the flag in school every day, and I meant it. Those are the ideals that I pledge allegiance to, not what the people are doing to me and family now, and by gum, I'm going to go out there and show them that those ideals I pledge allegiance to *are* valid." There was again another outrage, they were put in a segregated outfit of all Japanese-Americans and they were sent to Europe and a small number were sent into the Pacific Theatre. Talk about friendly fire. They were *really* in jeopardy in the Pacific Theatre. The 442nd Regimental Combat Team emerged as the *single most* decorated outfit to return back to the United States. The other irony from that period is the American outfit that opened the gates to the Dachau Concentration Camp, the Nazi death camp, was a Japanese-American outfit, the 522nd Field Artillery Battalion. This was hushed up and they were told not to talk about it until a white regiment came in. This information came out later in history. But the Japanese-Americans received the second highest medal at the time when they return from Europe, the Silver Star. Six years ago Congress requested the Pentagon to review the record of Asian-American soldiers from the Second World War, veterans who had received the Silver Star. After doing considerable research, the Pentagon said, "Indeed, there are twenty-two Asian-Americans who should have gotten the Medal of Honor," the highest military recognition that the Government can give. Twenty of those were Japanese-Americans. Of them, one is Senator Daniel Inouye.

Representing the Museum, I had the honor and the privilege of being there at the White House when President Bill Clinton awarded the Medal of Honor to seven surviving veterans; the others have passed on. Their widows, sons, or their grandchildren received the Medals of Honor in their name. It was deeply moving for me. Senator Inouye has an empty sleeve, but he's still vigorous. The other six were very feeble; one was on crutches, another had a cane and his steps were very unsteady — they were in their eighties. It was stirring in that they were getting the recognition and that they were still alive to do it. The following day the Pentagon inducted the recipients of the Medal of Honor into the Hall of Heroes and that evening there was celebratory reception. We heard not only from the recipients, but also from the widows and the family members of those who had passed on. It was a profoundly emotional experience and I feel very privileged and exhilarated to have been able to have been a part of that. That too is another commentary about the glory of this system. It was slow in happening, it was tardy, about fifty years too late and many of them were not able to receive it themselves. But it's happened and it was a profoundly moving experience.

Thank you for sharing that, I appreciate it. I understand that you ran for City Council in the 1970s. How did that come about and can you tell us how you got involved and where that's taken you in the meantime?

I think again that it's the internment experience that's behind the whole thing. My father, as I said earlier, deeply believed that we need to be participants in this democratic process. With his guidance, before I could even vote, he had volunteered me in the Adlai Stevenson campaign. I found it a lot of fun! Here are all these people who talk issues and ideas, but we also make signs and there are plenty of potato chips and Pepsi-cola — free! So, for a teenager it was fun experience, but also one that starts giving you an awareness about the importance of participation. So, I've been a volunteer in various campaigns.

In 1973 we had a mayoral election in Los Angeles and our City Councilman, Tom Bradley (the first African-American to be elected Mayor of the City of Los Angeles) and I was involved in his campaign, as was my Father. We had fundraisers for Councilman Bradley in our home. He was elected, which meant that there was this vacancy in the councilmatic seat that he had occupied. I never really planned to run for political office, but I am a political animal and I had been involved in various political campaigns. When that vacancy in my councilmatic district happened many of my political activist friends came up to me and said, "George, you ought to run for it. It's your district and you've got a track record in the political arena." I said, "Well, I've never been elected, I'm there as a volunteer." And they said, "No, you have a lot of supporters there and you have one great asset; you're known from your *Star Trek* association. We can build a campaign and a support base for you." They were very persuasive and, as I said, I am a political animal, so it was not an unattractive idea! They talked me into it. I did throw my hat into the ring and I must say I enjoyed it. It was a really invigorating, energizing activity to be offering yourself as a representative for the people in your district. To go door-to-door in your neighborhood, to hear what their concerns are, to know what issues concern them, and there's great diversity of opinions and sometimes conflict of issues and how to resolve them. That's the role of a politician and I found that engaging as well.

However, the very thing that they told me would be as asset also turned out to be a great difficulty — *Star Trek*. It was in reruns at that time and the local station that was running *Star Trek*, once the campaign was on, ran an episode in which "Sulu" was on the air for fourteen minutes; he was a part of the show, visible on the screen for fourteen minutes.

Somebody sat with a timer, apparently.

They do that — particularly lawyers! There were sixteen candidates running against me for that City Councilmatic seat; all sixteen

George Takei gives the famous Vulcan salutation at a *Star Trek* convention. PHOTO COURTESY OF ANTHONY WYNN.

of them demanded equal time for that station that was running *Star Trek*. Legally they had to give it to them. And so they had to give one whole boring night of time, fourteen minutes to sixteen candidates, who came on for those fourteen minutes to say, "My name is Joe Smith and I feel this way about education..." or "My name is Mary Jones and I feel this way about taxation..." They were able to talk as themselves, on issues, based on an equal time claim on my fourteen minutes as "Sulu" saying, "Aye, aye Sir, Warp Three" and piloting that starship. A fictional situation, fictional characters, words written by someone else; not my words! And that was supposed to serve as the equal-time basis for these candidates to talk as themselves.

How frustrating!

It was an *outrageous* situation. And, that station, in order to avoid giving a night a week to them, pulled *Star Trek* from being rerun. But the outrage of that is, I didn't become an actor to run for public office and actors make up a significant portion of the demographic of Los Angeles. The motion picture community should have a representative voice in the councils of Government. Because I, as an actor, chose to run for public office this station was forced to pull the rerun of *Star Trek.* I may be, as an individual, be willing to forego my residual payment, but because of a decision that I made I am imposing an economic penalty on my fellow actors; the people that wrote those scripts; the directors that directed them; and the residual payment makes up a significant portion of the annual income for people in my community. So I am imposing an economic penalty based on a political decision that I made, which was also unfair to my colleagues. Unfortunately, legally, that had to be inflicted on them. I felt terribly about that. There's a real inhibitor for people in my profession to exercise our full citizenship rights and responsibilities.

So in the intervening years it really hasn't changed. The rule still exists and that would happen again today?

It still exists and could happen today. People always cite Ronald Reagan. Well, Ronald Reagan — the bulk of his career was before 1960. It was since 1960 that the residual payment agreement between the producers and the Screen Actors Guild was signed. Very interestingly, Ronald Reagan is known in history as the President who opposed labor; particularly the Air Controllers strike when all the airports were practically shut down. Well, the very first Screen Actors Guild meeting that I attended was back in 1958 when I first joined the union. I went to my first meeting and the big issue being discussed there was whether the Screen Actors Guild should strike or not strike on the residual issue. I went to that meeting and the President of the union was leading us in a chant of, "Strike — Strike — Strike!" Guess who the President of the Screen Actors Guild was at that time? None other than that flaming labor leader: RONALD REAGAN, leading us in that chant! I wish I had a strip of that film. That's a piece of history! He was a labor leader as a President of the Screen Actors Guild and he was one who helped us establish residual payment rights.

Amazing.

Isn't that ironic?

Yes, very ironic. Well, let's go back a little bit; I'm sort of curious what your first inkling was that you were interested in the acting trade. How did you get involved, what was your first role?

My Mother says that I made my theatrical debut in the maternity ward! I don't think you become an actor. You are born with these instincts, I guess. I remember from the time I was a child I used to love to gather kids in my backyard and do playacting; in grammar school I was appearing in school skits; in junior high school drama clubs; high school plays and all of that. That organic part of me was there from way back. I can't say I found my acting interest at "that point" or at "that age," it was there all the time. However, parents don't want to encourage that, as a profession, they say its fine to be interested in the arts, but not to commit your whole life to it as your life's calling. So my Father kind of guided me into my other interest in architecture. Like a good son I began my college career as a student of architecture at the University of California at Berkeley. But all during that time — I was an architecture student for two years — that gnawing "I woulda, coulda, shoulda" was there. Finally, I had to be true to myself and I decided "I'm going to be an actor. I'm going to give myself the opportunity to really be who I am." I guess if there was any point in time, it was two years after I'd been a student in architecture, I decided I've got to be true to myself.

What was your professional debut?

I switched from UC Berkeley to UCLA because they have a fine theater arts department there. I was doing a student production at UCLA and I was seen by a casting director from Warner Bros. studio. He plucked me out of that student production and plunked me into my first major feature film, *Ice Palace*, starring none other than Richard Burton and Robert Ryan. Two weeks on location in exotic Alaska! And two months back at the studio — a real big major studio, Warner Bros. — working with Richard Burton. Breaking into the movies was, to me, a piece of cake! So it was from the classroom stage to a major studio soundstage.

Around this time, as well, you appeared on stage and — I think I'm right in saying — it might have been your first professional stage production, *Fly Blackbird!*

It was a little bit after *Ice Palace*, it was a civil rights musical written by a professor at UCLA and the music written by Dance Department music professor Jackson Hatch; a collaboration between the two of them. The civil rights movement was something that I was a part of as a student at that time, so it was a kind of living reality in theatrical form. The story was about a group of young people in the civil rights movement and I was the only Asian-American in that group of African-Americans and whites involved in civil rights. It was a musical and it was great fun, enormously successful in Los Angeles, and we did that for almost a year. I don't think quite a year, about ten-eleven months.

Then it moved on to Broadway?

Yes, a Broadway producer bought it and — it was a woman she was going to produce it in New York. She said, "There are no guarantees, but you all were wonderful here in Los Angeles. If you come to New York and audition you will be considered very favorably." There were no guarantees, but it was very persuasive guidance. So a good number of us, more than half of the cast traveled on our own to New York. That was kind of wonderful, because, a lot of aspiring actors go to New York just by themselves, solitary, to take on the big city. What made it wonderful for us was we were already a family, a theatrical family, having worked together and lived together for about ten-eleven months in Los Angeles. We traveled together to New York and we were kind of huddled — it was in the wintertime, so it was cold — we did literally huddle and we auditioned. However, it was a whole different story. There's a whole kind of New York mentality and we were "Hollywood" actors, with a little sneer. "They're not *real* actors; they act in front of the camera." There was only one of us from the Los Angeles production that was cast. It was devastating because we thought it was going to be a piece of cake. My character was named "George." The character was patterned after me. We had a proprietarial sense about the roles that we'd played. I'm eternally grateful that we did have a "family" to cling on to in our dejection, disappointment; in our almost suicidal condition! In that big, bad, cold city; we're Southern Californians and there we are in December in frigid New York. It was a traumatic experience.

Did you stay on in New York?

I did. We were determined! Classic struggling actors — you load trucks, you cater parties, you type labels in publishing houses — whatever odd jobs are available so you can go and audition for plays. It was a classic struggling young actor's existence.

There's such a misconception, isn't there, about actors. There's sort of the thought that all actors are rich and...

(Laughs)

**They have multimillion dollar contracts, are doing big movies —
but in reality, that's not quite the case is it? Aren't the majority of
actors *working* actors?**

It's just like life, you know. The Ted Turners and the Bill Gates are
that small fraction of society, aren't they? They're the ones who get all
the publicity, but in reality, most of us live "normal" lives. Yes, when
we get paid we get paid well. But then there are all the non-paid
months in our lives that it's got to be spread over. Yes, it's a distorted
picture that people have of actors. Yes, there are the Tom Cruises
and there are the Tom Hankses who get those multimillion dollar
contracts. Mel Gibson got twenty-five million dollars for *Patriot*, and
that's what gets publicity. But the rest of us are there as working actors
and a good number, the majority — I've read recently that something like eighty percent of the membership of the Screen Actors
Guild — make less than ten thousand dollars a year, which means
that they all have other jobs. The classic syndrome for most actors
is that they work as waiters. In Southern California when someone
tells me that they're an actor, I tell them, "How nice — what restaurant
do you work in?"

**About acting itself, do you subscribe to a particular school of
acting. Do you consider yourself a Method actor, or perhaps a
Playhouse actor. How do you describe yourself?**

At the time I was a student actor, the big heroes were Marlon
Brando, Montgomery Clift, James Dean, and people like that who
come from the Actors Studio background where Stanislavski is the
"Bible" and Lee Strasberg was the "god" and they were the successful
"disciples." So the Method acting style was the thing that was so popular then. When you work with people like Richard Burton and you see
where he doesn't have to go through all those tortured contortions in
order to get into character — because he knows the character here
in the heart and intellectually, and because he's prepared. When the
director says, "Action!," he can do it appropriately for the camera or
when he's onstage and the curtain goes up he can generate it on cue
without having to go through that kind of contortion. I've been a great
admirer of what Brando did in films like *A Street Car Named Desire*
or *On the Waterfront* and I see the result of the torture that he went
through to get there. But I worked with Richard Burton and I see how
he's able to deliver, without that, by doing the homework and getting
the kind of classic training and having all the techniques of acting as
well. I heard a quote when Peter O'Toole was being interviewed. They

asked him, "That particular scene from that movie was *so* moving, how did you do that? And he said, "Well, I checked to see where the key light was and I began like *this* and on that moment when I wanted to get that glitter in my eyes, I looked up at my key light and I knew that the glitter was there." That's what affected the audience. There's a technique as well. So, rather than subscribing to any one set school of acting, or one set philosophy of acting — you learn from everything. In college I learned about the Delsarte method, which was a series of about eighty different poses. When you want to suggest sadness, there was a pose; and happiness; there's all these poses! Number 1, 2, 3, 4, 5 — the whole gamut of successful acting styles and philosophies and you take from it. I do use a little bit of the Stanislavski philosophy and I do use a little bit of the Delsarte, which is what Peter O'Toole is using; very technical. Just going and catching the key light in your eyes. And Burton's tremendous discipline and preparation before you can go on stage or in front of the camera.

One of your most famous film roles is in *The Green Berets*, of course, with John Wayne. What can you tell about your experience working on that movie?

John Wayne is an icon. He's gone now, but he's still an icon. He defines an image of what American macho manhood is all about. I grew up watching John Wayne movies and when my agent told me that John Wayne wants me for this movie he's doing, I was blown away! You never think of an icon and yourself together. When my agent said that he wanted to meet me, I was just flabbergasted and on cloud nine, but also a little terrified. This was again at Warner Bros. studio. I went for the interview with John Wayne and there he was, exactly like he was on film. He walked the same way, he looked exactly the same. That's not surprising, but I kind of thought that there might be some adjustment to make. When he started to talk to me, he talked just like John Wayne! I always knew him as talking to John Agar or Ward Bond like that. But he was talking to *me* with that same John Wayne flint and that pace that he has in his speech. It was a really strange experience and he said, "I like what you do on *Star Trek*." He'd seen me on *Star Trek* and that was why he asked me. In fact, the character that I played in that film was named "Captain Nim." On the set — we shot that on location in Georgia — he kept calling me "Captain Sulu." So he gave me my promotion before Starfleet did!

That's great!

(Laughs)

This leads into your role — I guess it's sort of seen as a break-through role — on *Star Trek*, of course, the role of "Sulu" in the original *Star Trek* series. It's the first time that an Asian-American appeared in a weekly television series in a non-stereotypical role. How did Gene Roddenberry come to consider you for the role?

It's Gene's vision — the bigness of his vision — and the bigness

George Takei signs autographs at a *Star Trek* convention in Dallas, Texas. PHOTO COURTESY OF ANTHONY WYNN.

of his courage and adventuresome-ness. Television at that time was characterized as "the vast wasteland" and indeed it was. It was all pap that was flowing through the "boob tube" to use another term. Gene Roddenberry thought, "Here is this powerful medium called "television" being wasted like that, I'm going to do something to give it more substance; at least make the effort." And he came up with a show — he knew that you couldn't deal with substantive issues on television and so he thought on that a lot and he came up with the idea of a science fiction series where maybe with the overlay of science fiction he might be able to address issues and get it past the so-called sensors in television program practices. So he came up with this idea, crafted a show, presented it to the networks, and was a good enough salesman to sell it. In essence, he saw the Starship *Enterprise* as a metaphor for Starship Earth and he saw that for this Starship to survive, it's got to find its strengths, its intelligence, and its survivability in its pluralism; strength in its pluralism. In order to communicate that, he wanted the crew of this Starship Earth to reflect the diversity and the capability of that diversity on the ship. The role of "Uhura" was specifically to be an African-American. In the pilot it was a man, Lloyd Haynes played that role, but when the series sold Lloyd Haynes became unavailable because he got *Room 222*, so Nichelle [Nichols] was cast. My character was specifically Asian, to represent the great diversity of this planet and that was in important point that he wanted to make. I was lucky enough to be considered, and cast, in that role.

The original series was cancelled after three seasons and I guess everyone sort of thought it was dead and gone at that point?

Not everyone. Dedicated fans glommed on to the show and saw that it was a substantive show with a philosophic approach, good science fiction, but was dealing also with issues like the Vietnam War, or the civil right movement, or the hippie movement. So those people — who are the ones that organized the "*Star Trek* Lives" campaign — it wasn't dead they said. It lives!

And that was how the convention phenomenon started in the early 1970s?

Right, in the early 1970s.

***Star Trek* then returned in syndication and also picked up steam that way.**

Right.

Then came the films, you returned...

But the films came as a result of that organizing. The "*Star Trek* Lives" campaign. It was started by a housewife in Los Angeles by the name of Bjo Trimble. It was her organizing skills and the network that built the movement, and the way in which they campaigned by putting on demonstrations in front of the NBC studios in Los Angeles and Rockefeller Center in New York that got a lot of media coverage. Certainly the *Star Trek* conventions helped her organize. It was because of that kind of activism that *Star Trek* came back as a major motion picture in 1979.

Was that a unique experience for you? What was it like to get back with the original cast again? You'd seen each other at conventions,

but to actually be back on the set, on the bridge of the *Enterprise* after those ten years — what was that like?

That first day is unforgettable. Frankly, we never thought that it would actually happen. Because of the fan campaign, they initially, I think it was 1974, they said they're going to begin doing *Star Trek* as a TV series again. We were given a start date of February 1974, if I

George Takei discusses *Star Trek*. PHOTO COURTESY OF ANTHONY WYNN.

recall correctly and as we got closer to February of 1974, they kept pushing it back: To April, then June, then maybe in the fall for a mid-season replacement. Then that idea was dropped and then we started hearing about a Movie of the Month; that was the programming style that was popular at that time. We thought that might be interesting. We could get a two hour chunk to tell a story and there would be a bigger budget for a project like that — and that came and went. There were so many ideas that came and went; we were getting a little bit cynical. Finally, when they said, "We signed Robert Wise," that legendary director, to direct the first *Star Trek* movie and there was a contract in hand — otherwise he could sue Paramount — we knew that this time they meant it. Even then there was a little doubt; maybe they're going to pay him off or whatever. But then they started contract negotiations with us and then we had wardrobe fittings and all that, so it became more and more real. But we really didn't fully believe it until that first day when we were on that set, that circular configuration, and all of us — familiar people from ten years back — were there together on that set working together, playing the roles that we'd played. It was magical. It was an absolutely unforgettable morning when we all gathered there.

It was the beginning of so many films; six motion pictures in all with the original cast. *Star Trek VI*, I know, you're particularly proud of and received a well-deserved promotion.

At long last! (Laughs)

You became "Captain Sulu." The opening of the movie is the *Excelsior* with "Captain Sulu" and the crew, how did you feel when you saw that for the first time?

We had a cast and crew screening and we shot the film, we knew the story; and yet it was *exhilarating!* You can get a feeling from watching the film, even it is with an in-house audience — cast and crew — that it was a great film. Because of that, I wanted to see it with a real audience. I knew the manager of the Chinese Theatre where it played and I got him to sneak me into a Saturday night screening the first week and I sneaked in and I was standing in the back of the theater when the titles came on and then the first scene comes on. The first shot of "Sulu" in the Captain's seat and the cheering that went up in that theater was beyond music. It was like a missile being shot off! It was a fantastic sound; it almost brought the theater down. The cheering that went on throughout that film! *Star Trek* fans who show up on the first Saturday night are very vocal, very physically demonstrative, and when "Sulu" rescues "Captain Kirk" and the cheering that goes on; it was fantastic. I wanted to have that experience of seeing it with a real audience at the legendary Chinese Theatre.

That was the beginning of what's almost become the "Captain Sulu" phenomenon.

(Laughs)

There have been books and audio recordings; then "Captain Sulu" was brought back for a special 30th anniversary guest appearance on *Star Trek Voyager*, an episode called "Flashback."

It's in the classic tradition of *Star Trek*, you know *Star Trek* fans are activists. It came back as a movie series because of the activism of this housewife, Bjo Trimble, in Los Angeles who had this impossible dream, this campaign, to make a major studio response to fans. But that's been the whole history of *Star Trek*; it's been the fans that gave life to the extension of *Star Trek* as a movie series. They were going to do the sixth movie, *Star Trek VI: The Undiscovered Country*, which was going to be released on the 25th anniversary in 1991. But by that time, the salaries of a couple of the actors had gotten "galactic" and the producer was trying to craft a way to bring it in on a more modest budget. The idea that he came up with was to do a Starfleet Academy

George Takei talks about his promotion to "Captain Sulu." PHOTO COURTESY OF ANTHONY WYNN.

story, a flashback to the days when our characters were back in the Academy, when of course we were much younger. So his idea was to cast re-cast all the characters with younger actors who resemble us. So he was planning on celebrating the 25th anniversary of *Star Trek* with actors who were never there at all! Well, when the fans got wind of that, again, they started writing in tidal wave proportions and Paramount got that message and that producer was off the lot. They came up with the right script, the best script: *Star Trek VI: The Undiscovered Country*. So activism and fan campaigns have directed, shaped, and formed this *Star Trek* phenomenon.

I want to get your impression of Asian-Americans in television and film today. Do you think there's adequate representation currently on television?

Well, you know, the word "adequate" is the key in your question. Certainly when I started out we were infrequently visible on the media and when we were, it was usually rather insignificant or significant unattractive roles. You had the villains, the servant, or the buffoon. So we've come a long way from then. However, last fall the networks announced their schedule of new shows for the new season and when we saw that, we were shocked. Because we should be aware of the rich diversity of America today and any major city, whether it's Kansas City or Portland, or certainly Los Angeles, or New York or Seattle or Miami; diversity is what defines America. America is on the cutting of the rest of the world in terms of defining our diversity. And yet the new programs that the networks announced were totally devoid of that. All the leads and the supporting roles, regulars, were all white. We began a campaign to say that the media has a responsibility — not for affirmative action or bending over backwards — but to reflect the reality of American society today. From the Asian-American perspective, particularly, what we underscored was: We've got many series located in Hawaii, all the way to when we first started and I did a lot of guest shots on *Hawaiian Eye*, a Warner Bros. series, and since then we've had *Hawaii 5-0, Native Son, Magnum P-I,* one after the other. Now let's look at the reality of Hawaii; Hawaii is a majority Asian-American. The movers and shakers in Hawaii are Asian-American. The Governor, the bank head, the hospital head, the police chief; all the people who make decisions are a majority Asian-American and yet that's never been reflected in the Hawaii locale TV series. The perspective of the TV series is defined by the lead. The story's always told from the vantage-point of the lead character, and leads have always been white male, not even white female. That's the history of it. When you do a series locale, something called *L.A. Law* or *L.A. Doctors* and it still portrays an unreal, absolutely an unbelievably white cast, it almost invites criticism. I think the African-American presence is a bit more visible, but still we need the perspective of series as determined by the lead role. To reflect the diversity of America we need to do some improvement there. The African-Americans have made remarkable progress, however, and compared to that Asian-Americans are way behind.

Do you foresee any improvement in future television?

Because of the noise that has been made, the networks have been embarrassed into adding a V.P. with the title of "Vice President of Diversity," and it's been a kind of artificial toe dance, but they have added diversity to some of the shows that formerly were just pure white. For example, *The West Wing* added the African-American Assistant to the President, that young character. That character was not there when they announced the series. They've added other characters to other series, but they've been afterthoughts, after they've been reminded that they're remiss.

I want to thank you — it's been wonderful and so much interesting information and experiences you've passed on and talked about. I really appreciate it.

Well, I've enjoyed this time chatting with you!

George Takei attended a special screening of *Star Trek VI: The Undiscovered Country* in Portland, Oregon to raise funds and awareness for Parkinson disease treatment and research. The following morning, he trekked to the television studio to sit with me for a ninety-minute interview. One moment stands out in relief in the studio prior to the cameras rolling. As we briefly discussed the various topics that I wanted to cover during our time together, I said, "As you can see, I want to talk a lot about your early life and career; I'm only going to ask a few *Star Trek* questions."

"Oh, thank *God* for that! he guffawed, and that unmistakable deep laugh filled the soundstage.

Since my interview with George, he made the decision to "come out" publicly as a gay man, giving an exclusive interview to Alexander Cho, editor of *Frontiers* magazine. He told Cho, "I've been 'open,' but I have not talked to the press." He continued, saying, "It's not really coming out, which suggests opening a door and stepping through. It's more like a long, long walk through what began as a narrow corridor that starts to widen." George and his partner Brad have now been together for more than twenty years. They were married on September 14, 2008 in West Hollywood, California, during the short window of time when same sex marriages were permitted in the state. Fellow *Star Trek* actors Walter Koenig [Chekov] and Nichelle Nichols [Uhura] served as best man and matron of honor, respectively, at the ceremony.

George has worked on a number of projects in the intervening years; including a lead role in the play *Equus,* guest-starring parts in several television series, regular appearances as the host on Howard Stern's satellite broadcasts, an appearance on *Celebrity Apprentice*, and work with anti-discrimination organizations such as the Human Rights Campaign. He returned to the role of "Sulu" to star in an episode of the internet series *Star Trek: New Voyages*, written especially for him by original *Star Trek* series writer D.C. Fontana, entitled "World Enough and Time."

A graduate of the State University of New York (SUNY), Oswego with a degree in communications and theater, Robin Curtis got her start performing in regional theater productions in upstate New York. That, in turn, led to her pursuit of work in New York City, where she landed a role in the musical *City Suite* and signed with her first theatrical agent. Not long after, a commercial for Oil of Olay introduced her to the camera, which led her to Los Angeles and work in television and film.

Robin's career in Hollywood began with the television film role alongside John Ritter, continuing as she landed a guest star spot on the television show *Knight Rider* and other shows, before winning the audition for a Vulcan character named "Saavik" in *Star Trek III: The Search for Spock.* While her association with *Star Trek* has brought her substantial recognition, it doesn't define her as a person. Robin has incredible intelligence, wit, and an infectious positive energy.

I first met Robin when she came to Oregon to appear at the first-ever *Star Trek* convention in Southern Oregon, held in the theater town of Ashland. She returned a couple of years later to headline a celebration in Portland marking a major anniversary of the franchise. She stands as one of the most professional, yet most accessible and down-to-earth *Star Trek* actors I've known.

To start off with, I'd like to hear a little bit about your childhood and where were you born.
I was born in New York Mills, New York, which is small village outside of Utica, New York. The best way to qualify it is to say that the mayor pumps gas at a filling station on Main Street! I had a very

Robin Curtis

"Where Were You When We Cast The Winds of War*?"*

idyllic upbringing, very sweet and generous, and I had very loving parents. Remember the moment in *Big* when Tom Hanks wants to go back and he offers Elizabeth Perkins the choice to go back with him and she says, "Oh, God, no — I couldn't go back and relive all of that again." For me, I would have been happy to go back to my childhood. It was quite lovely and I didn't suffer the kinds of disappointments and frustrations that most teenagers, or a lot of young people, go through with their families. I was pretty much a fan of my folks throughout my high school and college career, and beyond.

Do you have any brothers and sisters?

I do. I have two brothers, an older brother and a younger brother, which is a super position for the middle child who is a girl. They say middle children suffer, but I didn't lack for attention from all angles. I live near my older brother now. I'm in Upstate New York and I'm just south of Syracuse, in another small village, and I moved to this location because he lived here.

What kind of work did your parents do? Were they involved in the entertainment field at all?

My mother, yes, to some extent because she was a musician; and I suppose you could say my father was, although it wasn't his vocation it was his avocation. He was often the master of ceremonies at most social events with relationship to his work or country club membership — and when I say country club — please, please imagine something in the most modest sense. You know, an old farm converted to a golf course, that sort of thing. It was a very low key situation. My father was a very avid golfer as is my younger brother, so that part of lives — when I was a little older, in high school — was very significant. It was a big part of their social life, if you will. Anyway, my mother was a musician and performed every Sunday in church and conducted concerts at Christmas and that sort of thing; she accompanied soloists throughout the community. She was very active in the community in Utica. So that's where I got my love of music.

Do you sing? Are you musical yourself?

I do and yes, I am. I did the church choir, the school choirs, sang for weddings, that sort of thing. Music is really what got me on-stage; musical theatre. Once I ventured beyond that it was quite scary actually, those many years ago. Music, though, was really the foundation upon which I grew to love performing. I was very fortunate to be a big fish in a little pond. It was a bit different when I got into college; more competitive. I frankly don't know how it is I ever sought acting as a profession because I'm not competitive, I'm not aggressive, and I really would rather not knock on a door, and have never knocked on a door where I wasn't expected or invited. You know the myth is — or what people choose to believe is — that you have to love or want it more than anything. I didn't, I just didn't. I don't know whether that was partly survival or just a well-balanced approach toward life. You know, my career was never *all*. Not even close. Maybe perhaps that's why I didn't have mega-success. I've always wondered about that, about ambition; just how important it is. I have standards and I work hard, but I wouldn't call myself ambitious.

After college how did you find your way into show business? Did you start out in New York City?

I did and it was a very quick process of elimination; I didn't know how to do anything else. A dear female friend who was a year ahead of me in college, we did our last summer of dinner theatre in the Finger Lakes region, said, "Look, I'm going to go to New York. I've waited tables for a year in Syracuse and I've had it. I'm going to New York, why don't you come with me?" With the encouragement of another good friend who had already gone ahead to the city and had achieved a modicum of success in soap operas, a guy friend, invited me to take advantage of whatever he might have to offer to help me get started. So off I went! But you know, it wasn't something I set out to do. It was really kind of something that presented itself and I stepped forward.

Within months of arriving in New York I got an agent and began to audition for the camera which was a completely foreign object to me, and a foreign medium, and it took a while to get the hang of it because I was behaving as if I were on-stage and communicating to a big theatre. I had to learn to take everything down; way, way down to that kind of DeNiro method of acting level. (Laughs) Not something I was familiar with at all! It took me a while to get the hang of it, but within the first year of being in New York I got a commercial and I was off and running. It was simply luck and the acquaintance of certain friends, and the maintaining of those friendships beyond college that helped make all of that happen. I look back and call some people my "angels" because they stepped up and invited me to participate in something at a given moment in time and just by saying, "Yes" I was able to be in something four weeks later that somebody stepped into and saw in that moment in time and said, "Hey, would you like to be my agent?" It was these kinds of events that occurred and really it shouldn't be that easy! There's supposed to be more suffering. (Laughs) Everybody said that you have to suffer and I didn't suffer too badly. The rejection didn't affect me too much, either. I looked at it as if it were all a big pie and there were little pieces for everybody. If you have endurance, some tenacity, and just a little bit of talent — you'll work! At least that was my approach and it worked.

I was in New York for about three years, but it became clear that the kinds of auditions I needed to be on more frequently were happening in Los Angeles, not New York. So I very begrudgingly went off for a trial six month period and was ready to wrap it up and come home. I wanted nothing more than to come back home to New York and the East Coast. Then I got my first job, a movie of the week with John Ritter. That happened at the tail-end of my six month trial, and that was that — I couldn't in good conscience leave.

That was the movie *In Love with an Older Woman*?

That's good! You do your research well. Interestingly enough, the director on that film works a great deal now. His name is Jack Bender. He's directed a lot of episodes of *Lost* and other TV series. When John Ritter died, it brought a lot of memories back to me from that time.

Did you work with John a lot in the movie?

I did not. I only had two scenes with him and they were lovely, he was terrific, and the whole experience was just fantastic for my first time on film. It was a great way to kind of break in. The very next thing that I got was a *Knight Rider*. There I was, running all over the soundstage and very close-by locations with David Hasselhoff in that crazy car. Just one by one, little by little the guest appearances came and more commercials. I had already established myself as a pretty decent commercial actress in New York. That was important to do in L.A. or I wouldn't have been able to survive financially without getting a job of some kind. Thank goodness that I did have one of the best agencies in L.A. as my commercial agents, so they were a steady and supportive source of work for me throughout the time that I lived there.

I think I read that you did more than a hundred commercials?

It was something like that. I've tried to count, but it's difficult when you look back. I didn't do many; I didn't do hundreds, but I was one of those commercial actors that worked regularly and steadily. Three national commercials a year, approximately, but very rarely did I get a bomb that never ran or turned into anything; and conversely, I never got one of the ones that ran for *years* and made me $80,000 thousand dollars a year. But I was enormously grateful that it was a steady line of work for me.

My only rule was that I didn't do commercials for anything that went up an orifice! (Laughs) They could go down an orifice, just not up. They make people look so damned unattractive when they put anything to do an antihistamine or a nasal decongestant in…but look, who are we kidding here? If someone had offered me a hemorrhoid commercial or a post-nasal drip remedy, I'd have lowered my standards and done it! You're always so grateful for work; I don't think anybody with a healthy approach to the whole thing says "no" to work. And if you allow the idea to come in that work you've done is going to harm you in the future, then it probably will. I just never entertained those ideas. How can you fault somebody for wanting to pay their bills, anyway? Toward the end I did voice over work as well, but it never came to be a big source of income or a big aspect of my career. But I enjoyed it; that's why I mention it.

Your breakthrough role came with *Star Trek* when you were cast as "Saavik." How did that come about?

It was a very gentle and unexpected process. I went over to Paramount in 1982, in the first couple of months of that year. I had a general reading with Elza Bergeron who was the casting director at Paramount at that time. I remember when I walked in and she said to me, "Where were you when we cast *The Winds of War?*" That was a very nice thing for her to say in her assessment of me; her first impression of me. I made a big one — and that's good. You just hope that you make a memorable impression on casting directors. It may not always be a favorable one, but you do want them to remember you. Her comment really started us off on a very nice foot. More than a year later, a year and several months later, she remembered me from that meeting and invited me to meet her and Stuart Jensen, who by this time was also working for Paramount in the casting department. So I went to the meeting with them over a part the name of which I didn't know, nor the character's relationship to the plot; the project I didn't know. I was simply told to go take a meeting about a part in a film. I learned that it was a *Star Trek* film, but I had no idea what the character was. I remember saying, off-handedly, that I hoped it was an alien character.

So you were familiar with *Star Trek*?

A little bit. My brother watched it when I was young, very young. So I had that and just kind of the "iconic" knowledge: "Beam Me Up, Scotty" — that type of thing. I don't know that I actually saw an episode where he said it, but I had heard people say it.

I'm not sure that the phrase was actually ever used, in those words, on the show!

Interesting! Well, I wasn't a science fiction fan so I didn't seek out the reruns or know the films at all; I just remembered it from when it was first on television in the 1960s. I was young and I remember thinking that Captain Kirk always had women around him, I was very locked

A publicity photo of Robin Curtis. PHOTO COURTESY OF ROBIN CURTIS.

in to the whole female-male dynamic on the series and how romantic and lusty it was. As you can see, I was too young to appreciate the philosophy and all the marvelous ideas that Gene Roddenberry was trying to get across in his stories.

Back at the audition, I thought I would want to play an alien because I wasn't sure that if I was in some kind of preposterous futuristic other-planet kind of experience in the storyline that I could take it seriously if I were human. So that's what I was really thinking there! I thought it would be easier to go along and play pretend future if I were an alien. The meeting itself was brief, sweet, and nice; then they invited me back the very next day to meet Leonard Nimoy. That was the thing, I think, that made the difference. He and I had a very nice conversation and he asked if he could record the conversation with a video camera; I told him, "No problem." The relaxed nature of our meeting was recorded on film then he asked if I would read for him the material and he gave me some sense of what this character was about. I remember he used the phrase, "She has a thousand years of wisdom behind the eyes" with regard to the character's Vulcan nature. That stayed with me. I learned her name was "Lt. Saavik" and I didn't know the character, but at that point they were willing to give me more information. Up to that point it had all been very secretive.

I went out to the waiting room and studied some of the scenes between Kirk's son David's character and mine, and then went back in to read with Leonard. Again, this was all recorded. I only mention that, Tony, because the more common experience is to go back again and again. The room becomes more crowded, you aren't introduced to anyone and you are expected to re-create what you did the first time on the second visit; and the same on the third, fourth, and fifth times. It's generally a very repetitive and cumulatively very stressful process because the stakes seem higher each time, the room is filled with more bodies that you are not familiar with and it all seems very menacing and frightening; and you're just desperately trying to bring them what they want, give them what they want. All of that was eliminated by Leonard's use of the camera in that first meeting. At the end of my first meeting with him he shook my hand at the door of the office and I'll never forget what he said. He said, "I have no doubt that you can do this role. Now it's up to the powers that be."

I never went back again until the screen test. That was just about the most unusual thing I've ever encountered, frankly, and I've never encountered it since. Granted, I've not met with a lot of "A" directors, either; but you normally go for more than one meeting to get to a screen test in a major film when you're an unknown actor. Leonard saved me a great deal of wear and tear, and I enjoyed the screen test and was led to think that it was just an exercise in appearing to be fair — if I didn't fall down terribly, I was going to get the part. And I did.

This opened a whole new chapter for me, in that I didn't know what I had done that *worked* — because I didn't feel a kinship with Vulcans at all. I was a bit freaked out that I had been hired to do a job that I really didn't have the ability to do. It didn't come naturally to me at all to be self-controlled. I felt very robotic and it felt very unnatural; it felt strange. I remember shaking Leonard's hand the first day when work began and told, "You seem to think I know what I'm doing, but I don't!" He promised that he would guide me every step of the way and he did. I'm forever grateful for that. He directed me very myopically and that was fine with me! Some actors might be offended by the director giving them line readings or taking them aside before every scene; but I'm not one them.

You have no idea where your career is going to take you. I was joking with you earlier, you're just so grateful for work that you take a job with enthusiasm and gratitude that you're working at all and you're able to be a professional in your chosen profession. *Star Trek* for me has always stood oddly separate from my other work. I still to this day don't feel that I conquered that genre or that character. But I must say, that was just the first eight weeks of my experience with *Star Trek*. All the weeks and years since then have been so joyful. I have so loved meeting people from all over the world; I have loved the camaraderie and the opportunity to go out and meet people in the fandom of science fiction. It's been a privilege to do that and it's rewarded me on so many levels; there's too many to mention. My point is, the original experience was an acting job and I played a Vulcan — who would ever think that Robin Curtis, who cried at McDonalds commercials, would play a Vulcan? It's interesting to reflect on that, but the experience that ensued has far outweighed those original impressions.

Did the cast welcome you aboard?

They were always there to extend some encouragement to me or give a supporting word. They were just great! You know the people I'm talking about, like George Takei, Walter Koenig, Jimmy Doohan, Nichelle Nichols, and DeForest Kelley. They're all lovely people. I have to say, that I didn't really get to know Bill Shatner very well at all, because he was just…well, *separated* from everyone and was a little bit elusive. The others are all just great people, so approachable and very friendly; and certainly have been very kind to me.

Do you think there was added pressure on you knowing that another actress had already played the character?

None! Nope, that never factored in. It weighed on my mind only before the whole job began only because I don't want to think in my life that my fortune comes as the result of someone else's misfortune. Once I was able to ascertain to my satisfaction that it was Kirstie Alley's choice to do other things and wasn't interested in returning to *Star Trek*, I was at peace about it. Very wonderful things were happening in her career at the time so I was happy for her; I was happy for both of us! From that point on, from the point when the part had to be recast; Leonard Nimoy and Harve Bennett, the producer, took the tack that in their minds the character simply didn't exist before this moment. Leonard didn't make me feel, even for a second, that I was fulfilling someone else's beginnings or template for the character. And frankly, he didn't direct me even remotely like Nicholas Meyer directed Kirstie; so I think he chose the right route.

Was it easier when you came back to do *Star Trek IV: The Voyage Home?*

I think it was a little easier because I was a year and a half older and a little more relaxed with everyone; and also a little more practiced in that style of acting. But the militaristic bearing and the evenly cadenced sound of the language was always foreign to me. The characters in *Star Trek* don't speak in fits and starts; everything is well-pronounced and evenly distributed, there's no stuttering, no variance, no up and down the way there is in real life. So the more you practice, hopefully the better you get at controlling that tendency. A straight line across the heart monitor has never been me! I have a lot of enthusiasm and excitement about the most ordinary things.

***Star Trek III* gave you the opportunity to work with some interesting actors; one of them was Merritt Butrick who played Kirk's son, "Dr. David Marcus."**

A very talented chameleon and just a gifted individual; he was a very bright and witty young man. His death was a horrible loss before his time. He really was incredible to watch and to work opposite. I couldn't get over how he could transform himself between characters. It's such a shame that he's gone, I think he was only twenty-nine years old. I remember he was very playful, a very creative guy and I didn't allow myself to really enjoy him until close to the end of filming. I was so anxious about doing a good job that I wanted to be perceived as someone very serious. But, after several weeks, his tendency to sing and play and joke around finally broke down my reserve. I was so saddened to learn about his illness that he died of AIDS. You know, that was back in a time when all of that was kept very secretive and I felt badly that his family didn't allow there to be a memorial of any kind. It's a double whammy. Not only have you lost a friend, but now you have the family's attitudes about how he died coloring the loss and acting as if there's something to be ashamed of — when actually there's nothing to be ashamed about.

You're been involved in many causes over the years. Am I right to think you worked helping raise money and awareness for AIDS research?

The picketing I've done and the activism I've participated in has to do with either one of two subjects: choice and anything related to planning parenthood, and AIDS; whether it's AIDS awareness or money to fight AIDS, etc. There were times that I did the walks, the talks, held hands, blockaded, etc. for one of those two causes. I'm a liberal girl!

That's fine with me! Now, you later returned to *Star Trek* and you were in a two-part episode in *Star Trek: The Next Generation*. How did that come about and how much did your previous *Star Trek* experience help you in getting the part?

You know, that's quite a common question that I get asked at conventions. You might think there was a connection between *Star Trek III* and *IV* and *The Next Generation* — but there isn't. Not once in my auditions for the part on *The Next Generation* was I acknowledged as someone who had a history with *Star Trek*, which I found to be odd. I realized, from the first audition, that they weren't going to treat me any differently than anyone else who was being considered. I finally did get "The Gambit," a two-parter; but it wasn't handed to me — I had to audition. I had to go in for a callback and it was very tough while I was waiting to hear back.

When I did get the job, I believe the only time I met producer Rick Berman and Michael Piller was when we were all escorted over in a van from the set to their offices in another building. We were simply brought up there to have our "look" examined. It occurred to me as we were all escorted around that no one ever said to us, "Well, hello! Welcome; it's really great to have you guys on board." I went over with Julie Caitlin Brown and the other guest stars and it struck me as to how impolite the whole process was. It felt like we were made to stand around like set pieces and commented upon. But that said, I was absolutely thrilled to get the role and have such a meaty part! I worked for three weeks and to finally work with Patrick Stewart was really exciting. Those shows, I believe, really do hold up over time.

You spent twenty years in Hollywood and one of your last roles, before returning back East, was in a film called *Making Contact*. You called that film "a fitting finale to your career." Why did you say that and what led you make changes to your life at that point?

The film was something that friends of mine created and produced, and generated the money for. They hired me, among other friends of theirs, to make the film with them. So it was like *The Big Chill* out in the desert, without the funeral. It was an intimate, funny little sprig of a thing. I could never tell if it was funny, dramatic, or what! Really, though, the material was interesting. That's what made it fitting, because I got an opportunity to play a really juicy character among all friends that I love and that felt like a fitting goodbye. What better way to go?

The reason I retired not long after that was because I got reacquainted with an old friend from childhood and we decided to get married. In order to do that, I needed to move back East, so I chose that moment in time to retire. It just all made sense to me. I wasn't working as much as I had in the past and I had always promised myself that when the business didn't provide for me any longer, I would find something else to do.

Is there a "glass ceiling" for women of a certain age in Hollywood?

Oh, absolutely. Meryl Streep did the homework, years ago, about Screen Actors Guild statistics and women. I believe it was around the time of *Out of Africa* and Robert Redford was paid double what she was, yet it was *her* movie. She brought light, not just to the disparity for women at that level of the game, but the disparity for women throughout the industry. The fact is that in a majority of the films made the percentage of roles that are male has been increasing, so we have this situation of ever shrinking roles for women and a void, or vacuum, for women over the age of forty or fifty. And in what roles are there, there is this ridiculous gap in age between the male protagonist and the female counterpart who just looks inappropriate next to him. Pairings like Anne Heche and Harrison Ford — I'm sorry! It just looks ridiculous. But Meryl Streep laid out the statistics and challenged women directors and women writers to do something about it. I had no expectation that this was a line of work that would sustain me until I was old. *I thought, I will show up and keep my craft honed. I will be present and stay alert and on-point.* When the time comes and there's no work, it's not time to cry. It's the time to re-examine your direction and maybe choose a new one. I think maybe I grew up in a generation that was exposed to the idea that you don't have to have one career

Robin Curtis, in a publicity shot. PHOTO COURTESY OF ROBIN CURTIS.

all of your life. You might have two or three in you. So I was open to
the idea that there might be something else that I'd love to do.

Those factors all came together. I wasn't working as much after the
age of forty and I had an opportunity to leave Los Angeles and have
some personal happiness and kind of explore a new lifestyle. I went
for it. I now live in upstate New York on a pretty little lake. I bought an
1830's house about eight years ago. I must have been out of my mind;
a woman in her late forties buying an old house. I didn't know better
at the time, but now I do. I've become partners with a custom home
builder and we own our own little custom home-building company.
I have my real estate license, and so I'm an associate broker with a
real estate company, in order to sell the houses we build. So I wear a
lot of hats! I write our collateral and marketing material which allows
me to have a creative outlet. It's all about reinventing yourself in this
life and surviving in this crazy economy. I go out and make the occasional convention appearance which I love to do; I enjoy meeting all
the fans of *Star Trek*.

**Robin, it's been great to spend some time with you today!
I've very enjoyed talking to you today; this has been fun — and
eye-opening.**

Thank you, Tony, I've enjoyed it too.

Paul Carr grew up in Louisiana and his acting career began with a role in the New Orleans production of Billy Budd. By the mid-1950s, he was working on live television in New York City, including appearances on Studio One and Kraft Television Theatre.

He made his film debut in 1955 with a small role in Alfred Hitchcock's The Wrong Man. The same year, he portrayed a prisoner of war in the New York Theatre Guild production of Time Limit on Broadway. His film career continued with The Young Don't Cry starring James Whitmore and Sal Mineo; and he also appeared in the Warner Bros. rock and roll jukebox movie Jamboree.

Paul worked steadily on television in the late 1950s and early 1960s with guest spots and supporting roles in numerous Western series such as Rawhide, The Rifleman, and The Virginian. Later he appeared in detective, medical, and war dramas, including 77 Sunset Strip, Dr. Kildare, The Fugitive, and Twelve O'clock High. Other television appearances included Burke's Law, Combat!, Gunsmoke, The Time Tunnel, and The Invaders. He also appeared in such classics as Get Smart, Mannix, The Rockford Files, and Murphy Brown.

He may be remembered best, however, for his various appearances on science fiction shows over the years. He played the recurring role of "Casey Clark" on Voyage to the Bottom of the Sea, followed by "Lt. Lee Kelso," the USS Enterprise helmsman in the second Star Trek pilot episode, "Where No Man Has Gone Before." He also joined the cast of Buck Rogers in the 25th Century as "Lt. Devlin" aboard Earth Starship Searcher for the show's second season.

Throughout his career, Paul's first love was the stage. He appeared in nearly 100 stage productions on Broadway, off-Broadway and off-off-Broadway, as well as touring companies, stock, and in regional theatres around the United States. He received the L.A. Weekly Theatre Award for Best Actor in the Theatre East production of Manhattan

Paul Carr

"Don't Call Me Boy"

Express *and garnered a Dramalogue Award for his role in the Los Angeles Repertory Theater production of* Assassins.

I first met Paul Carr at a celebration honoring the 25th anniversary of Star Trek *which I produced in Portland, Oregon. He struck me as an intensely intelligent man, a person who spoke in measured tones. Paul seemed to truly enjoy meeting the fans of his science fiction work. It was a couple of years later when we were finally able to sit down and talk at length about his life and career. I picked him up at his hotel and as we drove to the television studio for the interview he asked me about the history of Portland and the surrounding area. He was particularly amused to learn that in the early days Portland was referred to as "Stumptown," in view of the numerous remnants left from the many trees that had been felled.*

We both enjoyed the interview and it was fun to see him become animated as he remembered his beginnings and later, his work with Alfred Hitchcock. It's an honor to include his final interview in this volume.

A good place to start is at the beginning. I'd like you to tell us a little bit about your background and how you got involved in acting. Was it always in your blood?

Well, I don't know if it's in the blood or not. It's a kind of funny story, though, because it's the opposite of what you'd ordinarily hear about someone's family. My father is more or less responsible for getting me into this business. He saw me in a stage play in high school and for some reason thought I had talent! I'm from New Orleans, originally, and at the time I was a kid there were three little community theater groups and he read in the paper that one of these groups was doing a play called *A la Creole*; I still remember the name of it. There was a part for a seventeen year old tough guy. I was seventeen, but I wasn't a tough guy! He said I should go and audition for it. I lived in a small community called Marrero just across the river from New Orleans, a suburb, and I didn't have a car. I said, "Pop, I don't want to get on a bus, then a ferry boat, and another bus, then a street car…" He kept insisting and telling me to go down there. So finally I said, "Ok, ok."

I had a friend who lived down the street from me, Wilson Bernard, who had a car. I went down and knocked on his door and said, "Wilson, why don't we go down to New Orleans Community Theatre. They've got a reading and I want to audition for this part." Then I added, "There's a lot of girls down there." So I talked him into it, we went down there and I read for the role and got it. That meant that

I had to get on busses, street cars, and ferry boats every day to go rehearse. But I fell in love with it immediately and I stayed with it from seventeen, on.

That's amazing. I've never heard of a father, or parent, actively encourage their child to become an actor!

I know! That's the unusual part of the story. He loved the idea of my being an actor and when I decided to become a professional, he thought it was great! I had to go to New York and studied there and went to the American Theatre Wing. I spent a number of years in New Orleans doing community theatre, getting involved with that group, and learning — I mean, it was a learning process, of course. There were things I had never heard of; I'd read plays in school, but I didn't know what it was to really be an actor. It was quite an experience when I was a kid.

You are also a musician, right? You loved music.

I loved music; I was a clarinet player and spent a summer at Julliard School of Music in New York. My intention was to continue on with music and become a professional musician. But that went out the window once I got involved with theatre! (Laughs)

Do you still play today?

Yes, I do. I don't play clarinet so much, but I do have a saxophone, a tenor, and it gives me a lot of pleasure to sometimes just sit and play it. I don't do it often enough, but I do enjoy it.

You went to New York to pursue acting. Did you audition for the American Theatre Wing?

No, at that point I had developed a small resume, I had done a number of plays and I got a letters of recommendation from directors of the three community theatres in New Orleans and sent those in. So based on my resume and the letters, I was accepted into the school.

That led to your work on Broadway and live television. What are some shows that you have memories of from that period?

The very first things I did were in live television. I was in class and a good friend of my teacher was a very well-known television director, named Vincent Donehue. He came into class, I remember, and hired our entire class to be extras and background for a show called *Goodyear Television Playhouse,* an episode called "Native Dancer" with Gwen Verdon. It was normally an hour show, but that one in particular was only a half hour because half of it had been preempted. All of the young people in the class were ballet dancers because Gwen's character was a young woman trying to become a ballet dancer. We had scenes doing the ballet exercises, and I was in one scene in a drug store sitting next to her while she had a scene with Jack Warden who was her boyfriend in the show. Later on, Vincent hired me and gave me an actual role. I played an NBC page — with Geraldine Page. That almost ended my career because I was so petrified having to walk in and say actual lines out loud to a real live actress! It was very

Paul Carr talks about working in early live television in New York.
PHOTO COURTESY OF ANTHONY WYNN.

funny. Keep in mind this was all live television. They did have a lot of rehearsal, you didn't just stand up and do it like you do in a lot of films today. There was a ten day, sometimes two or three week rehearsal period in some cases. You felt very secure by the time you got onto the stage to do what you had to do.

So in some ways almost like rehearsing a stage play, right?

In some ways, yes. Live television in those days was like that, it had to be; except for, of course, soap operas. Those were done live and with a minimal amount of rehearsal, as they are today. But they were live! I got hired to do three or four shows soap operas. I had a couple of scenes — thank God they were small scenes. I was absolutely petrified. I didn't feel prepared, I didn't know what I was doing; I was scared to death. The actor I had to work with, I was part of his gang, was an actor named Mark Rydell who's now a fairly well-known director. He was very popular on the soap opera.

You also worked with Hume Cronyn and Jessica Tandy.

Yes, I did. That was in *Studio One*, an episode called "The Five Dollar Bill." I played one of their two sons, Robert Mulligan directed it. It won a number of awards, it was a good show. I did a lot of live television. My biggest lead at the time was a show called "Box 701" on *Kraft Television Theatre;* I did a number of *Krafts*. Prior to that I did *Westinghouse Summer Theatre* with Madge Evans and Dick Foran — you wouldn't know those names! — but they had been fairly well-known movie stars for years and years, long before television. They were really very nice people and I played their son on the show.

Did you pick up a lot of your acting technique from working with these various stars in television?

Yeah, you do; you observe and you watch and start seeing things that they do and — it's not so much imitating — but watching their techniques. The techniques for film and stage are different; there's a very big difference. The basic reality is the same as you're dealing with the basics of human nature and the human condition in human beings, but the expression of it has to be a little more…well, there's a saying that the camera doesn't lie. It finds the truth — and it does. If you try to tell the camera something it will often reject that. It has to come in and find it and get that truth from you, whatever that might be. In a sense, when we talk about projecting on-stage you are generally taking whatever the germ of truth is, this character's truth, and putting it out there for the audience. You're not asking them to come into you. When you're on-camera you're going into them in a different way. The camera is reaching in and grabbing that and pulling it in and giving it to them.

I was lucky enough, once in my life, to have played *Hamlet*. I didn't quite know what I was doing, it was really "deer in the headlights" time, I thought to myself, *What am I going to do now?* I was lucky enough to have a very dear friend who had studied at RADA [Royal Academy of Dramatic Art in London, England]. He coached me a bit and I also knew an English actor name John Abbott who also coached me and they made me aware of the power and strength of Shakespeare. If I trusted Shakespeare, I was taught, I could ride on the words — and I did. I kind of took a deep breath and would just go with it and let it carry me to wherever it took me. I'm happy to say that I got very good reviews. Out of fear, I could do nothing else but trust in the words. It was like a surfer riding on top of the wave; you get on top of the wave and stay there until you get all the way to the beach! And I did.

There is some decent writing in television; now, I'm not putting that down. But as an actor you don't have time to explore all the possibilities of something, you just don't. They put the camera there, put you here and say, ''Action!''You better know your lines! If you know your lines and you get through it, chances are the director is not going to ask too much more of you than that. Oh, they may give you a few directions and repeat it three or four times, but you are never going to feel that it is totally your performance that is coming from you and your technique and your experience completely. If you don't have a decent director that you can depend on and you get lost in piece of material, that isn't very good — and we all have, anyone who's ever done television has done that — the next thing you know you're floundering around and your flippers are out of the water!

Did you ever follow a certain acting method, like The Method?

My training was primarily the Michael Chekhov Method, which they call The Method. Stanislavski's was called the System; when [Lee] Strasberg got a hold of it, they started calling it The Method. He claimed to be following Stanislavski precisely, but it wasn't really true. Michael Chekhov was from the Moscow Art Theatre and he studied under Stanislavski — Chekhov was one of the great pupils and Stanislavski one of the great teachers. I didn't study with him; I wish I had. My teacher was grounded in Chekhov's method which was basically Stanislavski. Later I studied with teachers from the Actors Studio. So I'm grounded in what is commonly, but mistakenly called The Method. It is really Stanislavski's system, more or less. But you know, you develop your own tricks and ways of doing those things as you go along, as you get more confident and you get to know what you are doing. The better you know your material the better off you are.

You went to California to work for the legendary Alfred Hitchcock, right? How did that come about?

No, I was actually in a play in New York at the time called *Time Limit* and I was with the William Morris Agency. My agent called and told me to go over to Warner Bros. where I met the casting director — who liked me and had me up for a role in an Alfred Hitchcock film. I walked in and there was Hitchcock. He looked at me and said, ''He's fine'' and I walked out and had the part! (Laughs) It was a very small role in a picture called *The Wrong Man*. I had to be picked up for the shoot and I had never been picked up in limousine before. I was just a kid in New York, an actor who had a job in this play and was studying. I was supposed to be picked up at eight o'clock in the morning in front of the Hampshire House and this great big black limousine pulls up. The driver sticks his head out and asks, "Are you Paul Carr?" I said, "Yeah," to which he replied, "Let's go." I was thinking, *let's go where? In a limousine?*

I was driven to the dockyards in Brooklyn, near Brooklyn Heights. Then we went to another location and I was put in a bus. Then I was told to get dressed. So I got dressed, they made me up, and then I sat in the bus! I waited and waited and while I waited I noticed that there were two other limousines sitting there and they were setting up cameras and people were wandering around. I had never seen anything like this in my life, I was fascinated. It wasn't like television, like live television, at all. Finally, it started to get dark and I was worried because I had to get back to the theatre by eight o'clock; I had an eight-thirty curtain. In those days most shows began at eight-thirty. It turns out that Hitchcock had been waiting, he wanted to get the shot of the sunset falling between these buildings and it was really quite a beautiful shot. We sat there, me thinking, *Well, we could have done this other stuff.* I guess he didn't want to. So he got the shot and then they hustled me into the building. My character didn't have a name or anything, I was just this young guy coming down the stairs about to leave the building when Henry Fonda and Vera Miles — charming, lovely people; wonderful people — would walk in the building and ask me where "Mr. Molinelli" was. "Yes, he's on the third floor," was to be my response; then I would leave. That was my line! I had one line.

So I was up at the top of the stairs and I hadn't met Fonda or Miles yet, and I was standing there waiting; people were running up and down these stairs in what was an old tenement building and they had the light coming from down the stairs around a corner. Now I swear to you this is true! All of a sudden there was this shadow, an unmistakable shadow; it was right out of the television show. I could imagine that theme song playing. There was no mistaking who it was; it was Hitchcock coming up the stairs. I hadn't seen him since I met him in the office. He walked up the stairs and turned the corner and I was staring right into his eyes. [Paul Carr does his best Hitchcock imitation] "What is your line!" he demanded. "They're on the third floor," I replied. There was a pause. Hitchcock exclaimed, "They're on the third floor, *D!* They're on the third floor, *D! Do you understand?"* I said, "Yes." He then turned around and walked back down the stairs — and that was the last I ever saw of him! I rehearsed the scene once with Fonda and Miles; they entered and I repeated my line, "They're on the third floor, D." Then they put me in the limousine and took me to the theatre. (Laughs) So that was my introduction to film.

Paul Carr remembers his experiences with director Alfred Hitchcock. PHOTO COURTESY OF ANTHONY WYNN.

But what an introduction — I mean, Hitchcock, Fonda!

I know; it was fabulous. Even one line; who cares? It was just wonderful. But it was some years before I came to California. I came out to do a *Matinee Theatre.* I was starting to get known in New York, had done some live television, but came out to California — got married, had two kids — so I stayed!

Then you made another movie called *Jamboree.*

That was in New York as well! (Laughs) Well, when I was still in New York, I did three fairly big movies, I guess. *Jamboree* isn't one I usually talk about very much! As I mentioned, I was with William Morris and they submitted me for this rock 'n roll movie, it had the distinction of being the second rock 'n roll movie ever done. I went to see the producers and the director about it and they liked me, so

I was hired. They asked me if I could sing and I didn't sing, I mean I wasn't a trained singer. The musical director was a very famous jazz musician named Neal Hefti, a very nice man and we got to be friends for a brief period while I was doing this movie. We used to hang out and we saw every musician in town, I met these incredible musicians that he knew. Anyway, he called me one day, early in the morning, and said he wanted to hear my voice because they wanted to be able to match my singing voice with my speaking voice. "Can't you sing at all?" he asked me. "Well, I sing in the bathtub like every-body else; but I'm not a trained singer." I said. He said, "Well, come on down to the studio, we're trying to find someone to match your voice. I can't find *anybody*." I told him, "Ok, I'll come down but don't expect too much!"

So I went down and sang something, I don't know what it was; "Happy Birthday to You" or something very simple. He said, "Oh, you're fine. You can sing fine." Next thing I knew, I was a singer and I sang a couple of songs with Connie Francis. We pre-recorded them and they were used in the film. I never thought of myself as being singer or that kind of actor. I played the lead in the picture and I was rather naïve about this whole thing and I had agents who should have warned me and told me what I was doing, that I could have made this grow into something else. But it was just a job and I didn't take it very seriously — I mean, a rock 'n roll movie? That's not what I knew the theatre to do, I'm an actor! But I had great fun doing it, met interest-ing people, and also got to sing with Joe Williams and Count Basie. It was fabulous! But I was just a kid and I didn't know what I was doing.

That's great! What was the third movie you mentioned?

It was *The Young Don't Cry* with Sal Mineo. I had a pretty nice role in that and it was shot in Savannah [Georgia], but was cast in New York.

He's an actor that died far too young.

Far too young. He was a nice man, a very nice man. My character's name was "Tom Bradley" and much of the film was set in, and filmed in an orphanage in Savannah. It was actually filmed on location there at the Bethesda Home for Boys. James Whitmore was also a lead in that picture. The director aimed for, and got, some real Southern authenticity in the movie. It was pretty well-received for a "B" picture and Sal Mineo was quite good in it. I enjoyed working with him.

Your television credits are pages long, you've worked in just about all of the classic Westerns: *Zane Grey Theatre, Have Gun — Will Travel, The Rifleman, Bonanza, Rawhide, Twelve O'Clock High,*

Gunsmoke, and on and on and on! Of your work in Westerns, what stands out in your mind?

There were some that I was really pleased with and felt good about. The quality of writing was often very good. Of course, it was sometimes terrible! There's no question about it, occasionally very bad; but often quite good. I did things like *Wichita Town* with Joel McCrea, you know, people like that. *Have Gun — Will Travel* was a pretty decent show. It was Lamont Johnson's first directing job and again, Dick Foran played my father. The episode was called "Young Gun." So twice in my life, Dick Foran played my father! That one was the first Western that I did. It stands out for me, not because it was such a great drama, or anything like that — it wasn't — but I learned to do the "fast draw" on that show. I had to be the fastest gun in the West! I told them, "I don't know which end of the gun to *hold,* much less get it out of my holster fast!" In the opening sequence, I'm standing on the classical Western street facing down a gunman that's coming after me. I keep saying, "Don't do it, Johnny, don't do it!" He finally draws and I out-draw him and kill him. Well, the guy that I "killed" was the guy that trained me in the fast draw. He was a very nice man and I spent hours with him. I had this big rig that I had to wear and had to learn how to get the gun out of the holster fast. Well after that, I ended up doing *hundreds* of those things! I kept being the "fastest gun in the West."

I've always said that if I write an autobiography I'm going to title it "Don't Call Me Boy." I must have said that line in a least fifty Westerns! I always played this young neurotic kid saying, "Don't call me boy! Don't call me boy!" I did so many Westerns, I don't know which ones stand out dramatically. There was a *Gunsmoke* I did that I really, really liked.

What was it like working with James Arness?

He was big! Arness was big. He was a very easy-going, laid-back guy. We'd go out on location and I remember after a shot he'd collapse under a tree and try to get fifteen minutes of sleep. These guys...I remember David Janssen saying more than once, when we were working on *The Fugitive,* what a killer it was to be the principal lead on a series. But he was wonderful. I probably had more fun with David than almost anybody. He was a great guy. I remember one time they were showing the Emmys and Janssen said, "They shouldn't give Emmys for best performances, they should give 'em to anybody who can last for twenty-six weeks *doing* one of these things!" These guys just worked their butts off. They'd be there at six o'clock in the

morning and not going home until eight o'clock at night and just
working all the time.

**Especially on a show like *The Fugitive*, David Janssen just about
carried the whole thing and was in practically every scene and
every shot of every scene!**

Yeah, that's right. He did. That's another show that I'm very pleased
with and I had a very good role in an episode with Tuesday Weld
called "Dark Corner." It was a pretty good show, a good script. I
actually did two *Fugitives* [the second was "Nightmare at Northoak"].

**Every actor has credits they prefer not to talk about; as a working
actor isn't it true that sometimes you just need to take whatever if
offered — even if it's not so good — if nothing else, just to pay the
bills?**

(Loud laughter) Oh God, is that the truth! Sometimes you take anything, commercials, "B" movies, look — I had two kids and I had to put
them through school, take care of them; I had to pay the mortgage and
pay for the food. That's life. If you want to continue to live a "normal"
life, you got to pay your bills! You sometimes don't have the luxury of
turning things down that you should have turned down. That was my
unfortunate mistake in a lot of things that I did that I shouldn't have
done. I could look down the list of credits that you're holding there
and say, "Oh, there's one; there's another one — shouldn't have done
those!" But you do what you need to do to pay your bills and you're a
professional; this is what you do for a living. You do the best you can
under the circumstances.

**Not to cast any dispersions on what I'd like to talk to you about
next...**

(Laughs) Ok!

**You were brought on to *Voyage to the Bottom of the Sea*; were
you hired by Irwin Allen?**

Yes, I was hired by Irwin. He loved me! I went in to see Irwin about
this role during the first year of the show; they were still shooting in
black and white then. There was a character named "Casey Clark"
and the script was not bad, it was a fairly decent script. Clark was a
seaman on the Seaview and I think the episode was called "Doomsday."
I remember the script had something about us crossing the equator
and at one point they think the world is being threatened by nuclear
warfare. Clark has a wife and kid in San Francisco and it getting hysterical about it: he wants to get back there and do something to help
them. He gets quite hysterical at one point; it was a very emotional

role. Well, Irwin loved that! He thought I was the cat's pajamas because I could get all emotional over something. That's my training — I'm an actor! That's what I'm supposed to be doing. So he kept hiring me and at one point was going to put me on as a regular, but ultimately decided it was going to cost them too much money — so he didn't. Then he kept bringing me back! Any time he had any emotional "thing" he would change the name of the character to Clark and I would end up doing it!

I heard that you ran into Irwin Allen in an airport?

I was meeting a friend who was a still photographer and was working on one of Irwin's pictures. I was at the airport to meet her and Irwin was on the same flight. He came off the plane and saw me standing there. His first words when he saw me were, "What the *hell* are you doing here?" Irwin was a very gruff kind of guy, he didn't mean it and wasn't really a bad guy, but he was always a little bit coarse and couldn't express himself in a gentle way. It wasn't in his nature just to say, "Hi Paul, how are you? Nice to see you; what are you doing here?" So I just brushed it off — it was another example of Irwin being Irwin. (Laughs) When I was looking for a job, I used to go in to his office — I wasn't on the show as a regular, just occasionally — and this was toward the fourth year. The story editor told me there was a part coming up that's I'd be really good for. I went into Irwin's office and said, "Irwin, there's this part coming up next week on the show that I'd be right for and he barked, "If ya do it, ya can't do any more! The guy gets killed!" I said, "Well, ok. I'll do it." I'm figuring, well, this is last year of the show anyway; why not do it and just go out with a bang. So I did it and then the show was picked up for another year! I thoughts, *Oh God, I've killed it! I'm not going to be able to do the show anymore.* It didn't matter to Irwin. He used footage of me from another show and put it into a new show! He was always doing stuff like that. He was a funny man.

You did a lot of Westerns, a lot of dramas; but you also did comedies like *That Girl* and *Get Smart*. Is doing comedy on television difficult on shows like that without an audience reacting to you? Is it different than comedy on the stage?

It's different than *life!* (Laughs) It's not comedy; I don't know why they call them sit-coms — situation comedy. It's a whole different technique of acting. It has nothing to do with any kind of reality, any kind of life; I'm sorry if I sound jaded. There's very little of it that I can watch — I can watch *Fraser*, occasionally. It becomes a technique that has to do with a certain kind of timing and things that the editor is going to do, and that the director is doing; and it doesn't resemble comedy on-stage or even in film. It's a totally different animal. They add lines to things that have nothing to do with it — where does that come from? I've only done a couple; I've never been really successful at sit-coms. The most fun I had doing a comedy was on *Get Smart.* That was a real comedy; that was funny stuff that they were doing. I mean, they were doing *funny, funny* things. A lot of the humor was coming out of the character and not just added-in lines buffed up with a laugh track. People would be standing off-camera on *Get Smart* trying not to laugh at what was happening. Don Adams was pure genius. Some of the stuff he would come up with was just comedy gold. He was hysterically funny. Later, I did a couple of sit-coms with audiences in attendance. One of them was *Murphy Brown.* It was the episode that [Vice President of the United States] Dan Quayle complained about, where she had the baby. I played the tobacco executive that she was interviewing and we had a very funny moment in the opening where she says, "Oh my God, my water broke!" And I said, "Oh God, I need a cigarette!" and jump up and run off-camera. Well, she broke-up because I ad-libbed the line — and they kept the line in! That was a little bit better; but again, they rely so much on lines and attitude overlaid with the laugh track. You're sitting there scratching your head, sometimes, thinking, *why did they put a laugh track in there?*

In the late 1960s and 1970s detective and police shows eclipsed Westerns in popularity and you did a lot of those, including *Ironside, Mod Squad, Mannix...*

About five of each of those shows! I got to know Raymond Burr and Mike Connors; those were fun shows to do. Ray wound up directing one and hired me to be in it because he liked me. It was a nice atmosphere on those sets, especially on *Mannix* — especially with Mike Connors. He is one of the true gentlemen in this business. He was always doing something to make you look better. He knew it was his show and his name was the first to pop up on the screen. So he didn't worry about it, he had no ego problems at all. I remember once he jumped in front of me, we were doing a scene — I was the guest lead on this thing and it was one of the better shows that I ever got. I'm collapsed, I've been shot or something like that and he's rescuing me; it's toward the end of the show. He moved in front of me, in front of the camera and I said, "Thanks a lot Mike, for blocking me from the camera!" He said, "Shut up! I just got you a close-up!" He was that kind of guy, just terrific to work with.

I have to admit that a favorite show of mine from the 1970s was *The Rockford Files*.

Oh, I loved that! That was the other great gentleman in this business — Jim Garner. It was always pleasant to work on a show with Jim; just to be there. He was always so affable and easy to deal with and talk to. If you want to rehearse something, or change something, Jim would say, "Oh go ahead, do what you need to do." It was just easy and you just felt comfortable. Jim worked so hard on his show, too; this was another case of an actor putting in an almost superhuman effort.

A few years later you joined the cast of another science fiction show as co-star on *Buck Rogers in the 25th Century*.

That role started off as a one-shot and then turned into a recurring role when they liked what I did. I joined in the second season and they kept me on. I guess there was a possibility that I would have been kept on the following year — but the show was cancelled, so we never got that far.

Is there any role that you regret not getting?

Every one that I didn't get! If I auditioned for it, I wanted it and went for it with my total self, as much as I could. You can look back in retrospect and think, *If only I had gotten that part instead of Warren Beatty*...I remember that George Peppard got one that I wanted; Robert Redford got one that I wanted. I used to get some of James Dean's old cast-off parts. So I don't know; that's the best way I can answer that.

I don't think I'd be let out of the studio alive if I didn't mention your involvement in *Star Trek*.

[Feigning ignorance] *"Star Trek?* What's that?" (Laughs)

Did Gene Roddenberry, the creator, hire you to play that role?

I'm going to tell my story that I tell to fans at conventions. This was the pilot episode, actually the second pilot, called "Where No Man Has Gone Before." A first pilot with different actors and with Jeffrey Hunter as the captain had been filmed, but rejected by the network. In a rare move, they commissioned a second, new pilot for the series. The director was a man named James Goldstone and I had worked for Jim a half-dozen times. He called me saying, "We've got a nice part for you on a science fiction pilot." I said, "Great, I'd love to work!" I love science fiction because you get to play with a lot of toys (laughs) — toys you've never seen before! I got the script and saw that I get killed and thought, *ah well, that's the way it is; it's part of the job.* I found out that the first pilot had cost too much money and had taken too many days to shoot; they had some trouble with Jeffrey Hunter — so the role of the captain was recast and now Bill Shatner was playing it. We got on the set and it was a seven day shoot. NBC had said that if the pilot could be made in seven days on a budget; you've got a sale. Everyone

Paul Carr discusses working on the original *Star Trek* episode "Where No Man Has Gone Before." PHOTO COURTESY OF ANTHONY WYNN.

was anxious to do everything right and be on time, and do everything they could do to make the show work. So we were working along, and we get to the scene where I'm to be killed.

So let me set the scene: the character of Gary Lockwood is going through some kind of force field turning him into a God-like creature who was able to telekinetically move things with his mind. We had him trapped on an asteroid and Shatner — Captain Kirk — says to me, "Lee, can you rig this thing to blow up? We'll blow this planet up if he tries to get off." So I'm rigging everything and getting it all ready to blow up, when kinetically Lockwood's character knows what's going on and after everyone else leaves, sends a cable up from behind a console, wraps it around my neck, and kills me. So I'm the first person ever to die on *Star Trek!* It's certainly a dubious achievement. And

I'm the only crew member to die on *Star Trek* who's not wearing a red shirt!

We're standing there getting ready to shoot the scene and I'm talking to Lockwood, "See, this is a fun show, I'm having a great time — I wish I wasn't being killed!" All of a sudden, I'm lifted totally off the ground, my feet are pulled up from under me, and Gene Roddenberry who was six feet, four inches or something like that, is standing there shaking me. My cigarettes — I used to smoke at the time — my pocket change, everything is falling out! Roddenberry booms, "Don't worry about it, kid, we're going to freeze you and bring you back!" But he never did! (Laughs) Oh, well; those are the breaks.

Paul, thank you — it's been great to talk about your career.

Thank you, Tony. It's been a lot of fun.

James "Jimmy" Doohan was born in Vancouver, British Columbia, the youngest of four children. At the outbreak of World War II, Jimmy joined the Royal Canadian Artillery, where his first combat assignment was the invasion of Normandy at Juno Beach on D-Day.

He led his unit to higher ground through a field of tank mines and took fire from a German machine gun: four bullets in his leg, one in the chest, and one through his middle right finger. The chest bullet was stopped by his silver cigarette case, and his wounded finger was amputated (on-screen he would normally conceal it).

After the war, Jimmy made his first CBC radio show appearance in 1946, later appearing with such other performers as John Drainie, Barry Morse, Toby Robins, and Ruth Springford. He won a two-year scholarship to the Neighborhood Playhouse in New York City, where classmates included fellow Canadian Leslie Nielsen, Tony Randall and Richard Boone. During this period, Jimmy continued his work on radio and television in Canada and the USA, and earned a reputation for versatility.

Jimmy always had a gift for using foreign accents. Auditioning for the role of "Montgomery Scott," Chief Engineer of the USS Enterprise on Star Trek, for Gene Roddenberry, Jimmy did several different accents. Roddenberry asked which he preferred, and Jimmy replied, "If you want an Engineer, you'll want a Scotsman!"

The interview with James Doohan was conducted just prior to the opening of Star Trek III: The Search for Spock and appeared in a Star Trek fan publication. Additional questions to Mr. Doohan are from a follow-up interview conducted in Los Angeles in 1996 and have never before been published.

James Doohan

"Honesty and Honor"

What do you like best about yourself?

I don't know. Does one really sit down and think, "What do I like best about myself?"

It's a hard question.

You're darn right it's a hard question. I suppose it's my ability to work hard. That will get you all sorts of places. The ability to work hard was probably implanted in me at a very early age, but then you really can't do anything about it. You can't create. It's like when my father was a chemist — he would make a move and write copious notes on it, then make another move and make copious notes on that, and it worked. He couldn't invent anything unless he worked hard. It's something that's there — in me, that's for sure. I suppose I rather enjoy that I'm interested in things. I see something that needs to be done and I do it. Also, another thing that I like about myself is that I am very happy with my children. I have six of them and I am very content with them. I had something to do with that!

Yes, you certainly did. Were you every sorry that you didn't do something else or have you been happy that you stayed with acting?

I've had thoughts like that, I can't deny it. What actor hasn't? But not in the last few years. I've been forty years in the business, you know. I don't think I'm unhappy at all.

Is there anyone in the business that you admire a lot?

I've never met him, but I must say that I think John Gielgud is probably the best actor in the world. I've never seen him where he wasn't just perfect. I don't care what it is that I've seen him in — a lot of small parts, but he's just fantastic. He is brilliant. He knows how to do everything. Another is — and I've never met him even though he was on *Star Trek* — William Windom. He's a great actor.

What is most important to you as a person, other than your family?

Honor. Honesty and honor. I think that is about it.

Has there ever been a role that you turned down that you wish hadn't, later?

Not really. I did turn down a very important and highly lucrative role, but I've never regretted it. It was to play the Canadian lead in *Howdy Doody*, a character called "Timber Tom." They picked me! They only had me in mind, then when I didn't come they didn't know what to think. I had just got myself a lawyer to act as my agent, and they really didn't have any agents in Canada in those days. So I got my best friend who's a lawyer and he told them what was going on. They got quite huffy that I had a lawyer. I wanted money and I wanted residual payments and I wanted this, and I wanted that! It wasn't that much more money, really. What you would talk of as a basic minimum here is what we were talking, plus fifty percent. Here you ask basic plus ten thousand percent. They said, "Well, he really didn't want to do it."

I've heard you say that you would like to play the lead in *King Lear.* **Is there any other part that you would like to do?**

There are lots of characters that I could sink my teeth into. Dustin Hoffman is doing *Death of a Salesman.* There's a great role and I would be good in it. I envy him doing it! *All My Sons* — that would be another play that I'd like to do.

Did any of your children want to go into the entertainment business?

I don't think so, not acting, anyway. They don't want all the hassle, but they are doing their own thing. One of my girls is a very good singer and an interior decorator. She gets into musicals and she also does sets and costumes and things like that. Also, my son Chris is a very good singer and has his own band.

How do you feel about science fiction in general?

To me, science fiction has some great stories, but it has to have a very good scientific background before I'm interested. I even complained to Gene Roddenberry and he said, "It's a science fiction program, right?" And I said I guess that I hadn't read that much because all I have to do is see a monster on the cover and I won't buy the book.

Did you enjoy working on *Star Trek III: The Search for Spock?*

Oh yes! It was really very nice having Leonard Nimoy direct. After the first three or four days we all looked at each other and said, "Hey, he's done his homework." He was super. He's an awfully nice guy to work with. There was only one period there when he didn't know what was happening and "Spock" was getting in the way. He was maybe just the tiniest, most minutely bit difficult, but nowhere near as difficult as some other people on the set. But then again, even I can get difficult!

You had a considerably larger role in that movie, didn't you?

Yes, but even if you have a few more words to say, that doesn't make it any more to act. If there's anything that I'd much rather do it's have a small good part, than a lot of words. That's the way it goes, though.

Do you ever get tired of *Star Trek?*

You know, a number of years ago I was complaining to someone about the problem of being typecast in Hollywood. I remember his advice to me, "Jimmy," he said, "you're going to be known as "Scotty" long after you're dead — so if I were you, I'd just go along with the flow." So I thought about and decided to take his advice.

What about hearing everybody saying "Beam me up, Scotty" all the time?

I'm not tired of that at all. I've been hearing it for about twenty years. I've heard it at seventy miles an hour across four lanes of traffic on the freeway! I hear it from just about everybody. It's fun.

How did you originally get the role of Scotty?

I went in and read for Gene Roddenberry. I did about eight different accents for him, and he asked me which one I liked the most. I said, "Well, if you want an engineer, he better be a Scotsman because in my experience, all the world's best engineers have been Scottish." I decided to give Scotty an Aberdeen accent, which was something I had learned that when I was sent over to England during the war. While I was there, I met this fellow from Aberdeen; and I couldn't understand one word he said! But I did learn that accent from him and that was the one I used for Scotty. The writers based a lot of the character on me. When they found out I subscribed to technical journals, they starting putting things like that into my character. Scotty is ninety-nine per cent James Doohan and one per cent accent.

Star Trek IV: The Voyage Home **is the most popular** *Star Trek* **film to date, as well as grossing the most money. Are you surprised that the movie was so successful?**

No, not really, because it was one of the best movies we did. I liked it! I think it has one of the best lines ever uttered in a *Star Trek* show — when Captain Kirk tells the crew, "Everybody, remember where we parked!" In many ways in seemed to be much like the old *Star Trek* series and it was the most fun to do. I really enjoyed the film's comedy. Filming in San Francisco was wonderful.

You worked with Leonard Nimoy again as director on *Star Trek IV.* **How did you like that experience?**

Leonard is a great director. I think that he really proved himself with those movies. He's a great guy and he's one of the best directors around.

If the right show came along would you want to do series television again?

You're darn right. I'd love to do a comedy series. I've been very successful in comedy on the stage, and I have never really done a comedy on television or in a motion picture. I'm very good in comedy. I was taught by a guy in the East called Paul Crabtree. I would ask him, "Why are you directing me so minutely?" and he would say, "Because that's the kind of part that I'd like to play." I loved him, he was great. I was probably older than he was, but he was a great writer.

When you start a role, how do you approach it?

I just let it grow on me. First of all, you have to get rid of your book. And I do that. In the days of live television, I used to pull a trick on everybody, especially the director. We'd block the play and I'd fain enthusiasm, "Let's do that again!" About the third time I'd start to get a few groans from some of the actors that didn't want to do it again. Some of the guys would say, "Son of a gun, I know what you're doing! There's Doohan doing his old tricks again." But I'd go home and know all of my lines from the whole play. That gives you time to think and you don't have to be carrying something around in your hand. It gives you time to mull over what a line really means and how to say it, because what would happen in the first day or two would be nothing like what happened ten days later. So I was glad that I was able to do that.

What kind of person is James Doohan?

He's too disciplined for his own good. But then that has come in handy many times. Being a hard worker comes in here. I think that he is delighted that he was able to meet a teacher who was able to show him how to be a good actor. I was there under him for about six weeks and I thought, "Wow, is that what he is trying to teach?" It was really like a white flash. You know, people talk about that; and this is about what it was. I don't think that anybody in my class had that feeling. I was a hard worker before that; and about three times harder after that. At that time, I didn't know if I wanted to be in the business or not. I had been given a scholarship and I wondered if I really wanted to continue. But I worked hard at it. The blinding flash to me was a part of — sort of a spiritual thing, in a way, but it was also the answer to my problem.

Do you write? Have you ever considered writing?

I considered it about forty years ago, but I tried and I'm terrible! The only thing that I'm going to do is write my biography and that's all.

What would you most like to be remembered for?

I suppose, also strangely enough, it includes the hard work — it's for the characters that I've created. Not just for "Scotty," but for the other characters too. A lot of people have seen me do a lot of things in my lifetime.

I spoke with James Doohan for the second time in Los Angeles at actor William Campbell's Fantasticon, a huge *Star Trek* convention that raised funds for the Motion Picture & Television Fund, in support of the old actor's home and hospital located in Los Angeles. Later, actor DeForest Kelley [Dr. Leonard McCoy] and his wife lived

Actor James Doohan and a young Anthony Wynn at a 1984 *Star Trek* **convention.** PHOTO COURTESY OF ANTHONY WYNN.

there in their final years. I had just produced Grace Lee Whitney's full length recording entitled *Yeoman Rand Sings!* and was attending the convention with her.

James Doohan, who was seated next to us to signing autographs, leaned over and asked Grace, "Can I steal your young man to help me out? I can't keep up with all these people!" Indeed, a huge line of fans had materialized and Jimmy was attempting to sell his photographs, sign autographs, and greet patrons all at the same time. So I scooted my chair over a bit to help Mr. Doohan and about that time a convention staffer appeared. "Will you bring me a scotch whiskey, straight up? Thanks." Grace made a disapproving face at the request and whispered to me, "Oh, why did he do that? He doesn't need it." The scotch soon appeared, but Mr. Doohan was fiddling with his ears, grimacing. "There's so much damn noise in here I can't make anything out." Soon, his two hearing aids were removed and were sitting on the table between us, near the glass of scotch. But the fans didn't seem to care at all, and Mr. Doohan settled in to sign several hundred photos that day.

Prior to his passing, Jimmy was able to fulfill two of the ambitions he verbalized in the interview. He wrote his memoir *Beam Me Up, Scotty*, published by Pocket Books, and also co-starred in the mid-1990s television situation comedy series, *Homeboys in Outer Space* as "Pippin," which was more than a nod to his role in *Star Trek* as "Scotty."

At the end of his life, Jimmy suffered from both Parkinson's and Alzheimer's diseases, diabetes, and lung fibrosis. He died on July 20, 2005 at his home in Redmond, Washington with his wife Wende at his side.

In May 2012, the Falcon 9 rocket was successfully launched into space from Cape Canaveral in Florida carrying the Dragon capsule filled with supplies for personnel on the International Space Station. The historic mission was the final test flight for the Space Exploration Technologies Corporation, known popularly as SpaceX, prior to flying humans into space. The ashes of James Doohan and those of 319 other people including Mercury astronaut L. Gordon "Gordy" Cooper, were in a separate canister, or the second stage of the rocket that separated from the main capsule. The cremains of all aboard were anticipated to orbit the Earth for a year, before descending and disintegrating in the atmosphere during reentry.

Marlene and Carol are Star Trek and science fiction fans and memorabilia collectors who have amassed a virtual museum of keepsakes and collectibles at their home in Portland, Oregon. Featured many times on television, they are also well-known up and down the length of the West Coast for their work on numerous Star Trek conventions.

Star Trek was the first science fiction show that appealed to women as much as it did to men. It's also a show that appealed to gay people, as well as straight. Why was that the case? Gene Roddenberry's vision was for the USS Enterprise to explore the final frontier, not conquer it. He imparted morality tales without moralizing. Week after week, the show confronted the specters of intolerance and injustice, and week after week his characters found a way to defeat them without ever becoming them.

From the beginning, Gene Roddenberry promulgated the idea that women alongside men would help to shape the future: Majel Barrett in the roles of "Number One" and "Christine Chapel," Nichelle Nichols as "Nyota Uhura," and Grace Lee Whitney playing "Janice Rand." Later, when Star Trek was in danger of cancellation it was a woman, Bjo Trimble, who stepped forward to lead the campaign — twice! — to save the show.

So, here is the interview with Marlene Daab and Carol Jennings. They have been my good friends for a number of years, and bring a different and unique perspective to the talk about Star Trek.

Marlene Daab & Carol Jennings

"We're Not Geeks"

First of all, and foremost, you're both *Star Trek* fans and big collectors — but let's start with you, Carol — what does *Star Trek* mean
to you?

CAROL JENNINGS: When you see a lot of the science fiction out
there you think about the future as "we're going to be in a nuclear
holocaust," a kind of *Mad Max* sort of future, as opposed to what *Star
Trek* presents: a positive future. It's a future where we're going to
explore, go beyond, and get past all of our differences. It's not going to
become just some terrible place to live — everything "turns out" ok!

MARLENE DAAB: Right. Everything is not post-apocalyptic. It's a
very positive future and we've learned to overcome racial differences,
cultural differences, everyone is pretty much accepted as they are.
The quest for personal wealth and the "gathering of things," if you will,
doesn't seem to be at the forefront in the future. It's more about getting
along with your companions and working for the good of humanity.
It's the acceptance of people for their gifts, but also accepting them
for their weaknesses; everyone has something to contribute, whether
they're black, white, in a wheelchair, big, little; it doesn't seem to
matter. Everyone seems to have a positive role, something definite
to offer.

Your answers have led right into my next question. Why were
you attracted to *Star Trek?*

CAROL: Gadgets! (Laughs) No really, there are two reasons, I think.
Firstly, I'm a space-baby; I was in Kindergarten watching the first man
step on the moon and now on television there are shows with people
living in space! That's the whole adventure part of it. But, then there's
the gadgets — there are really the best gadgets on *Star Trek!*

MARLENE: Some of those gadgets have made it into our everyday
lives. Flip cell phones, for instance, are communicators! There are also
many adults who have been influenced due to watching the original
Star Trek, influenced to go into such fields as engineering, communications, or medicine. Those very things they have seen as only fiction
in a TV show have been brought forth by them and made a reality
now. We have advances in medicine that are directly an imitation of
things we saw on *Star Trek.*

CAROL: And so many people in NASA, too, have been influenced
by *Star Trek.*

MARLENE: Again, the show was just a very positive influence on
a whole lot of people. That's what it was for me, too. It was fun, it
was an adventure; the gadgets were cool. The premise of the people

coming together to form a family of sorts and look out for each other, to become this cohesive working unit was a very positive thing.

How do you feel then that *Star Trek* is different from other science fiction series that have come before and come after?

CAROL: It's different because the story isn't so much related to "battling the monster," which is generally the premise in science fiction. In *Star Trek* the story is about the relationships of the crew. Of course, they do occasionally battle aliens, but it's the relationships and the characterizations that make *Star Trek* unique and stand out from other science fiction shows.

MARLENE: I have to agree that it is the relationships — the interaction — how the characters and their inter-relationships developed. We really did see that, not only in the original series, but also in *The Next Generation*. Now, this was not a tight-knit group to start out with, they were new people coming aboard the ship. From that beginning as strangers they developed over the years in the series to become a close-knit caring group of people who happened to be space travelers. In *The Next Generation*, the stories that were the absolute best were the ones that dealt with the characters, the personalities, how they interacted — their souls and beings — how they were as individuals and as a group. The character development was good and that came through in a lot of stories.

CAROL: The thing that has set *Star Trek* apart, with the exception of one of the series, has been the writing. It's been so much better than you generally find in a science fiction series. And the writing makes all the difference. The stories have substance; they're not just good guy/bad guy.

I've heard particularly the original series, but also to some extent the other series as well, as "morality tales."

CAROL: Yes. That's it. *Star Trek* takes the problems of today and puts them into a story that people can relate to. Take, for example classic *Trek* and the episode "Let That Be Your Last Battlefield" with Frank Gorshin. He played a character with the right side of his face colored black, the other half white, and the filming of that episode was right in the middle of racial tensions in America. His character was fighting with another character and the whole reason for the conflict was that his opponent was black on the left side and white on the right, therefore the opponent was inferior! The episode very neatly showed the stupidity of racial discrimination without being too preachy.

MARLENE: It was way of bringing current social events forward and presenting them, as you say, a morality tale, without the audience being beaten over the head. The story was presented and the viewers were allowed to make their own evaluation of it.

I suppose that's something that other shows couldn't do at the time.

Marlene Daab and Carol Jennings in *Star Trek* dress uniforms at the 2007 Science Fiction Hall of Fame Induction ceremony for Gene Roddenberry at the EMP Museum in Seattle, Washington. PHOTO COURTESY OF ANTHONY WYNN.

CAROL: I think they could have done it, but they weren't written as well.

MARLENE: Or didn't have as bold a vision.

CAROL: Gene Roddenberry had a bold vision in that he wasn't afraid to stand up and say what was right and what was wrong.

MARLENE: Or at least be able to come up with a way to reflect back to the public what was going on in the present, but telling you in such a way that they could see those kinds of prejudices were wrong.

CAROL: Even in *Next Generation* there were episodes like "The Outcast" with the androgynous race where one of them falls in love with Commander Riker. For me, this story represented gays in our society; you have the one who loved somebody the community said they couldn't. It was another story that pointed out an issue of that time.

We're sitting for the interview in this marvelous room in your house that's full of gadgets, memorabilia, toys, and just everything *Star Trek*-related! It reminds me of a dealer's room at a convention, only better. As you know, conventions have now become a big part of the *Star Trek* mythos. Marlene, when was your first convention experience?

MARLENE: My very first one was in Eugene, Oregon. It was held at the fairgrounds in 1975 and the special guests were two actors that you've interviewed, George Takei and Grace Lee Whitney. My next convention in 1976 was here in Portland and Gene Roddenberry was the guest there. So those were both very memorable experiences.

CAROL: Mine was in 1990 here in Portland with Patrick Stewart. I was new to it and had no idea that those things existed. I was completely awestruck and the dealer's room had all the gadgets! That's how I first got hooked. It was a small convention, intimate. I went to a mega-convention in Seattle shortly thereafter with William Shatner and Leonard Nimoy and I didn't really like it. They were on a stage and I couldn't really see them. I thought it was waste of my time and money.

Most *Star Trek* conventions today are the big mega-cons with thousands of people that can cost an attendee several hundred dollars to attend. What do you think of the evolution of conventions?

CAROL: It's bad.

MARLENE: I think it's bad too. Even though there are thousands of people that still attend, I think the prices you pay and the fees paid the celebrities are very overpriced. I know that as celebrities they get paid a lot of money for their performances, for their autographs, for their appearances and things like that, but I still think its way too much money for the average person. I would like to see the prices come down a bit.

CAROL: It used to be that you paid to get into a convention and included in the price of admission were autographs from the attending celebrities, if, of course, you were willing to stand in a long line of people. So it used to be that the actors — the stars — were more accessible and were looked up to by young fans. Now with the extreme high prices that all of the actors charge at conventions for autographs, they're priced themselves right out of the market for many fans, and particularly the young children.

This leads into my next question. Perhaps in part due to the rising costs in attending conventions, both of you started volunteering to work at conventions and events. What was the first convention you volunteered at and how did all of this begin?

MARLENE: We had friends who were dealers and would travel to conventions. We initially started working with them, assisting. Then

Marlene Daab and Carol Jennings in their famous *Star Trek* memorabilia room which has been featured on several television programs. PHOTO COURTESY OF ANTHONY WYNN.

we actually worked a convention for them when they couldn't make it. We took the merchandise and worked the show by ourselves. It was a lot of fun! We enjoyed it and we liked working the crowd. Over the years, at so many conventions, we would see so many people who would sit back and not interact with fans. Well, when we were working we stood up, talked to the people, showed them items and actually conversed with them! It was really something that we enjoyed. So, having done that with our friends, and for our friends, we got the opportunity to work here in Portland at a local convention where we worked at the booth of Richard Arnold, who at one time had been an assistant to Gene Roddenberry. Richard has turned that experience of working for Gene Roddenberry into a living. He works as a consultant to Creation Entertainment, a company that hosts some of the largest *Star Trek* conventions around the country. He works at some of these conventions giving presentations and talks about his experiences working with Gene Roddenberry. At the Portland convention he had a table of items he was selling and he needed assistance there at the times when he was on-stage periodically. The next year we worked directly for Creation at one of their merchandise tables.

CAROL: So, at the point we were on their volunteer list. **You were becoming trusted volunteers for these people.**

MARLENE: Yes. Our names were being recognized as people who they had worked with before. So, when we found out about the Creation conventions being held in Las Vegas...

CAROL: They cost a lot more than we could afford!

MARLENE: Since there are two of us, everything is doubled! It wasn't possible for us to be able to afford to go to the convention and take advantage of having the best seats. If you're going to go, you might as well get the best seats and all of the fringe benefits that go with it. But we simply could not afford it. We decided then, to see if could cash in on what little recognition our names did have with Creation, and work as volunteers. We've been volunteering now for nine years in a row at the annual Las Vegas *Star Trek* convention, held every August. It's been wonderful and we've met people from all over the world.

CAROL: Its fun for us to volunteer for the conventions because we are more social, well more sociable — and we're fans! So it's not as if we're dealers who are only there to make money and looking at the fans walking by, saying, "Oh boy, there goes another geek..." We see people from around the world and now, after several years, it's like "old home week." There are so many friends that we've met.

MARLENE: For us, it's not a business venture. It's totally for fun; it's four days of being a kid again.

CAROL: There's one guy who's been there every year and he dresses as a Klingon very well. Sometime at conventions costumes aren't the best, and perhaps some folks shouldn't try to be Klingons — but there are others who take it seriously. And this guy is one of the ones that does it well. But one day during the convention he was out of costume and riding in a mobility scooter. It was then that I noticed a tattoo down the side of his arm of the Twin Towers and a fire department symbol. It turned out that he was one of the firemen who was hurt in 9/11 and the Las Vegas convention is one of the highlights of his year. Due to his injuries from that day, he not always able to walk well and he had to retire from his job. But he still makes a tremendous effort every year to come to the convention, to see old friends, and enjoy *Star Trek*. I find him to be very inspiring.

At these conventions you've met a lot of actors, performers; name a few that have made a particular impression on you for one reason or another.

CAROL: We were volunteering at the photo booth, where the celebrities pose for pictures with fans. It moves along very quickly, the fans have 15 seconds to walk in, sit down, the camera clicks; they get up, and go. For this session, it was Avery Brooks [Captain Benjamin Sisko of *Star Trek: Deep Space Nine*] posing for pictures with fans and he was very popular. The lines were out the door! When people would come in, he'd say, "Hi, I'm Avery — what's your name?" The person would respond, they'd shake hands, the picture would be snapped, and the fan would be ushered out the door. Well, the next day, Avery Brooks was signing autographs and the fans were telling us that Avery would look up, recognize the fan, and greet them by name! He remembered who most of these people were from just a fifteen-second meeting. And there were hundreds of fans who had had there pictures taken.

MARLENE: Now that's quite a memory! But beyond that, it's a gesture from a performer to his fans that says "You're important to me. I'm here because you put me here and I'm going to appreciate that." It was amazing.

CAROL: Marina Sirtis [Commander Deanna Troi of *Star Trek: The Next Generation*] is another actor who is great with fans. I have heard her interact with fans and she has said, "I'm here because of you. Thank you for my house, my car…" (Laughs)

MARLENE: It's performers like those, who actually thank the fans; those are truly the ones that stand out to me.

I've heard you talk, too, about a special celebrity couple that you've come to know at the conventions. Who are they?

MARLENE: Ellen DeGeneres had a television show a few years back called *Ellen* and in the show her character owned a bookstore and to draw more customers into her shop, she hired two performers to come in and do some evening performances. She found this really bad vaudeville-esque team to perform. We happened to catch that episode, then not long after were off to Las Vegas for the convention. Well, low and behold, none other than those two performers were sitting at a table in the autograph area! Their names are Charlie

Brill and Mitzi McCall. We went up to the table and started to sing the theme song that they had performed on *Ellen*. Part of it goes, "Enthusiasm! Enthusiasm!" On the show, they'd sing, then tell a joke — then sing the tune again, and tell another joke. Of course, they knew immediately that we had seen *Ellen*, and loved it. It turns out that they are not only a performing couple, but Charlie is an actor who appeared in the original series episode "The Trouble with Tribbles." He also appeared in archive footage, thirty years later, used in the *Deep Space Nine* sequel "Trials and Tribble-ations." He played the character who was the Klingon who had been surgically altered to look human. But it was so fun to meet them and we'd see them in the hallways of the hotel, where we'd all burst into song! It was just a great way to meet these people and talk to them; they were so approachable and very nice.

To my mind, there are very few series where fans actually know who the creator is, and who also have a reverence or respect for that person. What are your thoughts about Gene Roddenberry, the creator of *Star Trek*?

CAROL: The Great Bird of the Galaxy! (Laughs) I think that Gene Roddenberry had a vision and he was strong enough and passionate enough to see that vision through to reality.

MARLENE: Gene was a pioneer with his ideas. He forced us to look at ourselves maybe in a little bit of a different light, as a society. He was a humanitarian, interested in the betterment of mankind and ever hopeful that the future of humanity would be one that will turn out positively. In the 1960s he gave important roles to Asians, women, Blacks — not to mention a Russian on the bridge of the USS *Enterprise* at the height of the Cold War! He wanted to show that humans could work together, that we had gotten past the difficulties of the past. No one else was really doing that at the time.

CAROL: Gene Roddenberry took risks in showing how things could be; things that weren't that way at the time. *Star Trek* made history with television's first interracial kiss between Captain Kirk and Lieutenant Uhura [William Shatner and Nichelle Nichols].

Let's move into a little more of a personal area, if we could. When did you both meet, and where, and did *Star Trek* have anything to do with that?

CAROL: Yes it did!

MARLENE: We met through a mutual friend who also was a *Star Trek* fan and thought that we would all just hang out together and have a good time. Enjoy a mutual hobby, similar interests, and that sort of thing. I think we really surprised her when the two of us really hit it off and became a couple — and have been ever since. That was 1992.

CAROL: We met on March 27, 1992. It was at my house and I was hosting a *Star Trek* sleepover! (Laughs) There were several of us, part of a geeky little club.

Marlene Daab and Carol Jennings pose in their Star Trek memorabilia room. PHOTO COURTESY OF ANTHONY WYNN.

MARLENE: In November 2003 we went to Victoria, British Columbia in Canada and took advantage of their marriage laws and had a wedding. It was wonderful, it was very nice to be able to do that. We had a wedding planner who helped us to get our license, cake, champagne, witnesses — it was very small, but very meaningful. It's too bad that we had to go to a foreign country to do it, but we were able to do it nonetheless.

Congratulations!

MARLENE: Thank you.

CAROL: Thanks.

What does it mean to be gay and fans of *Star Trek*?

CAROL: I think that *Star Trek* fans are a group of people who are, in the vast majority, accepting. That's part of the attraction to *Star Trek* if you're gay, because there is such acceptance. When you live in a world where you're not accepted, it's fun to have this "fantasy world," this group of friends, where you *are* accepted. One of the couples we see at conventions every year are Dutch and are actually the first gay couple to get married in Holland. Not only that, it was a *Star Trek*-themed wedding! They are two men that we see every year in a place where we all connect. There are a lot of gay *Star Trek* fans and I think that it is the acceptance. When you have politicians, parents, the church, or whomever, telling you that you're "evil" and going to "hell"; you have *Star Trek* that is essentially saying that religions are a thing of the past, that everyone is accepted. Fans also identify with each other, with the characters on the show, identify with the stories; and you've got this place where you can go where you feel safe and accepted. It's a good feeling. Gene Roddenberry created a special symbol, the "IDIC," which stands for "Infinite Diversity in Infinite Combinations." That is the real core of *Star Trek*.

George Takei, who played "Sulu" in *Star Trek*, has been in the news. What are your feelings about that?

MARLENE: Well, I think it's wonderful! I think many fans knew already that he was a gay man...

Intuitively?

MARLENE: Yes. It wasn't a big surprise when we heard that he came out. Even though we might know, intuitively, there still is a good feeling that we have toward someone coming out because that means they've reached a point in their life where they feel more comfortable with themselves, and they can feel comfortable in being honest with their fans.

CAROL: There is no way that he could have come out earlier in his career. He would have a hard enough time because of his Asian heritage in getting acting work, due to all the stereotyping. It would have been doubly difficult being Asian *and* openly gay; it would have hurt his career. I think it's very brave of him and I'm proud of him. It's a scary thing to come out and it's even harder when you're a public figure. You don't know for sure how people are going to react. But I think, too, that *Star Trek* fans like him even more because he had come out.

You've been featured on a number of television programs and even took part in a live broadcast from your home when the last *Star Trek* movie debuted! Now I heard that you were interviewed for a new show. What can you tell me about that?

MARLENE: William Shatner has been filming a documentary for television about fans; not only about *Star Trek* fans; but fans in general of all kinds. Extreme fandom, if you will. He was at the Las Vegas *Star Trek* convention and film crews were there with him, following him around. They were near the booth where we were working and wanted to talk to me since I was a volunteer. So a number of the volunteers were interviewed en masse, as a group, and asked us about our work volunteering and about being fans in general. We're looking forward to being able to see that and see how we came across.

Our time is about at an end, but I have one last question for you; something a little more lighthearted. Do you think there is a difference between "Trekkies" and "Trekkers" and do you have a preference as to how people should refer to you?

CAROL: There's no real difference. It doesn't really matter to me. It's just semantics. I suppose the people who are more classic *Star Trek*-oriented tend to refer to themselves as "Trekkers" and *Next Generation* fans tend to call themselves "Trekkies." It's really the ideas and ideals behind it that makes someone a *Trek* fan.

MARLENE: I tend to agree with Carol. There really is no difference. We're all geeky in some way, on some level. But to be clear: we're not *geeks*! (Laughs) We're all fans, we're all loyal; we have been for years and years — and we will continue to be. Call me a "Trekker," or call me a "Trekkie"…just don't call me late for dinner!

Thanks for the great interview!

MARLENE: It's been our pleasure.

CAROL: Thank you.

Armin Shimerman was born to immigrant parents and raised in a small farming town in New Jersey, moving to Los Angeles when he was sixteen years old. In an effort to help her son meet new people there, Armin's mother enrolled him in a drama group and, as they say, the rest is history. Upon graduation from the University of California at Los Angeles, he was chosen as one of only eight apprentices out of a field of nine hundred at the prestigious Old Globe Theatre in San Diego. Armin appeared prominently in many regional theater productions for the Tyrone Guthrie Theatre, the Mark Taper Forum, the American Shakespeare Festival, the New York Shakespeare Festival, and the Indiana Repertory Theatre.

Following a move to New York, Armin landed roles in the Broadway production of Richard Rodgers' last musical, I Remember Mama, Broadway with Chris Sarandon and Teri Garr, Saint Joan with Lynn Redgrave, and Joseph Papp's acclaimed production of Three Penny Opera with Raul Julia.

Armin then returned to his adopted town of Los Angeles and he found recurring roles in two CBS series: "Pascal" in Beauty and the Beast, and "Cousin Bernard" in Brooklyn Bridge. His other television credits include roles on such television series as L.A. Law, Married: With Children, Civil Wars Seinfeld, and Leverage. He also appeared in the recurring roles of Judge Moskin on The Practice, and as "Principal Snyder" on Buffy

Armin Shimerman & Kitty Swink

"It's Hard to be a Method Actor and be a Ferengi!"

the Vampire Slayer. *Armin is perhaps best known for his role of "Quark" throughout seven seasons of* Star Trek: Deep Space Nine. *He has been married to actress Kitty Swink for more than thirty years.*

Kitty Swink was born and raised in Portland, Oregon and is a gradu-ate of the University of Oregon. After moving to New York, she appeared Off-Broadway in The Great Nebula in Orion, Augustus Does His Bit, *and* The Lugosi Trilogy. *It was in New York where Armin and Kitty first met and were married.*

Kitty has appeared in numerous television shows, including Judging Amy, Chicago Hope, Party of Five, Star Trek: Deep Space Nine, Any Day Now, Providence, Without a Trace, Crossing Jordan, Leverage, Harry's Law, *and several Movies of the Week. In Los Angeles, she has appeared in Last* Summer at Bluefish Cove, The Indecent Exposure Cabaret, *and the Women in Film One Act Theatre Festival. She is a member of the Matrix Theatre Company where she performed J.B. Priestley's* Dangerous Corner, *for which she was nominated for an Ovation Award, and won a Garland Award for Outstanding Performance by an Ensemble.*

You were both together in a wonderful two-handed play, A.R. Gurney's *Love Letters* which just ended its run. Is this the first time you've worked together?

ARMIN SHIMERMAN: No. We've done *Love Letters* before and we've also performed in movies together. We were a husband-wife team in *Like Father, Like Son*...

KITTY SWINK: Don't blink, you'll miss us! We also did *Love's Labors Lost*, we like to keep the love theme going.

ARMIN: We did the *The Garry Shandling Show* where we got cast separately and they didn't realize they had hired a married couple, much to their surprise, until about halfway through the week when they realized were a couple.

KITTY: They kept saying, "You guys carpool, how cute!" To which I replied, "Well, it's because we're married." I've also done a couple episodes of *Star Trek* but they never let us work together, they thought that was too dangerous."

ARMIN: But you weren't a Ferengi!

KITTY: No! I was too tall to be Ferengi.

ARMIN: Yes, right you *are* too tall to be a Ferengi.

You would have made a fun Ferengi!

KITTY: I would have been the giantess of the Ferengi race! I'm a very tall girl.

You both received wonderful reviews for *Love Letters*; do you think it's easier or more difficult to work together as a married couple?

KITTY: You know, even when we're not actually shooting something together we work together because we never do a project that we don't rehearse with each other; we're each other's best directors and critics, so I think it's just a nice extension of how we live our lives.

ARMIN: We enjoy working together. We have a great rapport; it's why we've been together for eighteen years.

KITTY: No honey, nineteen.

ARMIN: Well, the first year didn't count. (Laughs)

KITTY: Oh!

ARMIN: Maybe it was the last year that didn't count! (Laughs)

KITTY: Ohhh! (Laughs) I'll remember that.

ARMIN: We enjoy working together and when I'm working on my books, Kitty is over my shoulder and giving wonderful notes.

KITTY: Thank you.

***Love Letters* has really become an American classic, hasn't it?**

ARMIN: I think so, yes.

KITTY: The language.

Your characters, Andrew Makepeace Ladd III and Melissa Gardner are just so well-written. What have these roles brought to you, to your portrayal?

ARMIN: Well Andy is a bit of a stick in the mud; I have some of that.

KITTY: Just a little bit.

ARMIN: He eventually learns that the relationship with Melissa gives him more of a sense of life going on, and gets him away from his "nose to the grindstone" attitude. That's been an education that I need to re-live every now and then, just to remind myself to not be so much of a workaholic. It's helped a great deal.

KITTY: Melissa's a free spirit, but lets that free spirit take her too far. She has dangerous problems with that. You know, that's always good to revisit in your life. Whatever is your greatest strength can also be your greatest weakness. What I think is the greatest thing about doing this play, for us, is that the language is so wonderful. Armin and I both love language and are excited about introducing other people to the beauty of language. That's been a real ride for us.

ARMIN: The theatre is the last bastion of language as far as entertainment; films and TV are really about images. You can watch a show for an extended period of time and not have any dialogue in it whatsoever and still be incredibly well entertained, but you can't do that in the theatre. There is something wonderful about language; language has been with us forever. If we're not careful, it may just disappear. We have it now in novels, we have it in stage plays; and it's a precious asset that we have to make sure is always rediscovered and re-experienced.

I really agree with that.

KITTY: Thank you. I'm glad you do.

You mentioned something to me before, before we started, about the relationship of the audience and the actors. Can you tell us a little more about that?

KITTY: I think that's why so many actors love to work in the theatre. When you're in front of the camera there's maybe five objects in-between you and the actor you're working with. It's not about rapport. When you're on-stage it's not just about the rapport between the two of you, but the audience becomes a character and they come to life with you and if we don't come to them and they don't come to the party with us, it's an empty experience. But when you're all working together its cathartic in an almost mystical kind of way, which I know sounds funny. Even if you're doing something just slapstick-y and silly, you're partners. The audience laughs and you ride the wave of the laugh, then you give them the next one and they give you the next... It's a wonderful, almost athletic, experience.

ARMIN: It's in the very classic sense of community, of people work-ing together. The actor's job is to go through a catharsis on-stage and by the actor going through that catharsis the audience gets it as well. If the audience doesn't have the catharsis, then ironically the actors don't have it either.

By all accounts and from the reviews you've gotten for *Love Letters*...

ARMIN: There was a lot of catharsis going on! (Laughs)

KITTY: (Laughs) The audiences here have been really fun. They've come wanting to have a good time, wanting to be moved, wanting to laugh; and we've done it together. It's been fun.

You both have a love of the classics, of William Shakespeare and George Bernard Shaw. What was your first experience doing some of these classic plays on-stage?

ARMIN: For me, I'm the Shakespeare-lover. I was introduced to Shakespeare in high school when I was cast as Claudius in *Hamlet*. I was bowled-over by the language and by the power of the play and it became a lifelong passion. When I graduated from high school I went to college and sought a degree in English and I took a major specialization in Elizabethan Studies, and it was what I graduated with. When I graduated from college I went directly into a Shakespeare company in San Diego and for many years as an actor I worked primarily in tights doing classical plays, whether they were Shakespeare

Actors Armin Shimerman and Kitty Swink talk about their beginnings in show business. PHOTO COURTESY OF ANTHONY WYNN.

or Moliere or Shaw. It was my passion; it is what I was most in love with until I met Kitty.

KITTY: [To Armin] Thank you, sweetheart.

ARMIN: And I'm still in love with Shakespeare; I'm still in love with Kitty!

KITTY: He really is the finest Shakespearian actor that I know, and I know a lot of actors. He's really wonderful. Wonderful!

ARMIN: I've really been fortunate enough to also teach and the technique I teach is all about language; about a lost art that the Elizabethans studied all the time and we don't study so much: it's called rhetoric. If you understand the principles of rhetoric, especially Elizabethan rhetoric, then you understand perfectly why Shakespeare wrote the way he did. If you say the language the way the rhetorical principles tell you how to do it, it becomes amazingly clear. People who can't understand Shakespeare all of a sudden do.

There's a big debate going on between scholars about who Shakespeare really was. Do you have an opinion on that?

ARMIN: I don't. Whoever wrote the plays, wrote the plays and I'm thankful for it. I think the debate is simply because academicians really can't stomach the idea that a non-university student could have written all of these wonderful plays, had these enormously universal thoughts...

Or even that an actor wrote these plays?

KITTY: (Laughs)

ARMIN: ...or that an actor wrote these plays.

KITTY: That's a different story, entirely!

ARMIN: Understand that being an actor in Elizabethan times is similar to being an actor in porno films today; they had the same sort of bad connotation. So yes, it's hard to believe that somebody like that wrote these plays. It's a lot easier to try and find someone who has the academic background and might fit into the round hole that supposedly is Shakespeare. But I like to think that it was sort of somebody who didn't go to school and was just brilliant.

Beside acting on-stage and in television and films, you've branched out — you're the author of two books...

ARMIN: And I'm writing a third; some of it today.

Your most recent book is *The Merchant Prince*. Can you tell us a little bit about that?

ARMIN: *The Merchant Prince* came out of a wonderful situation. There's an actor named Peter Jurasik, a friend of ours, who was on *Babylon 5* for many years.

KITTY: He also played "Sid the Snitch" on *Hill Street Blues*.

ARMIN: Exactly. A publisher came to Peter and talked to him about the idea of co-writing a science fiction novel with a science fiction writer and they wanted to do a series of these books. Peter agreed to it and this publisher called up Peter's agent and asked, "Do you have any other science fiction actors that we might put together with our science fiction writers. Luckily for me, I was one of the actors that they had in the stable and they hooked me up with a wonderful man named Michael Scott who lives in Dublin, Ireland. The publisher brought Michael out to Los Angeles, it was his first trip to L.A., and we were in a hotel room for three days where we worked on the outline of our book *The Merchant Prince* and we came up with a great story. As I told you, I'm very much interested in Elizabethan times and Elizabethan characters. They asked me, "What do you want to write about?" I said, "I want to write about something Elizabethan." They replied, "Well, that makes for a very hard science fiction book." But Michael had this wonderful idea. He knew of this character called "Dr. John Dee" who was Elizabeth's astrologer. He had the largest library in England; he was

Armin Shimerman pauses before answering a question. PHOTO COURTESY OF ANTHONY WYNN.

a spy; he claimed to speak to angels and developed a language he called the "Enochian" language which he supposedly used to speak to those angels; he also was a very famous mathematician and just a well-respected and fascinating guy. Michael introduced me to this historical person and he began to write; he wrote the first chapter.

Now, I believe that the publisher didn't expect me to do much more than work on the outline. But he didn't know...(Laughter)...he didn't know that I had done some writing when I was younger and was fascinated with writing. And I had some time on my hands! So when Michael sent me the first chapter of *The Merchant Prince*, I didn't much care for it. I re-wrote the whole thing! Michael liked the re-writes — and that is how we set up the relationship. He would send me a pretty sketchy chapter and I would flesh it out. Almost all the dialogue that our leading character has is written by me; almost all of the descriptive passages are written by me and in the end I would say that I wrote about 45% of the novel and Michael wrote about 55%. We had great fun doing it and it was all done on the internet emailed back and forth between L.A. and Dublin; it took us two and a half years and we came up with what I consider to be a very good novel, we've gotten very good reviews on it. I hope everybody will get a chance to read it and lets me know what they think about it.

Your first book was a *Star Trek* book, *The 34th Rule*.

ARMIN: *The 34th Rule* ironically, came out first but was written second. It was started through two friends of mine, David George and Eric Stillwell. We were trying to pick some ideas for episodes of *Deep Space Nine* and we had about four or five episode ideas that we took in to the producers and pitched. "Pitch" meaning that we're trying to get them to buy these ideas. They didn't buy any of them. We were very disappointed when we left the meeting, very disappointed. Because I had written *The Merchant Prince*, I turned to both of them and said, "Why don't we write a *novel* about the Ferengi idea?" Eric didn't have enough time to do that; but David, who had always wanted to be a novelist, did. So David and I sat down and expanded the idea that we had and wrote it in a rather quick time. We wrote it in about nine months. When it came out it became the best-selling *Deep Space Nine* novel, ever. We got terrifically good reviews and I think our novel sort of changed the way that *Star Trek* books are written. This book is not really about a ship fighting somebody or trying to combat with some strange alien; it's really about people, much the same that *Deep Space Nine* is about.

I thought that *Deep Space Nine* was fascinating from the standpoint that, especially in stories dealing with your character of "Quark" and the Ferengi, they were focused on families and relationships, which was interesting.

ARMIN: We did. Certainly one of my main relationships on the show was my relationship with my brother. We dealt with that. *Star Trek* is really a metaphor for things happening to us in the twentieth and twenty-first centuries.

KITTY: Gene Roddenberry's original pitch on the classic series was "*Wagon Train* to the stars."

ARMIN: We went much further than that. We tried, even though it was comic relationship about two brothers, we dealt with a lot of things that brothers and siblings have to deal with. I thought we did a good job of that.

KITTY: And you dealt with unions, sexism, homelessness; it's a really lovely show.

Going back a bit, Kitty, I'd like to ask you about your background. You went to the University of Oregon, but when did you first become interested in becoming an actress?

KITTY: I think as a small child, but then at Beaverton High School on the Westside of Portland I was in a lot of plays. I worked backstage, I worked on-stage; anywhere I could because I was fascinated with theatre. I went to the University of Oregon and when I graduated, worked at a bank in the daytime, at a dinner theater at night, and sang telegrams on my lunch hours and on weekends to save money to go to New York because it was important. It's what I wanted. You can't do it unless you are willing to push that hard. It's a real struggle and you have to want it that badly.

ARMIN: Kitty's life is indicative of many actors and actresses who just have a calling and they follow that calling. Often it means leaving home; it means studying, and suffering for long periods of time. Luckily for Kitty she had success but there are a lot of people who aren't as lucky.

Sometimes it means working in other jobs other than acting...

KITTY: Oh, absolutely! Even at a point in our lives when we have both worked a lot and have been successful, done Broadway shows, done television; I've been on a soap — we had a year where things were really tight and we were making money as actors but not enough to pay our mortgage. Armin was teaching and I became a calligrapher. I was doing calligraphy for all of these society and Hollywood weddings which was very strange. A producer I had been a recurring character for in a show called *Almost Grown* came to a wedding where I had done all the calligraphy, and when I worked for him later on another show he said, "Well, I thought you had given up the business." I replied, "No, I was just trying not to lose everything that we had worked so hard to get." Fortunately we don't have to do that anymore. [Kitty knocks wood]

So you made it to New York.

KITTY: Back then, New York was everyone's first choice for theatre. Now I think there are other choices: Chicago, Seattle, and Minneapolis. I initially worked in regional theatre, but I sort of accidentally became a kind of nightclub chanteuse. It wasn't at all what I had in mind! But it was a lot better than being a waitress.

You were still entertaining audiences.

KITTY: Yes.

ARMIN: And she was good!

KITTY: Thanks, baby! It's because you used to like it when I sang Hoagy Carmichael to you.

ARMIN: I did like that! It was my favorite.

KITTY: I was acting still and going to class, I still studied — it's important, you always study.

Do you still sing?

KITTY: Every once in a while. I don't as much as I used to but I do sing some.

ARMIN: There isn't much call for singing actresses in Hollywood. There is in New York and other cities, but in L.A. they don't need that many singing actresses.

That's too bad. I keep hoping that musicals are going to make a comeback in films one of these days...

KITTY: Oh, me too.

ARMIN: I don't think you should hold your breath!

KITTY: This guy [pointing at Armin] did two Broadway musicals and can't sing, and he was fabulous in both of them.

ARMIN: I had a very lucky situation. I did Richard Rodgers' last musical and the character I was playing had a song in pre-production, a very nice song, but when they heard me sing they realized that I *couldn't* sing. But they wanted me anyway, even though I couldn't sing!

KITTY: You were fabulous in the show!

ARMIN: I was *great* in the show!

KITTY: Well, I can say that because I wasn't dating you at time I saw you perform.

ARMIN: They hired me anyway, even though I couldn't sing, and on the first day of rehearsal the director — very sheepishly — came up to me and said, "Armin, we love your work, but we're going to take the song away." I was more than happy to give it up.

KITTY: But then he got it back!

ARMIN: Yes, what happened was the character was so popular in the play that it was strange he didn't have a song. Richard Rodgers wrote his last song for me and a lady named Elizabeth Hubbard. It was very, very funny, but it didn't have an ending. The first three quarters of it were boffo, they were great! It just didn't have an ending. So when the show finally opened, the song left as well.

That show, of course, was *I Remember Mama*.

KITTY: Or, for those of us who saw it, *I Dismember Mama*. Liv Ullmann is not a musical comedy performer.

ARMIN: She couldn't sing any better than I could and she had seven solos! (Laughs)

KITTY: You were good, George Hearn was good.

George Hearn is wonderful, isn't he?

ARMIN: George Hearn introduced us.

KITTY: He also talked me into proposing to Armin.

[To Kitty] So you're the one who made the proposal?

ARMIN: Oh yes, Kitty made the proposal.

KITTY: The first time. Then he proposed three months later.

ARMIN: You see, being regional theatre actors as well as Broadway actors, we were in many cities the first couple of years of our relationship. When Kitty proposed to me, I was in Minneapolis; and when I proposed to her, she was in Indianapolis.

KITTY: We were in this funny, but nice, hotel with the whole cast on opening night and there was a lounge singer who said, "Oh, Hey! I just heard that Armin and Kitty are going to get engaged tonight. Armin's proposed to Kitty and I want to sing a song that will be — *your song!*" Then he started singing, "Don't go changin'...*Hey! Hey!*" At that point, all of us got up and left — eighteen people up and gone! (Laughs)

ARMIN: Then she made me get down on my knee and do it right later on in the evening. [To Kitty] I must have done it right; we've lasted a long time.

KITTY: [To Armin] A long time, even if you can't remember how many years. (Laughs)

There's a seeming myth about Hollywood that divorces may be more rampant than in the rest of society. Is that really true?

ARMIN: Yes, it is true. I think it is just what we were talking about, which is that people are separated for periods of time. When you go off and do a film from anywhere from three to six months you're away from each other for a long time and that puts a real stress on a relationship. Even if you're doing TV and you're coming home every night, the hours are extremely long. What happens is you don't see the other person all week long because you get up so early and come home so late that the other person is usually asleep. It puts a great stress on a relationship to not see each other for long periods of time. Also, if you're successful as an actor; or even if unsuccessful, for both these things — makes the person going through that stress enormously unstable. You have to be careful to root yourself in reality when you're doing this.

KITTY: I'd like to say that our friends, for the most part, are long-married couples. Rene Auberjonois, who played "Odo" on Star Trek, and his wife have been married thirty-seven years, I think. Andrew Robinson, who played "Garak," and his wife have been married for more than thirty years.

ARMIN: Both of those relationship were started in the theatre and weren't necessarily "Hollywood" marriages.

KITTY: I do think that if you're one of those people who's, say, twenty-three and just plain beautiful and you're kissing a different girl in a show every week, maybe that could do it.

ARMIN: That could be seductive.

KITTY: We do a little bit of that, but not much.

ARMIN: That's the great thing about being a character actor!

You don't mind being called a character actor?

ARMIN: Oh, God, no! That's what I am! I'm very happy to be a character actor. God, I'd be a miserable leading man. There's no shame in that whatsoever. I'm very proud to be a character actor.

KITTY: Me too.

Kitty, you've done a lot of episodic television; you've been in just about all of the top shows on TV.

KITTY: One year I was on five shows and they were all cancelled; three of them before they aired, and two of them while I was on the set.

ARMIN: I begged her, "Don't show up on *Deep Space Nine*, please! Please stay away from our show!" (Laughs)

KITTY: If it was a bad show that season, I was on it! It's really terrible.

One show that you can be really proud of is *Designing Women*. It's a classic episode of that series called "They Shoot Fat Women, Don't they?"

KITTY: This was at the end of the bad year we talked about earlier and I had worked as calligrapher for Gerald McRaney and Delta Burke's wedding. I went to the audition and I was supposed to have been the other sort of "hot" girl in high school, while Delta was *the* "hot" girl. Now she was heavy and I had all these lines about her being "the poster child for the Save the Whale Foundation" and just awful things; and she had been so lovely to me. Of course, on the set I felt just awful and she was really sweet about it. Annie Potts was an old friend and she was really sweet about it; but it was embarrassing. The night we taped, Gerald McRaney came to support Delta. I had a scene in the bathroom where we're all diss-ing Delta and she overhears us. I started crying and the director yelled, "Cut!" Harry Thomason, who was producer of the show with his wife Linda Bloodworth-Thomason, was directing that episode. I started to walk off the set. Gerald McRaney was there saying, "You didn't write it, don't worry about it!" He put his arms around me and the two of us cried. That was so sweet. Gosh, that was a long time ago.

ARMIN: There are nice moments like that on TV, usually backstage.

KITTY: You usually don't want to say those kinds of things about somebody you really care about, but it was a funny episode. She won

Armin Shimerman listens while Kitty Swink describes her experiences working on *Designing Women*. PHOTO COURTESY OF ANTHONY WYNN.

the Emmy for it. It talked about an important issue, which Delta has been very brave about.

Armin, you've done some teaching and different work in the theatre; what are your feelings about Method acting? Are you a Method actor, or do you subscribe to another philosophy?

ARMIN: It's hard to be a Method actor and be a Ferengi at the same time! (Laughs) No, I'm by no means a Method actor. There are basically two main schools of thought for American acting techniques. One is certainly The Method. The other is called the Neighborhood Playhouse technique. I am more a member of the Neighborhood Playhouse technique than I am of The Method. A Method actor, for the most part, tries to conjure up memories of things that happen in the past and by use of those memories, create a performance. The Neighborhood Playhouse technique says, rather, that you build a character with characteristics and you think about those things, and then you get all of your life from the other person. So, as I respond to you now — I'm responding to what you are giving me, what Kitty is giving me, what the camera is giving me. I respond to that, so I'm always working in a partnership. If you want to define the two, the Neighborhood Playhouse is about partnership and Method acting is about soliloquy.

That's very interesting. I've never heard it described like that.

ARMIN: That's my take on it.

Armin, you've been associated with several hit series to date, including *Brooklyn Bridge, Beauty and the Beast,* and of course, *Deep Space Nine.*

ARMIN: There's a lot. But there was a long fallow period when I was seriously considering looking for another occupation altogether. *Brooklyn Bridge* came out of the blue; I didn't audition for it, somebody just called one day and said, "How would you like to like to be on this program *Brooklyn Bridge*? I was only supposed to be there for one episode, but fortunately one of my lines was that I was a cousin to one of the leads and this was a show very much about family. There was a cousin's club — and because of the cousin's club I got more and more to do and I ended up doing a season of Brooklyn Bridge. They went on for another season, but that's when I began *Deep Space Nine*.

KITTY: A lot of the people on that show are still very dear friends.

ARMIN: Yes, in fact the lady who played my cousin and the mother of the two boys, Amy Keno, we are all business partners together in a small hotel together in Palm Springs.

Of course, Marion Ross was on that show.

ARMIN: Yes, and she was just a wonder. She never came out of character! We all know that Marion Ross doesn't have that Jewish accent, but she never dropped the accent — ever — during the day and was the character all day long. She indeed might have been a Method actress! She was a wonder to work with, and a dream.

And then there's *Beauty and the Beast*.

ARMIN: Yes. That was a wonderful program and I was on it for about two and a half years, playing a character called "Pascal," who was a pacifist and a communicator. Although I had been doing TV before that, I was rather uneducated about how you work on TV. The truth is, when I worked on *Beauty and the Beast* and especially watched the work of Ron Perlman, who was the lead, I learned a great deal about how one works on TV. It's a much different medium than working on-stage, which is what my primary experience was. It taught me a great deal about the camera, about performance on TV, about what to focus on, and it gave me a great sense of success. I was on a very good program and as I watched I learned from my choices and I got better as the program went on.

Was there a feeling of "family" on that show?

ARMIN: Yes, and in fact some of my dearest friends are those from the *Beauty and the Beast* cast. Ellen Geer, who runs the Theatricum Botanicum; Roy Dotrice; David Greenlee; and James Avery, who was the second lead on *The Fresh Prince of Bel-Air*.

KITTY: He calls us Mom and Dad!

ARMIN: We have stopped traffic with this huge man, a huge Black man, proclaiming, "MOM! DAD!" Everyone around turns and stares!

Your first experience with *Star Trek* wasn't *Deep Space Nine*, was it?

ARMIN: No. While I was doing *Beauty and the Beast*, I got an opportunity to play a talking prop on *Star Trek: The Next Generation*. I was a big *Star Trek* fan and this was a very small part. There's a given in Hollywood: if an actor appears on a TV show, he or she cannot come back to that TV show for about three or four years, because the producers don't want the audience to confuse the old character with the new one. Usually they need that length of time for the audience to forget that you've played so-and-so. I was aware of that rule and I said to them, "I'll be glad to do this part, but only if you'll continue to consider me for other parts on *Star Trek*. Now I had a great deal of make-up on in this small role. Luckily for me, two weeks later they were bringing the Ferengi on for the first time on *The Next Generation*. That, as everyone knows, also requires a lot of makeup. Since they had just had a short character actor for this prop part — me — I was fresh in their minds. So they brought me in to audition for this Ferengi character. There was a little of *Richard III*, a little bit of my Shakespeare background went in to that Ferengi character and I was hired for the part. I became the prototype for all Ferengi that followed.

You then spent a total of seven years on *Deep Space Nine*.

ARMIN: Seven years on *Deep Space Nine*, four episode of *The Next Generation*, and I had the honor of being the guest star on the first episode of *Star Trek: Voyager*.

KITTY: He was the first one to play the "hat trick."

ARMIN: The "hat trick" is appearing on all three shows. [*The Next Generation, Deep Space Nine*, and *Voyager*]

Your makeup...

ARMIN: My makeup. (Laughs)

That's a lot of years...

ARMIN: That's a lot of years in rubber, yeah.

KITTY: He had more facials than most women I've known! (Laughs)

ARMIN: It was very difficult to wear the rubber head and the mask. It was claustrophobic, it was hot, and it was disorienting. One of the ironies is that the Ferengi had such huge ears and the actors who played them were made deaf by the makeup. It was a little like having your hands over your ears while you talk; you could hear but it was a faint sound. On hot days it was enormously hot inside the makeup. It was very, very difficult. But Kitty gave me a great piece of advice when I was about half way through and complaining about the makeup a great deal. I always wanted to be on *Star Trek*, I was happy to be on *Star Trek*, and she said to me, "If you want to be a Knight, you have to wear the armor."

That is so apropos.

KITTY: After all those years of wearing corsets, high heels, wigs, and makeup I was so pleased that he had to do that. I didn't know it would be so bad, but I was sort of tickled by it. Is that mean? Yeah, I know its mean.

ARMIN: She's a feminist. (Laughs) And so am I. Ironic, since "Quark" is such a pig!

You worked with Ron Perlman who had a lot of makeup on *Beauty and the Beast*.

ARMIN: Absolutely, much worse than mine was. My makeup time was about two hours at the end, but Ron's was about three or four hours. In fact, Ron Perlman was the first person I called when I got the job and I said to Ron, "How did you do it? How did you endure those two and a half years in that much makeup?" Ron very wisely replied in his low-pitched voice, "Armin — think of the money." (Laughter) Often I did, because it made for a lot of overtime.

This has been a wonderful interview and we're nearing the end of our time. As a last question, what do you see as the future for "Quark"? Do you see a future on television or film? Perhaps further book adventures?

ARMIN: Certainly there will be further books. But I believe Quark — and he's not going to like this at all — I believe Quark's dead. I don't think we'll see Quark again, except maybe on book covers.

KITTY: I think he's wrong. While we don't think there will be a *Deep Space Nine* movie, there may be movies of mixed casts of the different *Star Trek* casts.

ARMIN: On the last day of shooting, as they took the head off for the last time, there were two voices in my head. One was a very loud voice, saying "At last, at last! Free at last!" But there was also a small, tiny little voice, "Don't kill me! Don't kill me!" I don't want to kill Quark off; maybe he will rise again.

I'll keep my fingers crossed for that.

ARMIN: Thank you.

Thank you so much, both of you; this was a great interview.

KITTY: Thank you.

ARMIN: Thank you, Tony.

Eric Stillwell began his journey to Hollywood as a production assistant on the Hallmark Hall of Fame presentation of Promise, *a television movie starring James Garner and James Woods filmed in Oregon. He followed that with positions as production assistant and script coordinator for* Star Trek: The Next Generation, *production associate on* Star Trek: Voyager, *and script coordinator for the feature film* Star Trek: Insurrection.

Following his work at Paramount Studios on Star Trek, *Eric worked for six years as Vice President of Operations for Piller², the production company created by* Trek *scriptwriter and producer Michael Piller. He also served as associate producer on USA's* The Dead Zone *television series, and ABC Family's* Wildfire *series.*

Eric co-wrote the Next Generation *episode "Yesterday's* Enterprise," *a fan favorite, and briefly took a turn before the camera as a Klingon extra in* Star Trek VI: The Undiscovered Country. *He went on to co-write the* Star Trek: Voyager *episode "Prime Factors" with David R. George III, and collaborated with both George and Armin Shimerman to write the story upon which the* Star Trek: Deep Space Nine *novel* The 34th Rule *was based.*

Currently, Eric works for the FOX Broadcasting Company in the Alternative Entertainment department, where he works on shows including American Idol, So You Think You Can Dance, The X Factor, *the* Primetime Emmys, *the* Annual American Country Awards, *as well as other specials and reality shows which air on the FOX television network. Eric and his wife Debra reside in Burbank, California.*

Eric, I've been looking forward to the opportunity to interview you for quite a while. As we begin I should disclose that we've

Eric A. Stillwell

"Star Trek *Changed My Life*"

known each other for a few a years. I think we first met in about the eighth grade in woodshop class at Jefferson Junior High School in Eugene, Oregon.

We were making cutting boards...I think I still have one!

Let's just jump right into things. Your career so far has been interesting, as a lot of it has been related to *Star Trek*. What are your first memories of *Star Trek*, when did you first see it and what attracted you to the show initially?

My father was in the Air Force and he was stationed in Idaho at Mountain Home Air Force Base. I was in the fourth grade and one of my friends at school, Brett, and I would always hang out after school and ride our bikes around and go to each other's houses. Except, whenever his favorite was on, he couldn't leave the house; he was addicted to a show called *Star Trek*. One day I was over at his house and it was time for *Star Trek* and he insisted that I stay and watch the show. I even remember the exact episode, "Return to Tomorrow" — the one with "Sargon." I don't know what hit me about the show, other than at that age I was interested in the space ships and aliens; but possibly being the competitive person that I am, it may have just been because he was into it. Before that time, I don't think I had any hobbies or special interests other than hanging out and being a kid and doing whatever kids do in the fourth grade! I started watching it every single day after school because it was always on a three o'clock, right after school.

One day there was an announcement that the station from Boise, which was carrying the show, had decided that for the next six months they were going to replace *Star Trek* with *Perry Mason* reruns. I was just beside myself! So I started a letter-writing campaign. Now, mind you, in context, *Star Trek* was already cancelled and new episodes were no longer being produced. These were just reruns of *Star Trek* that were in syndication, as the show had gone off the air in 1969. Writing a letter to a TV station and sending a petition was kind of ridiculous for a cancelled show, but I remember getting a letter back from the TV Station Manager promising that it would be back on in the fall and he sent me two black and white still photos of "Kirk" and "Spock," which I think I still have somewhere. In 1975 my dad retired from the Air Force and we moved to Eugene; that's when I started attending Jefferson Junior High.

This is around the timeframe, isn't it, that you were getting catalogs in the mail; catalogs from Majel Barrett's company.

Yes, I was definitely a subscriber to Majel's *Star Trek* fan club magazine and to Lincoln Enterprises, her company. I was desperately looking for other people that were interested in this "strange, new discovery" that I had made and I felt like I was one of the only people in the whole world who had ever heard of *Star Trek*, which was obviously not the case. So I was overjoyed when I found out that Gene Roddenberry's wife ran this company called Lincoln Enterprises, which sold *Star Trek* paraphernalia. Then in the mid-1970s they started a fan club to help promote the new *Star Trek* TV series which was being developed, the *Star Trek* II project. In the late 1970s this morphed into *Star Trek: The Motion Picture*. They started doing newsletters and had pen pal lists — in the time before the internet where you actually had to sit down and write letters to people — and one of my longest-running friendships in my life was with a girl from Baltimore named Barb Watson. We were both obsessed with *Star Trek* and started writing back and forth all the time. I can tell you right now, the internet makes life much easier than it was back in the 1970s!

Barb was the one who, through her creative efforts to get me to respond to her postcards and things, created this persona that she was a Starfleet commodore at a "starbase" somewhere and she was trying to track me down because I was a starship captain and wasn't responding to her communications, or something! So I got into this whole persona thing of being a starship captain and sending her my mission reports from deep space. That's about the time you and I created a local fan club for *Star Trek* in Eugene. We continued the role playing idea of having a starship and having all the local members of the club being crew members on the ship. We thought we were the only ones in the universe who were doing anything like that, until a publication came out called *The Star Trek Catalog*. In the back, there were lists of fan clubs and one of them was this Starfleet club based in Texas. So you and I looked into it and wanted to get more information about it, but it seemed that it was basically defunct. But the gist of it apparently was that there were hundreds of local fan clubs like the one we had created in Eugene that were going on all over the country, and all over the world, that were loosely linked together through this international organization. When we tried to participate in it — we were the USS *Republic* — it became obvious that there wasn't much going on and if we wanted to do something that we would have to take it on ourselves.

That led to you eventually, not too much later, virtually running the organization.

A kind of a coup! (Laughs) I just learned, recently, for the very first time that according to the Guinness Book of World Records, Starfleet holds the title of "Largest science fiction fan club in the world." It's still going after all these years!

Eric A. Stillwell at home. PHOTO COURTESY OF ANTHONY WYNN.

Am I right to say that lead to you contacting Gene Roddenberry, the creator of *Star Trek*?

Yes, I'd say that my primary contact was through his assistant, Susan Sackett. I didn't have any formal contact with Gene directly until later, but Susan was quite supportive of the fan club. I think the high point came when *Star Trek II: The Wrath of Khan* came out and *Starlog* magazine ran a little article about the fan club. We were flooded with inquiries and new memberships and ended up with about three thousand members at the time.

You decided to attend the University of Oregon in Eugene and major in political science. I'm curious about what led you to make that choice, as opposed to say journalism, writing, English, or some other field?

Well, there was no math requirement! I discovered in high school that math was not my forte, especially by the time I was senior and taking algebra II or trigonometry, or whatever it was. For some reason — and I can't explain this — but from the time I was very young, even before I was *Star Trek* fan, I was always fascinated with politics. In 1972 I was interested in the whole campaign between McGovern and Nixon, and thought the political dimensions were so fascinating. One of the things I wanted to do when I was a kid was to be President when I grew up! But politics was always just a sideline hobby; even though in high school I was involved in student government. I had these really ambitious goals of going to the Air Force Academy, becoming an astronaut and being part of NASA because of my interest in *Star Trek*. I discovered that I really had no aptitude for math or science (and I was much better at writing, history and stuff like that), which really came when my application to the Air Force Academy was rejected. So I decided to go to the University of Oregon and the first thing at orientation I was asked, "Ok, what are you going to major in?" I didn't even know that we had to think about that the first year that we were at the University and I guess a lot of people will just put undeclared, but I'm never one for putting off a decision so I looked at all the requirements and saw political science and thought, "Well, hell, I didn't even know you could major in political science!" So that's what I chose — with absolutely no goal or intention of applying it to any real life job. I just wanted to get a college degree and get done with school.

Your first official credit listed is the television film *Promise*, with James Garner and James Woods. I'm wondering how that came about; I understand it was filmed in Oregon?

It was filmed mostly around the Salem area and near Triangle Lake. At this point in my life I had already graduated from the University and moved to Los Angeles to pursue an entertainment career. My first year in California was a dismal failure and the only bright point during that time was the opportunity to work with [actress] Bibi Besch on a series of performance workshops that she was teaching. She had appeared in *Star Trek II: The Wrath of Khan*. Bibi was a very inspirational person and I learned a lot from her. Other than workshops, I really had nothing else to do with the entertainment industry while I was down there. After the first year I basically ran out of money and my roommates started moving out, so I decided that it was time for me to come back to Oregon and regroup.

I read about a Warner Bros. movie that was part of the Hallmark Hall of Fame productions, with James Garner and James Woods, so I started calling the offices down in Los Angeles and asking about getting on the project as a production assistant, or anything. Be a runner, be a volunteer; whatever. They kept saying, "Well, we'll see..." Finally when they came to Oregon, they told me that "When we get up to Oregon and open our production office, why don't you come and see us." I was very persistent, which was one of the things that DeForest Kelley had told me as career advice when I met him at a *Star Trek* convention. He said, "Persistence is the key to success in Hollywood." I went up to Salem where the production office was and found out they would let me spend the day and read the script, hang out, and see what it was like. But the fact of the matter was, for insurance reasons, they couldn't use volunteers on the set because if something happens to you and you're not covered by insurance, the production would be liable. The location manager, though, needed some help drawing maps to locations, helping the crew to know where the locations were and since I was a local person and familiar with the area, he wanted to keep me on but he didn't have enough money to hire me. So he paid out of his own pocket for me to say in a motel in Salem, and provided my meals, so that I could help him out.

The production office was kind of impressed with that, so they wanted to try and help me out. The production coordinator got me a job on the second day to be an extra in the show. That particular day they were shooting a scene in Dallas, Oregon, which is one of the places I lived growing up when my dad was in the Air Force. We only lived there half a year when he worked at Adair Air Force Base, before it closed and we moved to Colorado. It was fun to be back in Dallas where I lived in kindergarten, to be an extra in this scene with James Garner. On the third day, I found out they had fired one of their assistant directors and they didn't want to wait to fly someone up from Los Angeles, so they hired me a production assistant on the show. It was a pretty cool experience and, ironically, the last day of production after we wrapped, I was driving home to Eugene and I heard on the radio that Paramount had announced that they were going do a new *Star Trek* series. The production crew for *Promise* was going to fly me down to Los Angeles with the crew for the production wrap party, so I thought this would be a great opportunity to drop in and see Susan Sackett at Gene Roddenberry's office, quickly type up my new resume with my one movie credit on it, and make sure that I was going to be part of the process. It was a very exciting time. I eventually got a call from Bob Justman, one of the producers on *The Next Generation*, asking me if I could come in for an interview for *Star Trek*.

He was also a producer on the original *Star Trek* series in the 1960s.

Right. So I went in, had my interview and he was great. It was a very odd interview because he didn't really ask any questions, he just talked for half an hour about what the whole business means, how much work it involves, and the best ways to get into it. I remember him saying, "If you're interested in being a producer, the fastest way is to be a writer." I kept thinking about that for a long time because I had always been very proficient at writing and in school always received A's in all my written reports. Even though that's not quite the same thing as writing fiction or writing for television, I thought that since I at least had an aptitude for writing that I could try to apply it to this process if I really set my mind to it.

I went back to Oregon and waited to find out if I was going to get the job on *The Next Generation* and I got this lovely letter from him basically saying that I was one of the top finalists, but in the end they decided that the few people they would hire were people who had previously worked at the studio in some other capacity — like working in the mailroom, in the page department, as a tour guide, or whatever; because those people had more familiarity with the studio, executive buildings, the sound stages, and all that. So I got it into my mind that what I really needed to do, if I wanted to work on *Star Trek*, was go find myself a job at Paramount that would be a stepping stone to working in production. I moved back to Los Angeles and I just kept trying and trying and trying to get a job at the studio. I finally got it August 1987, when I was hired by the guest relations department to be a studio page.

What exactly does a studio page do?

In the time before 9/11, when they still gave studio tours, primarily we gave tours to the general public, VIP guests, producers and executives at the studio. Also there were jobs for pages during the live production of shows, sitcoms like *Family Ties* and *Happy Days*, other shows like *Solid Gold*, *The Arsenio Hall Show*, and all these things that were being produced at the studio with live audiences. They needed pages to coordinate the live audiences and do crowd control. I did all of the those things for several months and during that time I made a pointed effort not to go to the *Star Trek* soundstages, or go bug the people in the production offices, because that's the last thing they want to see; some annoying *Star Trek* fan bumming around all the time. I never really did that because I thought that would just turn them off.

Then it just kind of fell into my lap one day; my boss in the guest relations department said that there was going to be a screening for one of the new shows that Paramount was producing. They needed pages to do door duty, have the guest lists, and check off all the people that were coming to the screening. He came to me because he thought I would be interested in it, because it was for the new *Star Trek* show that was coming out in September. I thought, "Wow, that would be so cool!" He said that one of the perks is that after you check everybody in and get everybody seated, you can stay for the screening. Pages were allowed to sit in the back row at the premiere of whatever new show or movie was being screened. I was floating on cloud nine at that point. This was the cast and crew screening of the pilot episode "Encounter at Farpoint," the first time that most of the crew would see the completed first episode of the show. And I was going to be part of that!

That night I was standing at the door checking off names, because everybody had to be on the guest list to get in; Paramount was very secretive about those things, they were paranoid about information leaking out. One of the guests, of course, was Bob Justman and his wife. When Bob walked up, I didn't even think he would remember me from all the people that he interviewed, but right away he recognized me.

"Eric! What are you doing here?"

"Oh, I'm working on the lot now in the guest relations department."

"Really?" he said. "How long have you been here?"

"About two months," I replied.

He seemed quite surprised, I think because he hadn't seen me hanging around or bugging anyone. Then all of a sudden, here I am right on the lot. He introduced me to his wife, saying all kinds of complimentary things. I do remember one other interesting thing, I have to say, which in retrospect is kind of funny. I really didn't know who all the other people were who worked on the show. One guy came up and I couldn't find his name on the guest list so I wasn't going to let him in. It was Rick Berman! It didn't mean anything to him, I was just some nameless page who didn't know who he was. Later on, it became obvious to me that he was one of the most important people involved in the production; I was glad that he didn't remember that moment!

The very next day — I swear this is true — I came into work dressed in my page uniform put all my stuff in my locker and my boss sent me to work my shift. Afterwards, I came in and he said, "Eric, I forgot to tell you there was a phone call for you." I said, "Who was it?" He replied, "Oh, Bob Justman's office called and wanted to talk to you." It was six or seven o'clock in the evening by this time, but I phoned anyway, knowing that producers are working to all hours. Bob said, "Can you come over to our production office right away?" I said, "Sure!" and raced over to the production office. He told me that one of the production assistants had been promoted and they needed to find a replacement. Obviously, they were looking for someone on the lot who was familiar with the studio; it was just like my whole strategy was working! He asked if I wanted the job. So now I was faced with this dilemma: I was only working part time as a page and I was working a full time job for the city of West Hollywood in the personnel department. The very next night, my boss from West Hollywood was coming to see an episode of *Cheers*, but the *Star Trek* people were asking me if I could begin the very next day! Another thing was, when you become a page at the studio they know there is so much turnover and demand for hiring within the company when you're in an entry-level position, that you have to make a commitment when you sign up to be a page that you will stay at least six months before you except another position at the studio. The only caveat was that my boss knew that I had interviewed for the *Star Trek* job *before* I became a page and that I wasn't actively seeking the position. I thought, well, I can probably get out of it that way — because who's going to turn down a job on *Star Trek*, right? But then I said to the producer, stupid me, that I had this ethical dilemma and that I had made this commitment and I didn't know if I could get out of it. I remember Bob Justman looked at me, then yelled out to his secretary in the outer office, "Carol, bring in the resumes for this position!" She walked in with a stack of paper about two feet high of people who wanted to work on *Star Trek*. He looked at me and said, "Ok, this is Hollywood; screw ethics! Do you want the job or not? Well, the very next day I started at *Star Trek!*

What exactly is a production assistant and what does that job entail?

A production assistant is basically on the lowest rung on the crew. It's like being a runner and we actually had bicycles which we used to run errands all around the studio delivering memos, delivering scripts; anything the producers needed or wanted. The direct chain of command was that we worked for the production manager and his assistant is the production coordinator. Our desks were near her desk so she would be our supervisor and tell us to do this or that. There was also an in-box of interdepartmental envelopes that needed to be delivered to various studio executives or to Gene Roddenberry. The production was like a doublewide trailer facility that was somewhere between where the soundstages are and where the offices were for the writing staff, who were in the Hart Building. Paramount is fifty-five acres in size and there is a lot of distance to be traveled to get everything distributed. We were constantly running back and forth.

The irony of it all, too, on my first day as a P.A. (when I was still just starting to learn the ropes and remember everybody's names and trying not to screw up), the other P.A. told me that she was quitting and it was her last day! So I'm thinking, "Oh my God! I have to learn everything from her in a day!" When she finally told the producers, they were all freaked out and David Livingston, the Line Producer, asked me if I knew any women who would like to have the job. They were always totally politically correct on *Star Trek*. If there were two P.A.s, and one of them was a guy, the other one should then be a woman. I called my friend Heidi, who was also living in Los Angeles at that time, and I said, "Heidi! There's an immediate opening on *Star Trek!* If you want it you should come for an interview. The desks for the P.A.'s were in this big "bullpen" where everyone can hear everything that's going on and she was on the other end of the phone telling me, "Oh, I look like crap, my hair's messed up…," meanwhile I could tell that David was hearing my end of the phone conversation. He broke in, "What's the problem! Why is she hesitating?" I replied, "Well, she says she looks like crap…" And he barked back, "I don't care what she looks like! I just want to know if she can do the job!" So she came in for the interview and they hired her.

It was great to have one of my best friends there so that we could both be "lost" together! Eventually we devised a system where each of us had certain interests or preferences in different aspects of the production and we would divvy up the distribution responsibilities so that she was the one, for instance, who would deal with the wardrobe department and the props department, and I would be one who would deal with the writing department. That enabled her to hang out in the areas that she was interested in and the same for me. That's how you get the chance to meet people and develop relationships in the studio. We also shared a lot of responsibility for distributing things to the set and to the Executive offices. During that process you meet all sorts of people from the highest ranking executives in the studio all the way down to the guys in the print shop, and guys who build the fake rocks for the set. If you were interested in something like television production, that was a good place to start. I kept remembering, too, what Bob Justman told me about writing; so I became the unofficial P.A. for the writing department, even though that wasn't an official designation.

After the second season there was this weird situation where the script coordinator went on a leave of absence and never came back. Nobody ever heard from her and didn't know what happened or why she wasn't coming back. They eventually decided to eliminate the position, but then the script department became chaotic as far script distribution was concerned, because the script typist was taking on all the responsibility of both typing and proofing the scripts, as well as the distribution and everything else involved that this other woman used to do. I convinced Rick Berman's secretary that the position needed to be reestablished and that I should have the job! Ironically, right around the time they were trying to convince the producers to do that, the script typist had a shelf collapse in her office; you know, the kind held on the wall with brackets, and it crashed down on her face and broke her nose. She was off work and on disability, while the whole script department went into total chaos. I was basically keeping things going and I was just a P.A.! A temporary employee was brought in, but I was handling all the distribution and making sure the scripts were getting printed and doing everything that the script coordinator would normally do. So they reinstated the position and gave me the job.

This happened in the second season?

Yes, near the end of the second season. It was an interesting time for the first couple of years on *The Next Generation*. So many odd things were happening; there was a director's strike, then a writer's strike, and production was closed for a while. At the end of the season things were also interesting because they had decided to do a "clip" show to make up for lost time in production because of the strike and they didn't have enough scripts. So they thought they could do a clip show by just writing a very raw skeleton of an episode and filling the whole thing in with clips from the previously filmed shows. We were calling it "Riker's Brain" because it reminded us of that episode from the original series called "Spock's Brain." It was a lame episode where

Riker gets bitten by some vine on a planet and goes into a coma where he has all these weird flashbacks, dreams and nightmares. The art department had sent over a drawing of the medical device that Dr. Crusher would put on his head in the episode. It was exactly like the one from "Spock's Brain!"

Mike Okuda and all these guys in the art department knew everything about the original *Star Trek* series and could slip things through that the modern day producers would never even realize had anything to do with the original show. I thought that was the most hysterical thing, but then the producers caught on to the joke. They really didn't like doing an "homage" to the original at that time because they were still trying to prove that they could "do it" on their own. So it couldn't be called "Riker's Brain" and they needed a new title for it. I actually was the one who came up with the name "Shades of Gray," which is really kind of hard to describe but it was like the feeling we had; the episode wasn't black and white, it was just shades of gray. As one of the tasks, the producers gave me a rough outline of the script and instructions to find all the clips to fill in the holes. Literally, I had to go to post-production and go through all the episodes from the first two seasons that had been produced and transfer clips onto reels to show the producers in order for them to go through and pick out the ones they thought would fit into the story scenario. I literally spent one week, eighty hours, compiling these clips! After they picked the ones they wanted, I had to go back and find all the script files on the computer and transfer those scenes into the new script format for the episode so they could time it out.

One of the things you have to keep in mind is that this is the pre-Windows era in the computer world. It was all in DOS-based format where you're typing all these codes, D: this, or D: that, just in order to get a screen up in order to type a script and there were all kinds of other codes, like ALT C for characters, ALT D for dialogue and weird macros and stuff that we don't deal with anymore today. It took a lot longer to do a script in those days — you couldn't even put an entire script into one file because the computer would crash! The computers just couldn't handle huge megabytes of data in those days in a single file, or a floppy disk. Each Act in the script had to be a separate file and each time you printed the pages they had to be assigned a code to remind it that, "Act Three starts on page (whatever)..." There was a constant need to keep track of all this information and all these computer processes to get a script out. Of course, every five minutes the producers were asking, "Where's the script? Where's the script?" There's a lot of pressure involved.

I went to David Livingston after that eighty hour week and said, "I really think I should have a screen credit for this amount of work." He asked, "What kind of screen credit?" I replied, "Script Researcher, or something like that." That was agreed to and that's what became my very first screen credit.

When the second season ended and work began on season three, I'm sure you must have still been thinking about Bob Justman had told you. How were you able to pitch the idea of your episode, which was produced in the third season, called "Yesterday's *Enterprise*"?

It goes back to the strike which had prolonged the production hiatus during the second season. The strike was actually between the first and second seasons, but it made the second season shorter and the problems built up toward the end of the second season. During the extended hiatus we were off work for so long that I actually came back to Oregon for a month and stayed at my parent's house. That's when I started working on the first speculative script that I wrote called "Shattered Time." When I went back to Los Angeles, I showed it around to a couple of the producers and they liked it. The Unit Production Manager, Sam Freedle, really like it a lot and so he started telling people about it. Eventually word got to Maurice Hurley, the head writer during the second season, and he really liked it. So they were going to buy it. But the last person who had to sign off on it was Gene Roddenberry; and for some reason he decided to pass on it. Of course, at this time Gene was starting to kind of deteriorate and he may even have had Alzheimer's disease. People just weren't really sure where he was coming from some of the time. You couldn't put a lot of stock in some of the decisions that he was making; and, in fact, we later learned that other people were making a lot of decisions for him. So I decided to be persistent and work on another speculative script, but that didn't get anywhere.

I had met another writer named Trent Ganino and we had gone to a studio screening of *Star Trek V: The Final Frontier*. The movie was so bad! True fans couldn't help but show their unhappiness about it. I remember that he and I started talking about it after we left the theatre and finally we went to this twenty-four hour diner and stayed up until three o'clock in the morning complaining about how bad this movie was and basically decided that we could write a better movie! He had already written a spec script at that time called "Yesterday's

Enterprise" and I had already evolved this other story that wasn't really connected to what he had written, but the two ideas ended up being merged together. In essence, Trent had written a spec script about a ship from the future that meets up with the current *Enterprise*. There's no time alteration or anything like that, but our crew knows from its history banks that if they send the other ship back it's going to be in the middle of a battle where they're going to be destroyed. So the dilemma they have is — do they warn them and run the risk of altering the timeline by the other ship doing something different than they would have done? Or should they just be sent back blindly to their deaths without warning. It was an ethical dilemma that Picard had to deal with.

The kind of thing for which *Star Trek* is famous, right?

Yes. Now in the meantime, there had been an edict from Rick Berman that he wasn't interested in time travel stories. Of course, later on that completely changed! I had been developing this other story, which I told Trent about, since I had seen Denise Crosby at a convention where she had said that she was interested in coming back on the show. My idea was based on "The City on the Edge of Forever" from the original series, where the *Enterprise* could revisit this planet with the Guardian of Forever. They were there to pick up a Vulcan archeological team that had been doing research on ancient Vulcan culture. The Ambassador, Sarek, was going to come and meet the Vulcan team and bring them back to Vulcan. There's then some kind of accident on the planet that alters the timeline in early Vulcan history and Surak, the founder of the Vulcan philosophy of nonviolence and logic, is accidentally killed prior to the revolution in Vulcan culture. Now the timeline is altered and the Vulcans are like the Romulans — they've in fact teamed up with them in this warlike empire. Together, they wiped out the Klingons and are now on the verge of destroying the Federation. Sarek, on the *Enterprise*, wasn't affected by the time change and tries to convince Picard that the whole thing is wrong and must be fixed. Because of the time alteration, Tasha Yar is back alive, and Sarek decides the only solution, as he's the only Vulcan left who knows the way things are supposed to be, is to go back in time and *replace* Surak in history. I always remembered as a kid that I thought it was so weird that Surak, the founder of Vulcan philosophy, had a name that was so similar to Spock's father, Sarek. So I had hypothesized as a kid that maybe Surak and Sarek were the same person! This was my way of making that happen.

Then one day I heard a rumor going around the office that Denise has actually contacted the producers to tell them that she was interested in coming back and Michael Piller was soliciting ideas to figure out how they could bring her back to guest star in an episode. I thought, "Oh my God, I have to take advantage of this moment!" So I went into his office and said, "Michael, I have to talk to you." He said, "What? What is it?" I sat down and blurted out, "I heard that you're looking for a Denise Crosby story and I just have to say this before someone else does; I have an idea." He asked, "What is it?" I then told the whole story and told him I'd been working with Trent." Michael then told me that they weren't really big on doing anything associated with the original *Star Trek*. But he said, "Do you think there's some way you can combine your idea with Trent's and make it into a story?" I immediately said, "Yeah!" to which he replied, "Then go write it!" I raced back to my office to call Trent. "Trent, you're not going to believe this!" So Trent and I worked furiously to combine our two ideas and make it into a story, and that's how "Yesterday's *Enterprise*" came about. We decided that if we weren't going to be able to do the Surek/Sarek thing, we still wanted to keep the storyline where someone replaces somebody else to balance out the future. We decided the Captain of the ship would be a woman, which in Trent's script it wasn't, it was a guy. The character changed from Robert Garrett to Rachel Garrett and we decided we would somehow kill her off in order to create balance in her part of the universe. In the story, Tasha then finds out that she would be dead anyway if everything went back to normal, so she agrees to return with the others so they'll have a chance against the Romulans when they go back into the battle. Of course, the whole thing with the Romulans and Klingons got switched around, because we thought it would be cool now if the Klingons were the ones who got pissed off about something that happened and didn't align with the Federation. Our idea was that at the end Worf would be commanding officer of the Klingon ship that's attacking the *Enterprise*. The powers-that-be decided that was too over-the-top, so it was nixed. But still, I think that would have been a great twist!

The only dilemma we had was, we couldn't figure out was how the *Enterprise* crew in the future know that the timeline has been changed. We kept thinking, well, maybe Data knows because he's an android, or something! We couldn't really figure out how to fix that problem. We had this stupid idea, too, that a probe comes through the wormhole before the timeline changes and later on the probe is in the cargo bay and they go and find out that the records are different; but that became really convoluted and silly. In one of our story meetings, Michael Piller said, "What about Guinan? She's an alien and we don't really understand everything about her species. Maybe they can transcend time, somehow, and she has some knowledge of the time change." That worked out really well and added a great amount of dimension to

Eric A. Stillwell with actress Whoopi Goldberg in costume as "Guinan" during the filming of the *Star Trek: The Next Generation* episode "Yesterday's *Enterprise*." PHOTO COURTESY OF ERIC A. STILLWELL.

Guinan's character development, I think. Also, apparently, "Yesterday's *Enterprise*" was the only time where Whoopi Goldberg had to work for two days of production on one episode. Usually, they would just write some easy little part for her that would be shot in one day.

How was it for you being a fan working on, then writing, for *Star Trek*? As an insider, what's your perspective on the overall progression and advancements in the franchise?

It was a little bit weird going from being a fan to being a professional in the industry because you can get a little bit jaded. Just in the time since *The Next Generation* started there have been so many technological advances that are beyond people's comprehension, including the fact that we were writing scripts in DOS format! Now with the advancement in computers, you can whip out a script in a day; something that used to take a week. If you look at this over the history of *Star Trek*, you had the mimeographed scripts that were hand typed with manual typewriters and carbon paper sheets. If you made one mistake on the typewriter, you had start the whole page over. Can you image how many hours it took to write a whole script and get transcribed, mimeographed and distributed?

So the technology has advanced, but the people and culture really haven't changed. The true success of *Star Trek* lies in the character relationship and the human condition. That's where the heart and soul of *Star Trek* always has been since the very beginning. In the end, it doesn't matter how advanced the technology is, you have to stay true to the storytelling that is about the human condition. If you can do that, the technology just opens up vast opportunities to do so many amazing things. All of it depends on the creativity of the written word on the paper. That's where it all starts. Then you have to have the people with the vision and the creativity to take the words and bring them to life. There's only so many words you can use to describe an alien, but if you have someone like Michael Westmore who is a magician with alien designs you can do everything. You need all those creative people to make a script come to life. But you have to start with a script.

There are people like Ron Moore who worked on the show, and others, who *loved* the original *Star Trek*. They weren't hired on and had to go watch all of the shows for the first time. [Producer] Harve Bennett was one of those people who had to go watch a bunch of old episodes before he started writing. He did a relatively good job of it while he was around, but imagine what someone can do who really loves *Star Trek* and doesn't need to go watch those old episodes! You know, people who've already seen them forty times over and over. To me, that's exciting. Rick Berman wasn't one of those people and Brannon Braga wasn't one of those people. Michael Piller had seen and did appreciate *Star Trek* and he was a fan of *The Next Generation* before he was hired on the show. He had an interest in seeing what Gene Roddenberry's vision was for *Star Trek* and became devoted to it. He didn't come in, like a lot of writers would say, "Well, who cares what Gene Roddenberry thought? We're here now and we're going to do what we want." *Star Trek* has too much of a rich, complex history to just be treated like it's another franchise production to be pumped out in order to sell more toys and make the studio rich. It needs to be in the hands of people who appreciate and love it.

Your episode, "Yesterday's *Enterprise*," has been voted by viewers as being a favorite episode of *The Next Generation*; and probably second most popular time travel episode after the original series episode "The City on the Edge of Forever."

Yes, it's stood the test of time and in various polls is usually in the Top Ten episodes of all time. But a lot of the time it will come in second to "Best of Both Worlds" which was written by Michael Piller. Of course, Michael was my boss for many, many years and we had this competitive ongoing debate about who wrote the most popular episode of *The Next Generation*. I would always remind him that "Best of Both Worlds" was a two-part episode, so I had the most popular one hour installment! (Laughs) So, yeah, that show is something that I'm proud of and my sole claim to fame in the *Star Trek* universe!

Let me ask you about the period of time when you left *Star Trek*. I'm curious what brought that about and what did you end up doing after you left Paramount?

Well, one of the things I always tell people is, "Beware of your dreams, because they might come true!" (Laughs) Working on *Star Trek* was one of the greatest dreams I ever had and it came true; it was an amazing experience. But no matter how it's perceived, or how you try to explain it to people on the outside looking in, it's still a job; a sometimes tedious, often pressure-driven environment of working twelve to sixteen hour days. On Fridays we would sometimes be there until midnight or one o'clock in the morning. It's easy to understand, when you read some of the biographies of the original people, why their marriages all ended in divorce; their kids didn't know who they were, and so on. From Shatner and Nimoy on down, and even Gene Roddenberry, all of them went through these experiences where they spent so many hours at the studio that they barely ever saw their wives and kids. It's a very high-pressure world. In my case, one day Paramount decided that in addition to *The Next Generation*, a spin-off series called *Deep Space Nine* would be produced. Now it wasn't a surprise to me, I knew it was in the works, but what I thought was coming was exactly what did happen. They wanted as many people as possible to work on both shows simultaneously. Basically to work twice as hard for the same amount of money or perhaps just some minor increase in their pay. To me, it wasn't worth it. Now instead of working twelve hours a day, I'm supposed to work twenty hours a day doing two shows and make just barely more money than what I was making before! I was killing myself already and there comes a point where you draw a line in the sand.

An opportunity came to me to go to work for a company that ran *Star Trek* conventions. I would travel around and host conventions, deal with the celebrities and fans, and to me that was very appealing because I love to travel and I love to promote *Star Trek*. Since I was intimately involved in the show, I was perfectly qualified to do that. I did that for a couple of years. The company I was working for was smaller than Paramount, and there's always issues when you're working for a smaller company with about ten employees versus a company with four thousand! Everything from benefits to different expectations about hours is involved. In the end, I worked more hours doing conventions than I did working on *Star Trek* — because with the conventions we worked on weekends in addition to our five day a week part of the job. But I liked doing it, and it was fun doing that — for awhile. (Laughs) Then I realized that I really wasn't being paid for working eighty hours a week, even though I was working eighty hours a week! This led me to leave and form my own company and run my own conventions. So if I was going to work eighty hours a week, at least I was working for myself and doing what I wanted to do!

This was around the time you met your wife, Debra, right?

Yes. My company was called Horizon Conventions and our very first convention was held in Bellevue, Washington. Debra was living in Seattle with a roommate and while they were both nurses, they also both had an interest in entertainment. They had been extras in *Northern Exposure*, for example. They heard about the *Star Trek* convention and decided to go. That's where we first met, even though it was just a passing moment. Not long after, Debra moved to Los Angeles and it so happened that my next convention with Horizon was in Burbank. She heard about it and decided to attend with an out-of-town friend who was visiting. This was in the fall and it so happened that it was the weekend of the time change and they arrived an hour early. I was on-stage doing sound checks and stuff and since no one was there yet, we felt sorry for them and let them in early! My father was visiting, taking pictures of me, and he just randomly sat down in

Eric A. Stillwell and his wife Debra. PHOTO COURTESY OF ERIC A. STILLWELL.

an empty seat. Well, Debra and her friend Angie had reserved seat tickets and came into the hall to see where they would be sitting — and my father was sitting in her seat! He was the only person sitting in a room with three thousand other empty seats and in an odd twist of fate was seated in Debra's chair.

Debra later wrote me and volunteered to help out and I took her up on the offer. We had a little office in downtown Burbank and she started coming in to help out. Over the next few months we were planning a large convention in London, England, and she came along to assist. Over the subsequent months we started to date — and rest is history!

What was it like running your own shows?

It was a lot of work, but fun, and it was successful at the start, especially the convention we organized at the Royal Albert Hall in London.

That was in conjunction with a British promoter and it turned out to be a spectacular event. It featured the entire cast of *The Next Generation*. That was a fantastic experience and the biggest *Star Trek* event ever held in England. The event sold out with over ten thousand tickets purchased three months in advance. The London film premiere was held at the Empire Theatre in Leicester Square the night before the convention opened and there were thousands of *Star Trek* fans that gathered in the square. But that was also same the time *The Next Generation* was coming to an end as a television series and transforming to the silver screen as a feature film.

From a business standpoint, the problem that was unforeseen to me was that when *The Next Generation* left television and became a motion picture, and new episodes weren't being broadcast anymore. The television audience for the other *Star Trek* shows dropped almost fifty percent overnight. The television success of *Star Trek* was very critical to the success of convention business in the U.S., because it was a means of directly advertising to the viewers who were interested in coming to see their favorite actors at the conventions. So, if you suddenly lose fifty percent of your audience, you lose fifty percent of your business. Effectively, that put an end to a majority of *Star Trek* conventions in the United States. It went from some four hundred conventions a year to running twenty or thirty a year. For me and my small company, it was the end of the line. When the convention business went south, I went back to Paramount. At the time there was a situation where Jeri Taylor's assistant had left and I was temping for her.

Jeri Taylor was an Executive Producer, right?

On *Star Trek: Voyager,* yes. She actually created *Voyager* with Rick Berman and Michael Piller. I thought that there was an opportunity to work for her and then one night she called me in and said that Michael Piller's assistant had come to her and really wanted to work for her and she decided that would be ok. She thought it would be in my better interest to go and work for Michael, because she was planning to retire in a year. She knew that Michael would be around longer than that and in the long run I would have better opportunities working with him. I wasn't sure at the time that it was the right choice for me, but working for Michael turned out to be the best part of my career in Hollywood. Even after he left *Star Trek*, we spent a couple of years at the studio because he had a development deal working on features and other television projects. But because I was still a Paramount employee, the future was always tenuous. In 1999,

Michael decided he was going to leave Paramount and start his own production company. At that time, he asked me if I would go with him and help run the company with him. So for that last five years, before he died of cancer, I was the Vice President of Operations for the production company he started with his son Shawn. I was an associate producer on all the television projects he developed, including *The Dead Zone* and *Wildfire*.

While you were working for Michael, did you still have an interest in continuing to write? Because you had written another *Star Trek* episode, one for *Voyager*, right?

I sold a story to *Voyager* and I had also helped to develop a story for a *Deep Space Nine* novel that was published by Pocket Books, called *The 34th Rule,* with Armin Shimerman. It was a "Quark" story and was a very successful, best-selling novel. I did have an interest in writing, but my relationship with Michael was such that...well, Michael was a very exacting person when it came to his demands on writers. Just from my experience as his assistant and seeing how he related to other writers and how he had responded to some of the material that I had written for *Star Trek*, I could always tell who the writers were that he wanted to encourage and the ones that he wasn't interested in. And I think I fell into the latter category! (Laughs) He never said that to me, point blank, but I could tell from my own observation of how he behaved with other writers. Partly, I think it was that he depended on me for the other responsibilities that I had running his company and dealing with the day-to-day property management issues; phone lines, internet and all the things that I did as office manager and property manager. He really respected everything I did for him to such a degree that it was almost that he didn't want me to be successful as writer, because he'd have to find someone else to deal with all of the other stuff, you know what I mean?

I don't mean this in a callous or cynical way, because he really did appreciate me and my capacity and he let me know that I was very valuable to him in that capacity. But I just feel that he didn't really want to go out of his way to encourage me as a writer. That said, he would never discourage someone from pursuing their dream. You know, I just realized that maybe I didn't have a certain amount of...I mean, being around Michael is intimidating as a writer, because he's so disciplined and his life was so structured around his pursuit of writing. I just thought, "I could never be like that." He would write every single day and it was almost like military discipline in how he would devote a certain amount of his time sitting at the computer. Even if he was having writer's block and sweating blood, he was going to write something! And then re-write, re-write, re-write. I was kind of lazy as far as writing was concerned, so being the pragmatic person that I am, I realized Hollywood is full of thousands of people who have critical roles in the infrastructure of production companies and projects, people who aren't always going to be the writer, director, or executive producer. Michael was treating me well enough and paying me well enough so that my wife and I had a nice home with a swimming pool, hot tub, barbeque. I was living the Southern California lifestyle due to my position, so I was happy. I was happy with my job, I was happy with my life; and I decided, I suppose, that I didn't need to beat my head against the wall to be a writer. Writers who are successful in Hollywood can make millions of dollars and there's always that allure. One of the things I discovered early on is that money isn't enough of a goal or an objective to be a good writer. You have to want it bad enough that you would do it for free, to be successful at it. No matter how much money is dangled in front of you, it's not going to make you a writer if that's not what you really want to do. So I really came to a point of accepting my role and my contribution as a part of a successful team of people who were doing good things and was happy about that.

You mentioned Michael Piller's passing; I understand that you gave a Eulogy at his memorial service in Hollywood. Now that some time has passed, what would you like to say about him now? How should he be remembered generally, and to *Star Trek* fans?

It's hard to put into words all the things that a person deserves to have said about them. Michael was a generous and good-hearted producer who really believed in opening doors for other creative, talented writers. One of his goals, from the very beginning when I first met him, was to break down the barriers that Hollywood has created with all the legal fusses and lawyers at the studios that prevent writers from having access to writing for shows. Michael was the first one who opened the doors to freelance writers to submit scripts to *Star Trek;* even if they weren't professional writers, even if they didn't have agents, even if they were "nobody." They could be from anywhere in the world. Michael made that possible by convincing the studio to let him do that and at the time, in the 1980s and early 1990s, we were the only show in Hollywood that was allowed to do that. Even other shows at Paramount weren't allowed to have submissions like that! Through that process, Michael discovered a lot of really creative people and opened doors for writers who may never have had those opportunities; including Ron Moore, who had never written for any show and was considering joining the Navy! He became one of the most prolific and successful writers on *Star Trek* and then Executive Producer and Head Writer on *Battlestar Galactica*.

If you watch some of the biggest hit television shows that there are on television, almost every single one of them has a writer who worked for Michael Piller. I think that's his legacy as a producer. There's so much cynicism in Hollywood, for instance, the belief that anyone who is creative is a threat to you. It's always said that you don't want to encourage anybody who could be a threat to you. Michael never believed that, he didn't worry about things like that. If he believed in you, he would help you. He did that for me on numerous separate occasions.

Looking back, how does it feel to have been a part of *Star Trek?*

It's a wonderful sense of accomplishment and was a dream come true. Working for Gene Roddenberry and Michael Piller and being able to make a contribution to the franchise is something that I'm very proud of. I think one of the greatest gifts has been the opportunity to travel around the world and meet fellow fans. That's what I love, visiting new places and exploring other cultures. Debra and I have been to more than forty different countries because of the show and we have friends all around the world. When I say that *Star Trek* changed my life, it's not just a line; it really is true.

Well, I think this is a perfect place to end. I appreciate you sitting down to talk with me today, Eric.

You're welcome; it's been a lot of fun.

Born in El Paso, Texas in 1921, Gene Roddenberry spent his boyhood in Los Angeles, California, where his family had moved so his father could pursue a career with the Los Angeles Police Department (LAPD). Following in his father's footsteps after high school, Roddenberry took classes in police studies at Los Angeles City College, and headed that school's Police Club.

He later transferred his academic interest to aeronautical engineering and qualified for a pilot's license. Roddenberry joined the U.S. Army Air Corps in 1941 and became an aviator. He flew many combat B-17 missions in the Pacific Theatre and was awarded the Distinguished Flying Cross and the Air Medal. After leaving the service, he was a commercial pilot for Pan American World Airways (Pan Am). He received a Civil Aeronautics commendation for his efforts following a crash in the Syrian Desert while on a flight to Calcutta.

When Gene left Pan Am, he fell back on his early training as a policeman and joined the LAPD where he served from 1949-1956. Before Star Trek, Roddenberry wrote scripts for many of the popular television series of the 1950s, such as Have Gun — Will Travel. (His first-season episode "Helen of Abajinian" won a Writers Guild Award) and he produced The Lieutenant, a 1963-1964 series about the United States Marines.

Gene developed his idea for Star Trek in 1964 and was picked up by Desilu Studios because of Gene's description of the show as a "Wagon Train to the Stars." He gained his affectionate nickname of "The Great Bird of the Galaxy," after a mythical creature referenced in "Man Trap," the first aired episode of Star Trek. Following the end of the original series, Gene and Star Trek actress Majel Barrett were married in Japan in a traditional Buddhist-Shinto ceremony on August 6, 1969.

Gene Roddenberry

"Our Wealth is Our Diversity"

He went on to produce Star Trek: The Animated Series *in 1973 and brought the series to the big screen for* Star Trek: The Motion Picture *in 1979. He served as Executive Consultant on the subsequent five films featuring the original cast and brought* Star Trek: The Next Generation *to television in 1987. Gene Roddenberry died in 1991 at the age of seventy.*

Before his resurgence and renewed success with Star Trek: The Next Generation, *Gene consented to two short interviews for* Star Trek *fan periodicals wherein he answered questions about the original series and the films. The first interview was given at Oregon State University in 1983 to Eric A. Stillwell and took place after the release of the second motion picture,* Star Trek II: The Wrath of Khan. *Eric has kindly consented to allow his interview it to be published here in book form for the first time. The second interview, which follows, took place just a few months later with Anthony Wynn, following the release of* Star Trek III: The Search for Spock.

INTERVIEW #1

What was your reaction to the *Star Trek* motion pictures after they were released?

There were things I didn't like about both of them, and things I did. In the second film, for example, I was disappointed when the Ceti eel crawled out of Chekov's ear and Kirk immediately killed it with his phaser. You'd think by the 23rd Century that we humans would react differently to alien life that is unknown to us, rather than reacting with primitive fear and disgust. But overall, I think we're finding our way toward a motion picture format for *Star Trek*. The process kind of parallels the development of the TV series. We did the first pilot, which was rejected, and the second pilot was more popular. After that we had a successful TV format — close shots, emotion — but pictures are different. People expect a motion picture to be a happening.

How much creative control did you really have with the films?

Not as much as I did with the series. I still have a say, but I don't have the freedom I had before. After *Star Trek: The Motion Picture*, I told them I didn't want to be Executive Producer. The only way I could have the freedom I had before is if I could write it, produce it, and direct it myself. And man, I've been working on *Star Trek* for sixteen to twenty years!

Are there ever mornings you wake up and wish *Star Trek* would just go away?

Well, it does go away. I don't hear about it for weeks. Majel and I don't talk about it around the house that much. I've never made a great deal of money off it, but I've realized enormous profits in other ways. When they do a fly-by of Saturn, or land a Viking on Mars, I'm invited. I'm welcome anytime at NASA and the Smithsonian. I have friends who are professors at Cal Tech. We drink beer and consider the state of the universe until three in the morning. And sometimes stewardesses on airplanes give me an extra free drink. I wouldn't have any of that without *Star Trek!*

Some fans and critics were hard on *Star Trek* — *The Motion Picture*. How does that affect you?

I don't listen to critics; I don't even do it that much for the audience. I do things for myself. Besides, there are things about the first film that I have never told anybody. I see no need to go into it now, but I will tell you that *Star Trek: The Motion Picture* was essentially an unfinished film. In the beginning Paramount couldn't decide whether to make *Star Trek* a feature film or a TV movie. Then when *Star Wars* came out in 1977 — and thank goodness for that — the executives decided they were missing the boat. But then they rushed *Star Trek* into production and didn't give us the time we needed to do it right.

Why couldn't the version aired on network television in February have been released originally?

Well, Paramount had booked us into a corner and couldn't extend the release date. Theaters all over the country had already paid twenty million dollars for the December release and we had to be finished — we had no other choice. So don't blame Bob [Wise]. He's an excellent director and he's received a number of awards. Nobody can say he didn't know what he was doing, but he never even had a chance to show the film to a live audience before the release. That's unheard of for a major motion picture!

After the first film, Paramount said they wouldn't do a sequel. What changed their minds?

Money.

Can you tell us anything about *Star Trek III?*

NO. Only that the question of Spock will be resolved in a way you can't even begin to guess. Things are not what they seem to be. Most people don't realize that Spock was to die because Leonard Nimoy had decided the Spock character was a monkey on his back.

I understand his feelings, but he would only do the movie if they promised to kill Spock. That was his price.

He's denied that.

Well, fine, let him deny it. I only know what really happened. When they had that enormous reaction from the fans, and the studio had an opportunity to see how valuable the Spock character was, they all had second thoughts. Then they made up a story that it was a publicity stunt, and indeed it was — it worked beautifully as a publicity stunt, but that was not the original intention. There were never optional endings to the script. None of those stories were true.

Is there any truth to the report that Paramount plans to make eight more *Star Trek* movies?

They were probably quoting Paramount accurately. They've said to me that if the James Bond films could go on forever, *Star Trek* could. I've had a lot of struggle with Paramount trying to convince them that if they take away the essential elements of *Star Trek*, which are the authentic hero figures and the optimistic earth future, they could kill the golden goose.

Do you think those are the elements that made *Star Trek* so successful?

Star Trek is the only science fiction or look at the future that we've ever had in American literature that says, "Hey, we made it!" It's an optimistic look at the future — that's why it was so difficult to make. It's hard to come up with an exciting story based on that. If you've got a world falling apart you've got all sorts of things, you're scrambling fighters all the time. What a lousy life. *Star Wars* wasn't even about humans. It wasn't even in our own galaxy. *Star Trek* says we solved our problems on earth and can now give our attention and courage to challenging the unknown. The other thing is that people are hungry for images to emulate and the *Star Trek* people are almost old-fashioned heroes you can trust. If they say something, it's true. They do not lie, they do not steal, they believe there are some things in life worth a great deal of pain and effort, and, if you get your back against a wall, there are also some things worth dying for.

Do you believe in those values — and see us surviving as a species?

Yeah!

Do you think you'll ever produce anything again for television?

I doubt it. I'd rather do my creative work as a writer than as a producer, but I've got something called *The Flying Yorkshireman* which

I have in script. And I've got my outline now on a novel. I'd also like to do some comedy. I did that before science fiction, and it's similar in that it is one of the few forms in which you can really comment on society. But producing for television is different today. We thought things were tough when we were doing *Star Trek* seventeen years ago, but today it's just impossible!

Writer Eric A. Stillwell with *Star Trek* creator Gene Roddenberry.
PHOTO COURTESY OF ERIC A. STILLWELL.

Can you tell us about your novel?

Yes. I'm working on a story about an alien who comes to earth to study humans and send reports back to his home world. The character's name is Gan, and he takes on the form of a human and lives among us. I use the character to make an analysis of ourselves as humans. On Gan's home world things are much different from earth, and he must learn to adapt to the fact that whereas on his world people only eat complex molecular minerals and nutrients, on earth it seems that everything living spends all its time trying to eat something else that's living. There are many other human practices that Gan must learn to live with, and all of these things come out in the story.

Well, thank you very much for talking with us — and good luck on your novel!

Thank you.

INTERVIEW #2

When did you get the first idea that *Star Trek* would be viable — that it was going to become a television series?

Starting in the beginning, of course, what I was trying to do was to find a format in which I could write my comments. Television in the United States is terribly censored. You really cannot write about anything important; they'll take it out. They're afraid they'll offend someone! I thought of Jonathan Swift, who, when he wanted to write about crooked Prime Ministers, crazy monarchs, and all of that, decided to do Lilliput — *Gulliver's Travels*.

Science fiction actually is a marvelous place for comment. You can invent any place you want, any situation to make your comments. I'd always loved science fiction, always wanted to do it, and I thought I might be able to do it better than I'd seen it. To me, too much science fiction has been about gadgets and not enough about people. People are what drama is. It was really an attempt to make a statement about Vietnam, and against intolerance, and about things in life that I believe in.

As far as when we knew it was becoming popular — we knew almost immediately we would have a small group of people who loved it, but we never were able to get a good audience rating while it was on the air. My own father, the night *Star Trek* premiered on television, watched it, excused himself, went out, walked up and down the street and apologized to all the neighbors! Space travel in those days was considered wild fantasy, something nobody could do. I guess we didn't really accept it until after man landed on the Moon that we became popular. Star Trek began to draw two and three times as many people on its reruns as it did on its initial network broadcast.

Have you ever had to suffer any allegations of tokenism on the makeup of the *Enterprise* crew?

Oh, I suppose that's possible, but if you put yourself in my position you'll realize that, with only so many speaking parts you're able to have, that you have to divide it up. The one thing about tokenism we get that I don't agree with is often they say, "You don't treat women as equals in the show." What I think people forget was when we started the show, there was no such thing as "Women's Lib." The term had not yet been invented! Sexual equality was not widely believed. But *I* did believe in sexual equality and put a woman second-in-command of the ship in the first pilot, but the network would not accept it. The women were writing, "Who does she think she is?" There are many things I wish I could have done. I would love to have had a chance, had the series gone on, to talk about the equality of sexual lifestyles and all manner of things like that. But in three years you can only do so much.

In some countries, *Star Trek* is still censored for broadcast. How do you feel about that?

I made the show for what I thought was proper for the moral systems and value systems that I knew. My feelings are this: I disagree, for instance, with the BBC in England about "The Empath"; disagree very much. "Empath" to me was a beautiful story. There is hurt and pain in it, but overriding all the hurt and pain you have this woman who is drawing the hurt and pain onto herself and suffering herself, to save it from somebody else. If someone is to say to me, "You can't have suffering and pain," I say, "Nonsense!" Suffering and pain are a part of life. They should be handled and handled well.

I feel the same way about violence and sex. My objection to violence and sex is on the shows where it goes on for a while and someone says, "Well, it's going slow now, why don't you have a fist-fight or a shooting?" Then they put it in to raise the ratings. I believe violence is a part of life. For example, what I hate about violence are the cowboy shows or the other shows where grown men strike out and hit each other in the face for thirty minutes. And after hitting each other with all their strength in the face, they grin and they say, "Wow, wasn't that fun!" That's not how life is! If a grown man hits another man in the face, teeth crack, bones break, knuckles get bruised.

I think one of the reasons why people were willing to go into the last war, and into various wars, is that death is such a lovely thing in war, you know. (Puts hand over heart.) Giving all for my country! *But, that's not how it is!* I know. Men lie out there and scream their guts out for hours, in agony. If you're gonna do violence, do it *that* way. Then people will say, "Well, yeah, I don't want our boys to do that." And sex is the same way. I see nothing wrong with sex. I think it is a lovely thing. I think, however, you just don't bare all because the film happens to be going slow at that moment. At the same time, if you have a story where that is a part of the story, and necessary to it, and done well and properly, then I think it should be in. Those to me are the tests.

The reason, particularly in American television, you have so much sex and violence at times, or so much emphasis on it, is by taking away everything else you might write about — war, religion, unions, labor, management and all of those. All the writers have left is sex and violence to get a story going. To me, the true evil is the censorship that prevents us writing about those things.

I'll tell you a story about how my feelings go. There was a convention where, to my total surprise, a young lady came out nude, and she was billed as "The Costume NBC Wouldn't Let Mr. Roddenberry Use." (Laughs) I was startled. We got a very nasty letter from a mother saying, "My fourteen-year old boy was there and I think it was terrible to show him a nude woman." I wrote her an answer saying, "You have your rights to your own feelings about that and perhaps the convention organizers shouldn't have allowed it." But at the same time, I said, "I am more outraged at the people who came out in costumes with all kinds of zap guns and weaponry and those things, rather than a simple human body." That's how I feel about that.

Did you ever feel restricted by the characters once they'd been brought to life by the actors?

I was delighted to see the actors establish themselves, to bring life to the written word on the page. Although it says "Created by Gene Roddenberry" on the screen, the truth of these things is that I created outlines of what the characters do and then very fine actors like Leonard Nimoy and the others, came in and put their flesh and blood in it. One of the great joys of my business is the things the other creative people do, and this includes the people behind the camera, the design technicians and everyone. It's really fun working in the industry. It's one of the few places that gives lie to the old saying that "a committee never created anything." We sort of do work as a committee, except that you should have a fairly strong chairman.

Obviously, *Star Trek* hasn't dated in its appeal, but would you like to go back and possibly redo some of the technical things?

Oh, absolutely. Every year that goes by, *Star Trek* is going to look more and more like Jules Verne. There's no doubt about it — although we won't be hurt as badly as some shows. Don't forget, we didn't do a show so much on technology, as one on people. Basic things like feelings and so on don't change that much. As a matter of fact, when I did the show I knew there were a lot of things that were wrong. I knew that you could talk into the head of a pin and they would be great microphones, but in 1966 I cannot have my captain talking into the head of a pin, because I'm playing to a twentieth century audience. It's the same with many things. I know, for example (and I knew all along) that you would not have those posts — communications, engineering, and so on — on a vessel of that type. That, however, is what a twentieth century audience can relate to, and also gave me something for actors to do, and I needed actors! If I did the ship as it probably will be, totally automated, who are your characters going to be? Where is the drama? Computers make lousy stars! So you give up many things. The whole point of drama, the whole point of art, any art, whether you're talking about music, painting, sculpting, or whatever, is not what it is — *but what it says.*

There's a lot of places, a lot of shows we made where you sort of go, "Oh God, I wish I'd had a hundred dollars more that day." But it was made with good will and good intent. We screwed up too, as any normal red-blooded person does, but we tried. I think the public accepted the fact that we were trying. Popular art is not a bad thing. The only place I got real resistance, at first, was at universities. The tendency of some people there is to feel that television and popular art really are not art. But the truth is that it is. This damn tube out there being seen by hundreds of millions of people every night is much more powerful than so-called classical art. I wish classical art were honored and everyone was enjoying that, too. It's a powerful, powerful thing.

How do you feel about how *Star Trek* is developing in the films?

It's not developing exactly as I would develop it, but you see, I can't expect to bring competent producers and people in and say, "Produce it, but don't do anything without checking with me." I have to give them their freedom too. You understand that I fought this fight for *Star Trek* for so many years, and so many battles with the networks and with Paramount and so on — and I won — and I didn't care to go back on the movie battle and fight all those same old fights all over again.

The only thing I've told the people who are doing it is, "You can do it your own way, but if you violate certain things we put in it, like respect for life and that sort of thing, then I'll have a press conference and pull out, and damn your picture. It'll cost you many millions of dollars." People say, "What is your control?" That is my control. They will listen to me, but I will not use that frivolously. I won't do that because I don't like the uniforms they put on the people. I have to do it for important things.

How did you feel about the destruction of the *Enterprise* in *Star Trek III: The Search for Spock*?

I didn't like to see the *Enterprise* destroyed and I certainly would hate it if they came back using the "pregnant duck" ship they showed us. I won't stop them and I hope good sense will come back and give us an *Enterprise*. I'm afraid that many people making it now do not have my background love of vessels, or didn't read Hornblower well enough and realize his affection for his vessels. I think that they'll have enough sense, though, to realize that since the *Enterprise* model is sitting in the Smithsonian Institute that it might be well to at least keep that going for them.

Do you think Horatio Hornblower would have made a good space captain? He had an awful lot of self-doubts.

He did! And that's one of the traits that helped make him the captain he was. One of the first things I gave Bill Shatner to do was to go home and read the Hornblower trilogy and that played a part in his shaping of it.

What are your feelings about *Star Trek* fandom in general?

I must confess that I have an enormous affection for *Star Trek* fans, not because they watch my show, but I have known them now for eighteen or nineteen years and I have never had a bad experience. They're completely lovely, gentle people. I'm particularly fond of the ones at conventions I meet who are disabled in some way or other, because I know what *Star Trek* means to them. I was disabled as a child for awhile and I know what it is to feel, "Oh, if they could only see past my outside and see the loveliness that is in me." *Star Trek* represents that to them. Also, I've so many times been to fan conventions and places where, like in St. Petersburg, Florida, the *Star Trek* movement down there pours all of their profit, everything they can make, into a children's hospital, and things like that.

The thing I think outsiders don't understand is that *Star Trek* fans are not just kooky teenagers. Eight year old kids like it — but so do U.S. Senators and NASA scientists! Our fans come from everywhere and I think there's nothing wrong with people wanting to identify with something, someone. I'm the same way about Hornblower. You start a convention on that and I'll be there — and getting autographs! We all have a right to have our fantasies. Certainly if real estate agents, veterans, and all of those people can do it; why not us? Why can't we have our fun, too?

In your more reflective moments, do you sometimes think that *Star Trek* has changed the way some people look at the world?

Yes, it has. I don't know that it's in huge and significant changes. I can hope that some people have heard our comments on tolerance and respect for life forms and our comment that the one thing we humans must be afraid of it that society doesn't force us into looking and acting and thinking alike. I hope society — and I do see it now and then — is taking diversity to heart. Diversity is loveliness; the wonderful differences between us! The only thing we have to fear is sameness — our wealth is our diversity.

I think that's the perfect note on which to end.

Thank you for the very interesting questions.

Bonus Interviews

An alumnus of Carnegie Tech, Gretchen Corbett made her professional acting debut with the famed Oregon Shakespeare Festival. Her first New York stage appearance was in a 1967 revival of George Bernard Shaw's Arms and the Man. But she is perhaps best known to television audiences as "Beth Davenport" in The Rockford Files with James Garner from 1974 to 1980, followed up with several television reunion films in the 1990s.

Gretchen is also known for her role as the reluctant parallel-universe denizen June Sterling on Otherworld. She was also Resident Director of ASK theatre, where she worked on numerous staged readings and workshops of new works. She has played leading roles in prominent regional theatres across the country including the New York, New Jersey, Circle-in-the-Square, the Eugene O'Neill Festival, the Long Wharf Theatre, Seattle Repertory Theatre, and the Mark Taper Forum.

She returned to her hometown of Portland, Oregon and for ten years served as Artistic Director of The Haven Project, a non-profit organization that paired underserved children with professional actors to create original theater. Her local stage appearances have included productions for Portland Playhouse, Third Rail Rep, Sojourn Theatre and Portland Center Stage.

Gretchen has received lead actress awards for Happy Days, Molly Sweeney, It Had to Be You and A Lesson from Aloes in Portland and for The Fox and Voice of the Prairie. Other notable productions in which she has appeared include One Flew Over the Cuckoo's Nest and Angels in America: Millennium Approaches.

Gretchen Corbett

"I'm a Stage Actress — We Don't Do Hollywood!"

I've enjoyed your work for so long! It's a pleasure to be able to talk to you about your career.

Thank you! Thank you for asking me. I'm honored to be here.

I understand that you were actually born and raised in Oregon.

I was! Portland is my hometown.

And you went to school here?

I did. I went to the Riverdale School and then in high school I went to Caitlin Gabel, where we had a wonderful drama teacher whose name was Vivian Johannes and she really, or it, captured my imagination. Also going to the Oregon Shakespeare Festival; every summer our parents took us down there and we saw four plays in four days and so by the time I was eleven I had seen the Shakespeare canon. Then we started all over again! I just wanted to be up on that stage.

So, in school when did you give your first performance, or when was your first play?

I played "Mrs. Santa" in the second grade and I was pretty good! I did a commercial in the sixth grade, and I played the "duck" in *Alice in Wonderland* at the Civic Theatre in the third grade. I had one line and my line was, "When I find a thing, it is generally a frog or a worm; but the question is: 'What did the Archbishop find?' " Now, I can't remember lines that I did last week — but I remember that one! (Laughs)

Were your parents supportive?

Well, they were supportive of me doing all kinds of things, of course. There were four kids in our family and we did all sorts of things. Swimming lessons, piano, and — if you had to do a play — ok. I don't think anyone dreamed that that would end up being my profession, but it did!

In Oregon, the Corbett family name goes back a number of years, actually to the pioneer days. Let me ask about your Mother. She was involved heavily in civic and cultural activities. Can you talk a little about that?

Indeed she was. She was actually from South Carolina originally and then she and her family moved here when she was a young teenager. My Mom's career, after we left the house pretty much, was to work at Portland State University where she was the head of Student Affairs, which essentially, as far as I could tell she ran the college! (Laughs) That's what it seemed like to me. But she was on about a billion Boards of Directors in the community and it was important to her. The Arts were important, as well as health and youth. That was pretty much her passion and she felt like she could give to the community. She was a pretty feisty woman — people liked her! She wasn't the *easiest* Mom to live with, but she was smart, had a great sense of humor; she was a great lady.

Do you think you take after her at all?

Gretchen Corbett talks about her family background. PHOTO COURTESY OF ANTHONY WYNN.

Oh, man! You know, I never thought I was like my Mom at all, until she died, which was a couple of years ago. In kind of putting together something to say about my Mom at her service I realized that there was quite a lot about her that I had taken on, that I had learned about. She was very organized and ran things easily and well, and I think I learned that from her. There are probably some bad qualities, as well — do I have to talk about those? (Laughs)

No…(Laughs)

Ok! (Playfully wipes her brow in relief.)

Going back even further than your parents, you have ancestors that were involved in the history of Oregon, a U.S. Senator, and an Acting Governor of Oregon.

I didn't have anything to do with that, but…

I'm curious how it affects you today, as far as your involvement with community affairs — or does it have any bearing on things you're doing today?

You know, it probably does in ways that I don't really know about. When you're a part of a community you want to be actively involved in the community and do things that matter. Maybe that comes from my Great-Grandfather, I don't know. I have great admiration for the men and women that were my ancestors and my parents took a lot of pride in being ancestors from them. I wouldn't take such pride myself, I think, it's a different time, really that we live in. I do admire the kind of people they were and how seriously they took building a community in Portland that had a symphony, an art museum, and good theatre. They cared about that.

Back to your own career path: We've talked a little bit about school and about how you were involved in productions, but was there a specific moment when you knew — when you really knew — that you wanted to be an actress and that you wanted to be on the stage? Can you pinpoint it?

You know, I was just thinking about that not too long ago. As I mentioned, when I was young and we would go to Ashland I would always want to be up on the stage. But my Aunt Helen lived in New York and she came out to Oregon regularly. She took me to brunch at the Contiki Room at the Benson Hotel when I was about eleven or twelve. That was pretty special to me. In that conversation, she asked me what I thought I was going to do when I grew up and I said that I was going to be an actress. She looked at me and said, "Are you?" And there was something about the belief in what this child had told her, and that she believed me. It made me take ownership of it in a way that I said, "Yes." I didn't have a clue how I was going to do that, but that was a huge turning point for me and I knew from a very young age — *that* was what I was going to do.

Was your first professional job here in Portland, or was that part of the Oregon Shakespeare Festival?

I suppose it depends what you call professional. I think it's defined as an actor who belongs to a union and you have to be of a certain quality before they let you in the union or you are hired at union wages. Ashland, at that time, was not Equity. They hired maybe one or two Equity people. But I was working in Ashland in the summertime and it was through working there that I was offered my first Equity job in

Louisiana at the New Orleans Repertory Theatre. At that time there were three companies in the United States that were repertory companies, and there was a lot more money for the arts then. These were companies that were national companies of the United States. I was offered the role of "Juliet" in *Romeo and Juliet* and a whole season of other work. It was my first professional job and I went down there and

Gretchen Corbett discusses coloring her hair for Out of It, her first film. PHOTO COURTESY OF ANTHONY WYNN.

spent a year experiencing the South, and the bugs (laughs) — and the *humidity*. I had never known that before! It was playing to about twenty-five hundred people a night, eight shows a week, and I paid some dues and learned how to be "on the boards," as they say.

You can't beat that experience, can you?

No, it was great. I hope that any person who wants to be a professional actor really gets their roots down onto the stage because that's really where you learn what you're doing.

I read in an interview that you had a profound effect on a local drama teacher who saw you in a production of *Othello* at the Oregon Shakespeare Festival.

Good God!

You were quite young, I think about seventeen.

That was before New Orleans, I played "Desdemona."

You inspired her to go on and become a drama teacher because of that performance.

Wow. (Long pause) Just wow. Shakespeare is pretty extraordinary and pretty wonderful. He was a genius and it sure is fun to do Shakespeare.

You've been involved here with The Haven Project, a local theatre project working with kids. Do you think that today's children are learning Shakespeare and are familiar with the classics?

No, they're not. Our educational system is such that teachers don't have too much time and far too few resources. The kids we work with don't have too much familiarity with the classics and with Shakespeare. They may know that "to be or not to be" is a soliloquy from *Hamlet* and maybe some of *Romeo and Juliet*. We took some of our kids from The Haven Project down to Ashland last year and that was really cool. They totally get it; the loved it! They understand and can make the leap of the language a lot better than adults can; more quickly.

So from New Orleans, did you go to New York?

I did. I actually was going to go back to New Orleans for another season and I went to New York for a visit. June Havoc and I had been in *The Rivals*, a [Richard Brinsley] Sheridan play in New Orleans, and June said that when I went to New York I needed to meet her agent. So I did. He was like a Jules Feiffer character — he scared the daylights out of me!

(Laughs)

June Havoc, of course, has had a long career on the stage and is the little sister of Gypsy Rose Lee.

Yeah, a long career. She's a great old lady. She's wonderful. We later did another play together where I played an epileptic girl, *The Effect of Gamma Rays on Man-in-the-Moon Marigolds*. Back in New York I met another agent who sent me to an audition for a film. He had me come back to his office, taught me how to catch a cab, and asked me if I wanted to make a movie that summer. I wasn't quite sure and told him, "Well, I was planning to go to Europe." He asked, "But do you want to do a *movie?*" So I said, "Yeah, yeah!" It turned out to be a pretty low budget movie called *Out of It*, a black and white film about high school kids with Barry Gordon, Jon Voight and Lada Edmund, Jr. This was before *Midnight Cowboy* and Jon basically did the same character he ended up playing in *Midnight Cowboy*. He chewed gum all the way through it. They dyed my hair brown because Lada Edmund, Jr. was a babe and she had blonde hair. The director always got confused when two girls had the same color hair! (Laughs) I sprayed some "stuff" in my hair because I didn't want it to be brown forever and my hair went berserk! I tried to iron it and they were coming to pick me up — it was just a mess. The film was shot out on Long Island and that was the first time I swam in the ocean.

I never made it to Europe that summer and I didn't go back to New Orleans. While I was shooting that picture I got the off-Broadway show *Arms and the Man,* a Shaw play, and I played "Louka." While I was doing *that*, I got a Broadway show which was called *After the Rain,* a play with a British company. There were a few Americans, maybe three. Alec McCowan was in the cast — a wonderful, crazy man and I learned a lot from him. I was really a kid and so green. Nancy Marchard was in that company and we roomed together for that play. I remember when we closed *After the Rain* I was crying, just sobbing. I felt like I had lost all my friends forever. Nancy said to me, "You know, you always work with people again in this business that you want to; and sometimes you work with people that you don't want to." That was comforting, in a way. (Laughs) Thinking back, it seems to me that it wasn't long before I worked with her husband Paul Sparer again at the New York Shakespeare Festival, where I did "Joan la Pucelle" in the *Henry VI* trilogy. (Smiles) I may be one of the few actresses you know who's done the *Henry VI* trilogy *twice* in my life; once at the Oregon Shakespeare Festival and the other in New York. When *After the Rain* closed, I went on to do the Broadway play *Forty Carats,* working again with Nancy. So it was true. *Forty Carats* was with Julie Harris and it was a big hit. I was in that play about a year and a half total, including the pre-Broadway touring, before we came into town. We were on Broadway for over a year. Nancy, Julie, and I all became really good friends for a lot of years. That was really nice.

Forty Carats, I think, had an intriguing plot device. In the show, Julie Harris played your mother and she dates a man much younger, while your character — the daughter — dates a man twice her age; an interesting juxtaposition.

They were each other's dates, actually.

Was that sort of scandalous for that time period?

(Laughs) I think it probably was! Older woman; younger man. But it was comedy; a light Broadway comedy. People loved it.

You also received a good review from *The New York Times*. It's so interesting I have to mention it. It read, "Gretchen Corbett is an unlikely cross between Lauren Bacall and Bambi, and this is just fine."

(Laughs) My God! Oh, how your past comes back to haunt you! Oh!

The play *After the Rain* has a really interesting premise: It's almost a kind of science fiction story with a plot that's set two hundred years in the future.

Good for you, you did your homework! We all wore white, is what I remember, and the stage was a black shiny surface and you had to wear little muck-lucks when you were walking around so that you didn't make it dirty. It was very futuristic and we were on an ark, or a raft; something like that. It was weird and Alec played the leader of us all and he was a madman. My character got pregnant in this play and they put a pad on me, then the baby disappeared! I learned a lot from the director of that play, a man named Vivian Matalon. One of the best lessons as a young actor that I learned at that point was from him. Often when you're a young actor you think that you have to "do" something and so you try to make a "moment" out of everything. That director taught me, for instance, that if you're coming through that door with a birthday cake — just bring on the birthday cake. That realization made a big impact on me. I kind of got it that you can just "be." That's what acting really is. It's hard to do, but you don't have to "do" anything.

Another play you did was *An Unknown Soldier and His Wife*.

Yes, that was directed by Anthony Perkins, in fact, the first thing that Tony ever directed. We did that show in Philadelphia and here he was, a major movie star, directing this little play. He was a very dear and very nervous about doing it right. He was a very shy and private man. He didn't take to being a movie star very much. He was a very good spirit, and wonderful man.

Have you ever subscribed to any certain type of acting training, like for instance, The Method?

I do think it helps a lot if you're trained. The Method is just one kind of training, but all an actor has is their body — so it's important that you train your body and train your voice. There are ways of breaking down a script that are just pretty simple ways of understanding the way human beings go about getting what they want and the way to define a character. A lot of us have great instincts about acting, but without training — for me, anyway, working as a director, I can totally see the difference between a young actor who has training and those who do not. Most of the training schools and colleges use a pretty wide range of techniques. I don't subscribe to one in particular, I've kind of come up with my own way of creating a character. I don't even think about it anymore. It's all intrinsically intuitive. Usually when I'm playing a role and somebody asks me about a character, or motivations for a character, I can give you the answer. But I really hadn't thought about it until you asked me. (Laughs)

After your run in _Forty Carats_, you were in a production called _The Bench_...

It's about as interesting as its title! (Laughs) That was an off-Broadway show that lasted, oh I don't know — maybe a week?

Yes, several performances...but you did receive a good review in it. Well, the show didn't, but you did. (Laughter) I don't know if I should mention the critic or not, but it was Clive Barnes and he said, "Gretchen Corbett, bright and eager, confirms the promise of her performance in _After the Rain_."

It was a short-lived, pretty bad play. The review is nice, but it was a pretty miserable experience actually.

You worked with Michael O'Sullivan in that production?

Yes. (Pause) I'm trying to think if that was Michael's last play. He died shortly thereafter, anyway. He was a madman. There are a lot of madmen in the theatre!

Something I'm really interested in talking about is a production that you did called _The Survival of Saint Joan_," billed as a medieval rock opera. Can you talk about that?

I spent a year doing _Saint Joan_. Other singers performed the songs, which were staged up above us, while we, the actors, performed the dialogue. In the play, the tenor was my "voice," or Joan's voice. There were a lot of songs. It was as if Joan hadn't been killed at the stake, and the story tells what happens to a saint. It was pretty wild. We started up in Buffalo, New York, and it was a huge hit. Then they brought it into New York. But because it was such a hit in Buffalo, they thought they should make it better. (Laughs) So they recast it, except for me, with actors who were much slicker. And it didn't work, which was too bad. That was the same summer I did _Saint Joan_ at New York Shakespeare Festival in the Park and then I did [George Bernard] Shaw's _Saint Joan_ in Portland. There was a new professional theatre that was starting at Portland State University, I think called the American Repertory Theatre. They called me up and said they were starting their new theater and they would like me to do a play and I could do anything I wanted with any director I wanted. I thought that's how the world worked!

That's pretty good.

I thought that from now on someone would just ask me what I wanted to do with whomever I wanted to do it with. (Laughs) Oh dear. That's not how it works! But this was pretty great. I called up Nagle Jackson who was a director and performer, and a wonderful man, I had met at Ashland. Nagle said, "Well, we'll have to do *Saint Joan.*" You can hardly go wrong with Shaw. So that was my year of *Saint Joan.*

It was around this time that you made your second film, called *Let's Scare Jessica to Death*, right?

(Laughs) Yes, I did. I did a movie called *Let's Scare Jessica to Death!* My film career is pretty thrilling. I played a mute. But that's not how it started out. When I got hired, it was going to be a film called *Laurie* and that was the name of my character. But then they hired someone who was more famous that I was and she wanted the movie named after her. So they rewrote the movie and I ended up being this kind of apparition and ended up dead in the bass case, I think. I'm very proud of that. (Laughs)

You did find your way back to New York...

Yeah, that was my home!

You appeared in Henrik Ibsen's *The Master Builder*, which a critic called "A rewarding introduction to one of Ibsen's deeply layered and self-revealing dramas." E.G. Marshall, among other actors, was in this production. What are your thoughts about that play?

That was a really wonderful experience. Austin Pendleton directed it at the Long Wharf Theatre in New Haven [Connecticut]. Austin is one of the best directors that I've ever worked with. He's a man of great clarity and he's a wonderful actor, which you probably know, and he's really an actor's director. There was something about what Austin gave me in that production and I ended up feeling that I had created this role all by myself and I was completely clear about everything that I did. That's such a gift for a director to be able to give to an actor. E.G. [Marshall] was a trip to work with. We had long, long scenes together — half hour, forty-five minutes — if you know that play, the scenes go on forever. E.G. never *really* knew his lines. I had one of those young brains and I was helping him out. I realized just before opening that I wasn't paying attention to my own performance because I was so worried about helping E.G. out. So I decided I wasn't going to help him out anymore, I wasn't going to feed him his lines; I wasn't going to think about that. I was just going to do the scene with him. So opening night came and we're doing one of the interminable scenes and there was this long pause. He said, "Would you like some tea?" I had no clue where we were, but I said, "Certainly!" We walked all the way across the stage, got some tea, he poured it; neither of us knew where we were. It lasted forever. Finally, we were able to continue on. But that's one of the big memories I have of that show.

It was also during that production when Eleanor Kilgallen came

Gretchen Corbett remembers *The Master Builder,* **a Broadway play, with E.G. Marshall.** PHOTO COURTESY OF ANTHONY WYNN.

to see the play and offered me, for the second time, a contract with Universal Studios. Eleanor was the sister of Dorothy Kilgallen and a casting agent. The first time she offered it to me, I said, "Hollywood, ick! No, I'm a *stage* actress — we don't *do* Hollywood!" (Laughs) By the time *The Master Builder* came around, I decided that I *could* do Hollywood. I had gotten off my high horse and understood what unemployment was at this time I said, "Yeah, ok."

Did you have a low period around that time?

Well, I really don't remember specifically. But being an actor you're always facing unemployment. You don't know if it's going to be a month, or six months, or a year until your next job. It's the uncertainty of not knowing. There's a lot of that. So I accepted the contract at Universal.

In other words, a regular paycheck.

That's right. It was a big deal to me at the time. I went to California, but kept my apartment in New York, and I started doing every television show known to God or man. I was one of the last of the contract players and essentially they would put me in a show, they would charge for my services, and they would pay me my salary. So they made money off of me. That's what the contract system was about.

So were you more or less obligated to appear in whatever they asked you to? Did you have the opportunity to turn something down if you didn't like the sound of it?

I did turn things down, because a lot of the contract players didn't have the background that I did. So they were really pretty, but they weren't able to put the goods out. I got a lot of jobs. I turned down so many things; some that might have made me a very, very rich woman. Not that I regret not being one of *Charlie's Angels*, but... (Laughs)

You had a recurring role on *Ellery Queen*, which was a favorite show of mine.

I *loved* doing that show. I enjoyed the costumes, the scripts were really cool. It was very fun to do that show, the stars Jim Hutton and David Wayne, were wonderful. Oh, I did so much work at that time, really an astonishing amount of work. Typically on those episodic shows we'd shoot twelve hours a day on a script they gave us two days before if — if we're lucky — then you have to walk and talk so you don't block anyone's light. You've got to be in synch with the cameraman and the whole crew behind him, and on top of that you have to create a believable character while bringing life and truth to the words you're saying.

Of course, there is the series that everyone remembers fondly. You got the role of "Beth Davenport" in *The Rockford Files* with James Garner. How did this come about? Was it part of your contract, did you have to meet with producers?

Oh yes, I always had to read for things and actually Beth was just a guest character for which I auditioned. Maybe they had it in mind that it could be a recurring role, but maybe not. I'm not sure. The chemistry between me and the writer, and me and Jim worked really well. So the next season they wrote a bunch of them and had me recur, and it rolled on from there.

The relationship between Beth and Jim Rockford was just so good; the writing is great.

Beth was really one of the first smart characters on television. That's one of the reasons why I think people really responded to it so strongly. I certainly had a connection with the character and I'm pretty much a straight shooter, that's the kind of person that I am. It was a good connection between me and what the writer, Meta Rosenberg, had written.

What's it like working with James Garner?

Gretchen Corbett remembers working on *The Rockford Files* with James Garner. PHOTO COURTESY OF ANTHONY WYNN.

It's just like you would imagine. He's a sweetheart! He's a man that is deeply loved by the actors and technicians alike; everybody on the set. Jim really takes care of the people around him and he is a generous and sweet human being. He's pretty much "what you see is what you get." What you see on the screen, that's who he is. He's well-liked by both men and women, and he's a guy's guy, yet women still like him a lot. So there you go.

There were some other great folks on the show, too — Noah Beery, who was Jim Rockford's father "Rocky." What are your memories of him?

We called him "Pidge." That's his nickname. He's one of the sweetest, dearest guys who left us too soon. He was an artist and he made

Western sculptures, art in the style of Will James. He lived out by the beach and he was pretty shy, actually; a very gentle human being.

One of the others on the show was Joe Santos, who played "Lt. Becker" — you had a lot of scenes with him; and Stuart Margolin, who played "Angel."

Joe's a great guy, he teaches acting and he's still working. Stuart is a pretty wonderful actor, not at all like his character. He's also a director and has been directing a lot. He's directed *Rockfords* and he's directed films. He lives up on an island up off the coast of Canada. But Stuart is definitely *not* what you see on the screen!

Jumping a little bit into the future, *The Rockford Files* returned in the 1990s with series of films and you were once again a part of that. What was it like coming back to the role of "Beth" after a long gap?

I was like being thrown into a pool, but you can totally swim again. It was pretty odd, I have to say, that the camera operator was now the director of photography. The first day I just stood in front of the camera and I said, "You know, guys, I feel like we all have old-age makeup on!" It's what it felt like! (Laughs) So many of the same folks were back; both in front of and behind the cameras. It was so weird! But it was a lot of fun and we had a good time doing that.

You had a leading role in a short-lived science fiction series called *Otherworld*. What do you remember about that show and your character of June Sterling?

Oh boy. It was a kind of mix of science fiction and *The Fugitive*. I played the mother and our family, the Sterlings, had ended up in this future world, or other dimension or something, and we were being chased by a futuristic cop. That world had a lot of different areas and cultures, so each week there was something different we would encounter. I think we shot about thirteen episodes of that show before the network pulled the plug. I guess the network didn't really know what to with us; how to promote it. At that point, I think it was time for me to move on! (Laughs)

You returned to Portland [Oregon] and you've been heavily involved in theatre here. It's like you came full circle.

This is a great city, I love Portland. I then had my young daughter Winslow and I wanted her to have some roots. When you're in Los Angeles the roots all come out of the sand. She could go to school and really think of herself as an Oregonian. She has great pride in this state and loves to say that she's from here. We had family here and I wanted her to experience what that would be. I certainly had a wide range of family around me growing up and it gave me a great solidity in my adulthood. My parents, as it turned out, were in their last years and so it was a really great opportunity for me to get to care for them. Let's be honest, I was old for film and television. There's really a pretty short shelf life for a woman, the stage is much more forgiving. I've done plays all over and I really love this place. If something was to be offered in L.A., it's just a short plane hop away. In this day and age where you do your work isn't so important.

You've had some great successes on Portland stages and some wonderful parts. You played the title role in *Molly Sweeney*; you were in A.R. Gurney's *Sylvia*; you won a best actress award for *It Had to Be You*; and had raves for Samuel Beckett's *Happy Days*.

I've had a wonderful experience working for [director] Dennis Bigelow. *Happy Days* is essentially a sixty-four page monologue that was really true hell to learn! (Laughs) It took me about six months. The setting is unique; the character is in a mound of dirt, or sand. In the first act she's up to her waist and in the second, she's up to her neck. It's not the prettiest I've ever looked on the stage.

It's got to be a challenge; it must test your acting skills.

Yeah, well, I think it's really what you're thinking about, anyway. If you really are thinking about it, then the audience is right there with you. It's a very moving and funny play that Mr. Beckett has written. It was really an honor to work on it. *Molly Sweeney* was also a great play to work on, and *It Had to Be You* was a fairly silly comedy. I'm looking for something silly to do again!

We're at the end of our time, but I want to thank you for coming by to talk, it's been wonderful. I've admired your work for many years.

Thank you, Tony.

Corinne Orr is a Canadian-born actress and voice artist, a naturalized American citizen who now lives in New York City. By the age of 14 she was working at the Montreal Repertory Theatre and the Montreal Mountain Playhouse. She acted alongside such notables as Barry Morse, Christopher Plummer, and William Shatner in productions such as George S. Kaufman and Edna Ferber's Dinner at Eight.

With her solid background on the stage, Orr was hired for roles on CBC radio in such dramas as Laura Limited, and then moved to CBC television to portray the character of "Suzie Mouse" on the children's soap opera Chez Helene, a bilingual program devoted to teaching children English and French. Relocating to New York, Corinne began working there regularly on radio, television, and as a voice artist. She also began a lucrative career as spokesperson for a variety of companies in a wide range of radio and television commercials. In addition, she dubbed foreign films into English and, as a multi-voiced talent, she is in demand in the cartoon world.

Orr's animation credits include Ultraman, The Adventures of the Galaxy Rangers, and Marine Boy, voicing the characters of "Marine Boy," "Neptina," and "Cli-Cli." She also voiced characters in the classic Speed Racer television series, in which she portrayed "Trixie," "Spritle," and each of the other female characters. Corinne also made an appearance in the live-action adaptation of Speed Racer on the big screen.

In addition to commercials and cartoons, Orr has narrated children's stories, provided voices for several dolls, and recorded numerous books on tape. For eighteen years, she was the voice of "Snuggle the Bear" in Snuggle's fabric softener commercials. Our interviews took place in Victoria, British Columbia, Canada and Portland, Oregon.

Corinne Orr

"Looking for Adventure in My Own Way"

Welcome Corinne, it's nice to be here with you.

It's good to see you, Tony. We're here in the beautiful Empress Hotel in Victoria overlooking the harbor and glorious ships; it's fun, really fun.

I want to talk with you about your career and some of the things that you've done in your life. I'd like to start at the beginning. Where were you born?

I was born in Montreal [Quebec, Canada], but we lived in a little French town called St. Hyacinth until I was five years old. My brother and sister were in their teens and my mother wanted to live somewhere where they could find eligible people to marry. So we moved to Montreal — where they both did get married, by the way! I was much younger and had trouble at first because my first language was French, then I had to learn English. My mother gave me elocution lessons and I got hooked. We did a lot of poetry readings, bits from plays; I just loved all of it. My first play was *Alice in Wonderland* directed by Silvia Narzzano when I was eleven. He later directed the hit movie *Georgy Girl* with Lynn Redgrave. I remember a crazy pig running around on-stage!

It was at the age of fourteen that I started working professionally doing radio for the Canadian Broadcasting Corporation. I was in a show called *Laura Limited,* directed by a rather formidable man named Rupert Caplan. I was in total terror of him at all times! I think everybody was. I'm sure he was a nice man and things would be different today. I worked with wonderful people: William Shatner, John Colicos (whom I adored, because he kissed my hand when I was fourteen and no one had ever done that! I didn't wash it for days), Jimmy Doohan, Christopher Plummer, and Richard [Dick] Easton. Bill Shatner was wonderful to me. He would buy me lunch at this place called Murray's, a kind of cafeteria that no longer exists. I was just a kid and that was very kind of him. When I grew up and was 18, he used to flirt with me, which thrilled me to pieces! He was so devastatingly handsome. I have nothing but lovely memories of him.

I studied with Dick Easton at the Montreal Repertory Theatre who was nothing short of a genius. But the theatre burned down! That led me to the Mountain Playhouse and we did a lot Noël Coward. That's where I met Barry Morse, his lovely wife Sydney, and their children Hayward and Melanie. Tony, you worked with Barry much later on, but back then I don't even know if he knew I was around. I loved Barry and I was in awe of him. He is so bright, so full of fun, a great sense of humor; he's a delightful man. What I admire most about him is that he worked clear up into his late eighties — almost until the day he left us! He was an inspiration.

But then I was just fourteen or fifteen years old and hanging out — and loving it! Elaine Stritch came and did a show there and I just adored her. She was so kind to me. A funny thing; she used to run around naked! I had never seen anyone do that and I was in awe of it. She was such a darling, warm lady.

What did your mother think about all of this?

Oh, my mother was very much against my going into the theatre. "You'll never make a living!" and so forth. But my first love was the stage. I ended up going to Toronto where — let's face it — I just about starved to death. I don't know how I existed. I did a play with Jimmy Doohan there called *Every Bed is Narrow*. Another actor I met was Chris Wiggins. I remember before we went on stage every night he would take out his teeth! I found that quite fascinating. He did it to "throw" us, to scare us; he was very naughty. My cousin, Leo Orenstein, at the time was a famous director, but I think I only did that one show for him. Now, he and I are very good friends! But back then it was rather tentative. Really, I do not know how I survived that time. I just do not know!

You segued from radio into television in Canada, right?

Yes. I was hired for a show called *Chez Hélène* on CBC Television was which a children's story done in English and French and I played a mouse! The mouse was actually a puppet, but I was the voice. I was in that show for two years and there were three of us in the cast. The show went on for years after I left, but I don't have nice memories of Hélène Baillargeon. She was domineering and she tried to throw her weight around — and she had a bit of weight! To me, she was not an actress; she got the show through political means and through her marriage. But, that said, on *Chez Hélène* I *was* one of the highest paid performers in television in Canada, along with Robert Goulet, because I had a daily show. I made $7,000 dollars a year! Bob was certainly more famous than me and made more, of course. He was a genuinely nice guy and I liked him a lot.

I know that you left and went to New York; what brought about that move from Canada?

What happened is that I was doing a few commercials in Canada, but I couldn't live on what they paid. I know that Barry Morse talked about this in his book, how performers were paid just peanuts, really. I don't know how to explain it; it just wasn't a living wage. That's why so many Canadian performers have come to the U.S. Canada just didn't encourage its creative people. Now, of course, it's quite a bit different. Vancouver is a hot-bed of film and television and Toronto, Montreal; they're all on the map now. But when I was there, they weren't and you really had to go away. So I went to New York and I lived at the Barbizon Hotel for Women which was a totally fabulous experience! In those years, women like Grace Kelly stayed there. They checked

Corinne Orr remembers Elaine Stritch and her nudity. PHOTO COURTESY OF ANTHONY WYNN.

your bed every night to make sure you slept there — alone. No men were allowed above the lobby! There was a doorman there and in Canada I had lived in a house with my parents, so I didn't know about doormen. So I gave him a quarter, but I was really poor. I would try to evade him, to not give him a quarter; but he always found me! He almost bankrupted me with his lousy quarter I would give him every time he opened the door. (Laughs)

I was so poor, but I met a lot of nice guys who would take me to dinner. We would go out to eat at six-thirty or seven pm; then I would go out to dinner again with another guy at nine pm! I mainly remember eating. I really didn't know anybody there; but failure was not an option — I had to do something. So I got the yellow pages, looked up ad agencies and, believe or not, I started getting commercials. But I was making fifteen to twenty calls a day. People who didn't make it often wanted the work to come to them. *You* have to put out the effort, *you* have to call, *you* have to send the postcards, *you* have to send the letters, and *you* have to send the emails!

I'm a multi-voice so I could do kids, or anything. It was at this time that I also found Titra, which was a major dubbing company, and we did all of the very classy foreign movies into English. We dubbed them. They call it looping now. At that time technology was not as good as it is now and we had to go into this huge projection room with a screen like a movie theatre. In the back was the projectionist, then there was the director, the slater, and it was my job to fit my mouth into the mouth of the people on the screen. In other words, I had to match my lines, my words, with the movements of the character's mouth. Not always an easy task! Here, the greatest person is the writer.

This was when I met the director and writer Peter Fernandez. He was a genius at writing dubbing scripts, it was kind of like doing a jigsaw puzzle. If the word in French was "mais pourquoi?" in English it would be "my, but why?" Every mouth closing was called a labial, so we had to match the labials. We did Bernardo Bertolucci films and a lot of spaghetti westerns. Some actors would come in and do their own voices — Clint Eastwood was one. English actors like Joan Collins came in; she was lovely. But we dubbed all of the foreign-speaking people into English and I got to play every kid in all these movies! I played Claudia Cardinale in a movie. My favorite was an unknown film called *Sister Karate Street Fighter.* All I did was scream! I had no dialogue and I loved it because I didn't have to worry so much about the mouth movement.

In those beginning days, didn't you also do some television — including that famous series *The Nurses*?

That's right! I played very small parts and would get the "disease of the week." (Laughs) It was horrible! For two dollars, or whatever, I would walk around with whatever they were dying from that week. I was very thin and had good legs and also did some leg modeling at the time. Zina Bethune played the lead in *The Nurses* and she had heavy legs, so they would use my legs instead of hers. She just recently died; what a terrible tragedy that was. She was driving in Los Angeles when she saw an injured animal by the side of the road, which turned out to be a dead possum. Zina got out of her car to check on the animal and was struck by two cars and killed. What an awful way to go.

You worked on several notable animated series in the 1960s, beginning with *Ultraman* and *Marine Boy.* Tell me about those.

Oh my God, I had forgotten about Ultraman! You're right! But let me tell you, Marine Boy was such fun. I played "Marine Boy" and "Cli Cli" — a little imp; I don't know what he was! I also played "Neptina." Peter Fernandez directed me and when he would get unhappy, he

Corinne Orr talks about working on *The Nurses.* PHOTO COURTESY OF ANTHONY WYNN.

would call out, "Nep*tuna!*" I would get so mad. In the cast we had Jack Curtis, Jack Grimes, Peter, and me — it was a limited budget. So I would play all the women and all the kids. I hear now that Marine Boy is really famous in England because it ran there for ten years. I would like you to know that I never got one penny, because at that time the concept of residuals had not been put into practice. So I am poor, but famous!

So this leads me to ask about one of your most famous roles...
Snuggle the Bear! (Laughs)

Well, actually I was going to say *Speed Racer!*
Don't forget, there were a lot of other cartoons in the middle. *Princess Guinevere and the Jewel Riders; The Adventures of the Galaxy Rangers;*

and I did a thing called *Johnny Cypher in Dimension Zero*. I got that job by knocking on a door. The guy thought I was gutsy so he gave me a part! There were so many at that time that I truly can't remember them all. I also worked on a lot of features, like *Jack and the Beanstalk*.

When *Speed Racer* came Peter Fernandez gathered the same cast he had used for *Marine Boy*. Because we had such a limited budget, he wrote, directed, and played the parts of "Speed Racer" and his mysterious brother "Racer X." Jack Curtis played "Pops Racer," Jack Grimes played "Sparky" the mechanic, and I played "Spritle" — the crazy brother who lives in the trunk (with "Chim-Chim" the monkey) as well as "Trixie," "Mom Racer," and any other girl that came along, as well as the occasional man in crowd scenes!

Did you realize the impact this show would have on pop culture?

Absolutely never. I made $100 dollars a show and we did fifty-two shows; I thought I had landed in heaven. I've never seen a penny from it since! Well, that's not *quite* true. Now many years have gone by and it's become one of those "cult" series. I'm invited to sign autographs at conventions and we've done many auto shows. *Speed Racer's* car, of course, is gorgeous.

How many of your own personality traits did you put into "Trixie" and the other characters you played?

Well, how about "Spritle"? I'm naughty like him; he'd eat candy all the time, as you well know like I do! His mission was looking for fun and adventure. I don't stay in the back seat or the trunk, but I have traveled a lot looking for adventure in my own way. Now "Trixie" was something that I aspire to be. She was so totally wonderful. She flew her own plane, she was a race car driver — I can't do any of those things! She had a darling boyfriend, "Speed Racer," wow. She was a hot cookie there, I liked her. I could never be as wonderful as she is!

What does the "G" stand for on "Speed Racer's" shirt?

It symbolized a Japanese name, the Japanese name of "Speed Racer" which was Goh Mifune. The "M" on his helmet stands for Mifune Motors. You may remember that "Trixie" had an "M" on her blouse, too. That was for her Japanese name, Michi Shimura. But Peter called him a member of "Go" team. Of course, "Speed's" brother had the "X," so Peter named him "Racer X." Peter's solution for the "M" on "Speed's" helmet was to coin the term "Mach 5." He did other funny names, too; the one that comes to mind right now is "Fingers Clepto." He also came up with clever plots and worked to avoid violence. For example, when showing some race car bad guys you'd see arms and legs flying and people half-crushed. Then the dialogue would be something like, "Oh, they don't feel too well, but I hear they're coming out of the hospital tomorrow." (Laughs) So we didn't have any deaths. It was the same when he wrote *Ultraman.* The monsters would battle; it was such a cheap show, I look at it and just fall apart laughing. But the line after a battle would be, "Oh, I guess he'll feel better in the

Corinne Orr discusses her work on the classic series *Speed Racer.*
PHOTO COURTESY OF ANTHONY WYNN.

morning." Like I said, no one ever died. I played a mother and a child in *Ultraman.* I remember the line (quoted in character as a small child), "Mommy, I wanna spaghetti sandwich!"

I've heard something about how you played crowd scenes in *Speed Racer* and some of the other animated shows.

Long ago in radio, I did a lot of work for CBC Radio, we learned the words rhubarb — garbage are the sounds that are best for crowd scenes. So one of us would say "Rhubarb" and the other would be saying "Garbage," very quickly, and it would sound quite convincing. The engineer would lay the voice tracks over each other and particularly in dubbing, we would make up crazy lines, and often we would have to do it again because we'd say crazy things that didn't fit into the scene. Stuff like, "Hey, how 'bout a date tomorrow night!" in the middle of medieval castle; you know, something that totally would not apply. We had so much fun! But that was back when we were all working as an ensemble in the studio.

Of course, now you go into a studio alone and there is a little TV next to you. The engineers in the control room can do anything with your voice: push it sideways, move it up, cut off a breath — stuff we couldn't do before. So now when you go to work you do it alone, you do your lines — maybe three times each — and leave. You might never meet another person in the cast and it's kind of sad. I've done shows where I would have loved to have met the other cast members.

How difficult is it to act alone?

It's not easy. It makes the director more important than ever. I've been very fortunate to work with really good ones. I've worked for Disney, Kit Meredith, and as I mentioned, the great Peter Fernandez. To me he's the most brilliant director there is and I was very blessed to have been able to work with him.

You and Peter Fernandez did a wonderful commentary track on the DVD release of *Speed Racer,* too.

We had a good time doing that. I have to be honest, though. We've really been exploited left, right, and center. Not for the DVD commentary, but so many of our other things have been used without compensation. People really do think that I'm a millionaire and I'm not.

You mentioned Snuggle the Bear earlier...

Yes! I loved doing him. I played him in commercials for eighteen years at Screen Actors Guild scale. I got thirty-five cents in residuals per showing. In the beginning I made more money, but the last five or six years I made under $5,000 dollars a year. People would say to me, "Boy, you must be rich!" And it would kill me — I wasn't. Finally, I asked them for a raise and they said, "No." They really were not nice to me and I felt very under-appreciated. I created the voice of "Snuggle the Bear" and they just didn't have any feeling or caring for actors. As a result, they switched his sex; he's now a guy and runs around with supermodels! How this sells laundry products, I have no idea. But I wish them well.

You did a fun animated show for Disney called *P B J & Otter.* What do you remember about that?

Oh, I had a good time. I beat out twelve hundred people, including movie stars. It all happened based on a tape my agent sent to Disney. I never had a face-to-face meeting with them. They just liked me;

thought I was great and "bam," I was hired. I played "Shirley Duck" and "Wanda Raccoon." Fun characters! The Disney folks were really nice people and it was a great job.

Are you still as excited by the acting trade as you were at the beginning?

For the most part, I am. I think to be an actor you've got to want something more than just a mundane day-to-day job. You need to have a desire to fulfill your imagination, to explore literature, drama, and to give something more of yourself. I think all artistic people have a little something apart from the others, a little extra "umph" if you will. The real important thing is perseverance. I think poverty is great incentive! (Laughs) You have to go-go-go, and as I said earlier — failure is *not* an option. You get tremendous rejection in the arts. There are 400 people vying for every job. It's insane.

How do you deal with rejection?

Well, I will go to an audition for Product X and someone will ask me the next day, "What did you audition for?" And I'll say, "I don't remember." Maybe it's not that I *don't* remember, it's that I *don't want* to remember. I push it out of my head and go on to the next. When I do get it, I'm happy, of course. But I just immediately forget what I've auditioned for. If you don't, you start questioning, "Why didn't I get it? What did I do wrong?" The truth is that you did nothing wrong, maybe they wanted a brunette and you're a red-head; they wanted an old woman and you're young; they wanted a "nasal" when you're soft; who knows what they want?

Let me tell you the horrors today. They are so cheap now that I have had many auditions over the *telephone*. They fax you the script, you dial the number and there's just a machine at the other end and it suddenly it says, "Record." You're fumbling around momentarily, "Ah-ah-ah." Then you get your lines out and hang up, and you tremble. You're thinking, "Did I do it right? Did they like me? Do I get a second chance?" My last horrible audition on the phone I got a call on call waiting on the whole audition went to pieces. I was so frustrated! I just hate that. I don't know how they get any real sense of the line, or the character. The phone is not a true portrayer of your voice. My phone sure isn't! What with static, background noise, and whatnot. It's tinny. The whole thing is just very sad. The other thing is ageism in the advertising commercials. I was one of the top voice-over people in 1980s and I would do up to five a day. If I get four auditions a year, now, in commercials, it's a miracle.

Is that because the trend is to use more Hollywood actors now instead of voice artists?

That's absolutely correct. We hate that. I used to do children's recordings for a few hundred dollars and now they'll get some person who can't read or act, a so-called "star" who will make $7,000 dollars. For commercials they'll get a $100,000 dollars. You know why? The producer will be able to say, "You know who I had lunch with today...?" It's an ego thing. To do voiceovers you must study acting. You must! Even to make a flat delivery you need to have the technique to do it. The next thing you get is an in-born clock in your head. When they say thirty seconds, they do not mean twenty-nine. They do not mean thirty-one. You have to get a clock in your head and do it exactly on time. I'm pretty good at that; I don't know how. Maybe because I've been working for a hundred years!

Looking to the future, is there anything you haven't done that you would like to try your hand at?

I would say stage work — the stage is my great love. How could it not be for any actor? But I really do love cartoons. I think I'm so blessed. Anyone who offers me a job, I'll do it as long as it's union. Obviously, I've never cared for money or I'd be in another profession! The sad truth about acting is that the average salary is $5,000 dollars a year and eighty percent are out of work at any given time. So looking at those figures, it's a total miracle that I survived and made it, and that I've had a wonderful career.

It's been wonderful to talk to you today.

Thank you, Tony! You've been wonderful to be with.

A number of years ago I was in London, England visiting the actor Barry Morse, and had a little bit of spare time on my hands. Wanting to see a little more of that amazing city, I decided to take an organized walking tour; the best way, really, to truly see London. I've been on a number of walking tours throughout London at various times on different visits, but that particular one I believe was a tour of sites associated with the great writer Oscar Wilde.

One of the other people who had gathered for the tour was a striking woman in high spirits with auburn hair who introduced herself to me. "Hi, I'm Corinne; what's your name?" I replied in turn and before long we were off on our walk around London. The tour guide was very quick and the two of us ended up at the rear of the group. We had such an enjoyable time together that once the tour ended, Corinne asked if we should go on another walking tour! We sat down to rest on a bench for a moment, continuing to chat. I soon learned that Corinne was an actress from New York and in London on a sightseeing and "theatre" vacation — there to see several shows in the West End.

"What brings you to London?" she asked.

"Well, I'm here visiting a friend who's also an actor — you probably don't know him, but his name is Barry Morse."

"But of course, I know him!" she exclaimed in surprise. "We worked together on-stage at the Montreal Mountain Playhouse in Canada!"

Well, it was an amazing coincidence. She was from New York City; I was from Portland, Oregon — and here we were meeting on a walking tour in London, England! I soon learned that Corinne was actually *Corinne Orr*, the renowned voice artist and actress of the classic *Speed Racer* animated series. As it turned out, one of her very first jobs on the stage happened to be with Barry Morse and William Shatner in the play *The Man Who Came to Dinner* at the Montreal Mountain Playhouse.

That chance meeting between us on the pavement in London was the start of a friendship that has lasted over many years. It directly led to my membership in a wonderful New York City charitable organization, the Episcopal Actors' Guild. In turn, that membership led to the New York debut performance of my stage play *Bernard and Bosie: A Most Unlikely Friendship* at Guild Hall. As Barry Morse himself once commented, "Flukes and coincidences; it's amazing how they channel and divert our lives."

Born in London, England to a cockney family, Barry Morse began his career with performances as a boy soprano on BBC radio in the late 1920s. As a boy scout, he also acted in a number of amateur plays and productions in London's East End as a child. But it was as a fifteen year old school dropout and errand boy that he won a full scholarship to the famed Royal Academy of Dramatic Art (RADA).

Famed actress Dame Sybil Thorndike was one of several notables who reviewed his audition and later told Barry that they had found his presentation to be "curiously touching." At the time, he was the youngest student ever to enter the Royal Academy. He wrapped-up his work in RADA by starring in the title role of King Henry V, a Royal Command Performance for their majesties King George VI and Queen Elizabeth, patrons of the Academy, and also won their coveted radio-acting award.

Barry followed with runs in London's West End and in theatrical productions throughout the United Kingdom, as well as appearing on the BBC's earliest live television broadcasts beginning in 1937. Barry made his West End debut in a play called School for Slavery, and with Crisis in Heaven directed by John Gielgud. He continued working in many plays, on the West End and throughout England, including The Assassin by Irwin Shaw, in which he created the leading role and received great critical acclaim. He started his movie career playing stooge to the wry and dyspeptic comedian Will Hay in The Goose Steps Out.

He married fellow actress Sydney Sturgess on March 26, 1939 after a two month courtship following their introduction while working together in a repertory theatre company in Peterborough, England. Two children followed; daughter Melanie in 1945 and son Hayward in 1947.

Barry Morse

"To Everything That Was"

Barry and Sydney relocated the family to Canada in 1951, working in live theatre and on CBC Radio, as well as acting in the premiere television broadcasts of CBC Television from Montreal.

When the fledgling Canadian television service started regular broadcasting from their new radio and television headquarters in Toronto, the family settled there, and Barry devoted time to performing and producing the landmark half-hour CBC Radio series, A Touch of Greasepaint *and later,* Barry Morse Presents *on television, among others.* Greasepaint, *which ran for 14 years, explored the experience of actors through the ages and served as a rough draft for his touring one-man show,* Merely Players. *He is a five-time winner of Canada's Best Television Actor award.*

His theatrical background is extensive, including work in the USA, Canada, Australia, and the UK. He has performed on Broadway in Hide and Seek, Salad Days, *and the lead of Frederick William Rolfe in* Hadrian VII *for more than a year in Australia, on Broadway, and on tour. He directed the historic Broadway debut of* Staircase *starring Eli Wallach and Milo O'Shea, which stands as Broadway's first depiction of homosexual men in a serious way. Other notable stage work includes* Sleuth, Man and Superman, The Caretaker, The Voice of the Turtle, Merely Players, Bernard and Bosie: A Most Unlikely Friendship, *and several hundred others. In his lifetime, Barry performed every play of William Shakespeare and all of the plays of George Bernard Shaw; he also served as Artistic Director of the famed Shaw Festival of Canada.*

Barry starred in a number of television series, including The Adventurer *and* The Zoo Gang. *He also appeared in many popular miniseries presentations, including* The Golden Bowl, The Martian Chronicles, Whoops Apocalypse, Sadat, The Winds of War, War and Remembrance, *and* Icon. *However, he was probably best known to the public around the world for his series roles as "Lt. Philip Gerard" in* The Fugitive *with David Janssen and in the syndicated series* Space: 1999 *as "Professor Victor Bergman" with Barbara Bain and Martin Landau.*

The following interview consists of portions conducted by Anthony Wynn in London at the flat of Barry Morse in 2003 for a Space: 1999*-related website, a few additional comments recorded in an informal discussion in 2004, and a third brief interview in 2005 in Toronto, Ontario, Canada. Some of the questions are based on input from fans of* Space: 1999, *thus much of the interview consists of Barry's memories and discussion of that television series.*

How did your intense interest in George Bernard Shaw develop?

It was quite marvelous. It's the sort of unconventional series of happenings that one wouldn't think of putting into a movie script or a novel! As most people know, I was trained on a scholarship at the Royal Academy of Dramatic Art. Now I didn't really know much about George Bernard Shaw at that point, although he was a world figure

Actor Barry Morse and Anthony Wynn. PHOTO COURTESY OF MELODY SAUNDERS, *MELODY SAUNDERS PHOTOGRAPHY.*

and as widely known or as deeply popular as say, Winston Churchill or President Roosevelt; but I didn't know much about him or his works at firsthand. As a student at RADA, I came to know almost immediately that he was one of our Board of Governors and always deeply interested in the way actors worked. Being a playwright himself, he wanted to know as much as he could about how plays are prepared for presentation — how they are produced. So he used to come quite frequently, which many of our Board of Governors didn't, to RADA to see performances not only of his plays but of other people's plays, too.

In particular, he would come to rehearsals to give advice to us about playing his plays. I always remember the first time I actually personally encountered him when we were doing a production at RADA of Shaw's great little play *Androcles and the Lion*. The Lion appears as a character in this play and I was lucky enough to be playing the Lion. He came along to one of our rehearsals and in his exquisitely cut tweed suit, the kind of tweed suit he always wore, he laid on the floor of our grubby rehearsal room at the Royal Academy, this dusty wooden floor of the room where we used to rehearse. He lay on the floor on his back, waving his arms and legs in the air to show me how the Lion should behave as he put it, "When he wants his tummy tickled." So we became very much devoted to him because he treated us all — and we were just ignorant kids, I was a fifteen year old snotty-nosed urchin — as if we were his equals and contemporaries. He called me "Mr. Morse" and all that sort of stuff. He became instinctively, from our point of view, a deeply treasured friend.

How do you normally start your mornings?

It varies very much according to what I'm doing. In the old days, of course, when I was a youngster first working in repertory theatres, we had to rehearse every morning and we usually were called for ten o'clock in the morning. I was living in lodgings in those days and I would get up eight o'clock and have some breakfast, look at the script that we were currently rehearsing for the next upcoming play, in order to familiarize myself with the new character that I would be about to play and to start to learn some of the lines that were involved. Then I would get myself ready to go down to the theatre to have the first rehearsal, for whatever play it was. We would rehearse for about three or four hours until about one-thirty or two o'clock, at which point we would break for the afternoon.

If we were able to, we would take a little time to have a bit of plea-sure; going to the movies, or going for a walk or a swim, or whatever. We would turn up back at the theatre again at about five-thirty or six o'clock in the evening to prepare ourselves for the *two* performances which most times we had to give. This was in order to compete with the movies — we would do two performances of a full length play in the evening; one usually at six-thirty and the second performance at nine o'clock. So we weren't out of the theatre until about eleven-thirty at night. Then we would make our way back to our lodgings, perhaps have a late supper and get to bed, if we were lucky, some-where around midnight. This in readiness to get up again around eight o'clock in the morning to get prepared for the next day of rehearsal for next week's upcoming play and then to play two performances of our current production! So it was a hectic sort of life.

Later on when I started to work in movies and in television, the hours were totally different. During filming I had to be at the studio at eight o'clock in the morning which meant getting up much earlier in order to get breakfast and get myself tidied up and dressed, and down to the studio — wherever that was. For example in London, there is Elstree Studios which takes more than an hour to get to, or Denham or Pinewood Studios which are down in Buckinghamshire, which also takes an hour or more. Then, depending on how successful and how prosperous one is, the filmmakers would provide transportation and a car would come and pick you up. But before that when I was playing small parts and relatively un-prosperous, I would have to find my own way there on the train or the bus, or the combination of the two. So the travel time could be very substantial, leaving for the studio at a quarter to seven in the morning in order to make sure to get to the studio by eight o'clock. Shooting might go on until six-thirty or seven o'clock in the evening, so it could be eight or eight-thirty at night before I was back at home again. So we had very long days.

Let's talk about your series, *Space: 1999*, which by the way, was filmed at Pinewood Studios. What is your favorite episode from that show and why?

I think I'm at one with most followers and fans of the *Space: 1999* series because this question is quite often asked at conventions and meetings concerned with *Space: 1999*. It's very striking that a majority of people will tell you that their favorite episode is "Black Sun," a show filmed quite early in the series, where we're faced with imminent death. There's a scene in the show between Martin Landau and I, and we decided eventually that we would more or less improvise it. As I recall, Martin and I were having a glass of brandy and sitting there recognizing that we were going to be dead within the next half hour, or whatever it was. In one of the exchanges between us as we raised our glasses of brandy, Martin said, "To everything that might have been," and I replied, "To everything that *was*." That was the kind of high moment, as it were, in that episode.

What kind of brandy were you and Martin Landau drinking in the "Black Sun"?

Burnt sugar and water, as it always is when it comes from the prop department! People sometimes do imagine — and it has happened of course — that people do use real alcoholic drinks. In the matter of shooting a television series, when you may have as many as seven or eight different takes of one scene, you'd well drink yourself into insensibility and be flat on the floor if you drank real brandy! There's always been a convention that the prop department would supply a liquid, which in this case looked satisfactorily like brandy. If you sip it and react in the manner that you probably would if you were drinking a good old brandy, well then the audience is convinced that you are indeed drinking a brandy.

When you first got the role of Professor Victor Bergman, how much of it was shaped by you, by the producers, directors and the writers? Ultimately the actor adds something of themselves to the role and I'm curious as to how you shaped it.

It's not a question of adding something of one's self to the role, but something of what one perceives, or conceives, as the character that one is being called upon to play. With regard to the character of Victor Bergman, most people are astonished to learn (and even I was astonished to learn) that at the point when we started to shoot Space: 1999, we had only *one* script — which is an act of flagrant lunacy in my book! I thought that Lew Grade, who was the ultimate producer of it all, must be very, very crazy to embark on a series for which there was only one script. And in that one script, there was virtually no indication of the nature of the characters at all, beyond the fact that Victor Bergman was the oldest inhabitant and a kind of "Space Uncle." But as to what kind of character he was, and how he became the kind of character he was, there was no indication at all. All of that fell into my lap because I felt that we ought to have some idea as to our characters. I always remember that we had a meeting with the Andersons; Martin Landau, Barbara Bain, and I met with them just before we started to shoot. I was always the troublemaker, and I said, "Look now, can we please have a little discussion about *who we are*." Upon which one of the Andersons said, "Oh well, now the boots are going to be made by…" Oh my lord, I thought, *We've stumbled into trouble here.* And so, most of what emerged ultimately as the character Victor Bergman was what I invented or imagined.

I remember writing an imaginary biography of his background as I foresaw it and how he became the kind of person that he was. Of course, none of that was indicated in the script at all. My perception of Victor Bergman was that he was a much more eccentric sort of character than eventually he became. There was no indication in the script as to his background; where he was born, where he grew up, what sort of education he had, what his tastes were; all of those things that one wants to know about a character that you're presenting. So I wrote this biographical sketch about his background which I then passed to the Andersons, who as far as I know made no use of it at all. For one thing, I didn't want to wear those uniforms that everyone else had. He was not the sort of character, I felt, to succumb to appearing in a uniform. He was a senior world-class scientist!

Did you improvise the scarf that you wore in that episode?

I think so; yes, I think so. Because, there again so little attention was paid to the individual characters. So this was an opportunity to hint a little bit that Bergman was not entirely conventional in his tastes.

Were there any scenes filmed on Prof. Bergman's disappearance from *Space: 1999*?

They never explained it at all! I've grown weary of answering that question, from all sorts of viewers from all over the world who say, "Come on, they went on to a second series and Victor Bergman has just disappeared — nobody ever said a word about what happened and what caused his disappearance!" So I've grown used to saying, "Well I guess he fell off the back of the moon." No explanation was ever offered or given as to what happened to him or why he disappeared.

Can you share how you feel your character should have been written out of the series, if you had had a say in it?

If they are going to try and explain what happened to Victor Berman and why he was no longer around, they must go one of several routes. One could be that he simply died because presumably he was the oldest inhabitant of the crew. Another explanation might be that his artificial heart failed and he died. But a more imaginative explanation might be that they touched down somewhere on some or other outer planet in which he, Victor Bergman, became deeply fascinated by the lifestyle of these people who lived on this other planet, XYZ. He then decided that the rest of the crew must go on in their explorations and he would remain with the XYZ population. He would study the way they live because he felt that it was a rather superior way than the normal human race lived! That would have been an interesting development, wouldn't it? There are all kinds of other ways that his disappearance could be explained, but such a thing was never done in the original series. So it remains a mystery — what ever happened to Victor Bergman?

You were asked to write the Foreword for a new *Space: 1999* novel called *Survival*. What are your thoughts on that project?

Well, I was very touched and honored that in the course of their story the publisher, Mateo Latosa, invented the name of "Yendys" for a character that becomes quite significant in the life of Victor Bergman. That name is the reverse spelling of the woman who was very much the most important in my life for more than sixty years — Sydney Sturgess. It's a marvelous tribute to her.

Do you think a modern version of *Space: 1999* could be produced and successful today? Perhaps the name could be changed to something like *Space: 2099*...

It's always possible to produce more — and hopefully better — versions of any existing series, particularly in the science fiction genre, because it's a field that's expanding all the time and is never completely examined. They've done it with *Star Trek*, haven't they? But I would like to think that in any future production of that kind the individual characters should be paid more attention to. For instance, what do we know about Zienia Merton's character and what her personality was? (Aside from what Zienia brought to it, as she's a most engaging and attractive young woman.) We never found out anything really about her background and why she comes to be where she is and doing the kinds of things that she does; the same with Nick Tate, Prentis Hancock, and everyone else. We never found out very much about their essential characters and you don't need to go too far to look to find that all the best dramatic material in the whole history of mankind is based on human character. What human characters *feel,* what they try to *do,* and how they *respond* to what happens to them. You don't need to go any further back to look than the best example of all, your friend and mine, William Shakespeare! He doesn't have all that much in the way of explosions or lighting effects, or all those things which they try to cram into a show, but he does have an amazing variety and depth of human characteristics. That's what drama is all about.

Do you have fond memories of being on the *Space: 1999* set with the cast?

I enjoyed it all, I usually do. In a career which now has lasted more than 70 years, I've only very rarely had experiences where I hadn't been comfortable and happy with the set-up in which I was working. In this instance we were working with a charmingly professional bunch of actors, most of them much younger than me, and the general atmosphere within the shooting period was really very friendly. This, despite the fact that we were working fiendishly long hours in order to keep up with the calendar pressures of turning out a new show — if possible — every nine shooting days. Many of the followers of the series perhaps don't know that our first episode, instead the scheduled nine days, took twenty-six days! So we were running behind schedule almost from day one.

Did you have any hesitation in working with Hollywood actors Martin Landau and Barbara Bain? Since both came from *Mission: Impossible*, I wonder if cast and crew mistook their enthusiasm and proactive natures?

Oh, no. The fact that they had been successful Hollywood actors in another series was impressive in itself, but they are — as anybody who knows them would readily tell you — a couple of wonderfully relaxed professionals, with charming personalities, who don't have, as so many so-called Hollywood stars do, an inflated sense of their own importance or self-worth. They settled themselves down very readily amongst what was an almost entirely British cast and worked with marvelous equanimity with everybody in the unit. Of course, they were both of them experienced enough through their time with *Mission: Impossible* to know of the immense stresses that there always are in shooting a weekly television series. They were and are — both Martin Landau and Barbara Bain — first class real pros, as we always say in the trade.

Were there any guest stars on the show that you particularly liked or remember?

Some were very good, like the rest of the world, and some were better actors than others. Of those working as guests on the show, most of them were good. As you know, my dear old friend Peter Cushing appears as a guest and he was a long-standing friend ever since we were beginners. He and his wife were deeply, loving friends of my wife Sydney and me. And then there were other people like Joan Collins, she was a big name and was very disciplined and well-behaved. I can't remember, truthfully, any of them that were in any way difficult or objectionable. They all fitted in pretty well.

Did the show make a mark on your career personally?

In terms of enlarging my popularity and all that sort of thing, yes, I suppose it did. I always say that one of the most pleasurable aspects of that series was that it recruited an army of fans from all over the world, who I've met in the succeeding years, and it's rather touching to find that there's whole groups of people from all sorts of different countries who are brought together and bound together by a mutual admiration for this series. So, indeed, it had a value from my own personal point of view, in that way, in that I've been able in the 30 years since we shot that series to meet the "customers" — the audience — in all sorts of different parts of the world. In normal circumstances, it you do a single television show you're not likely to meet the audience in the same way and with the same friendship as I've been able to with fans of *Space: 1999*.

Barry Morse in a never-before-seen publicity shot. PHOTO COURTESY OF ROBERT E. WOOD.

Have you ever felt stereotyped at any point in your career?

I've always deliberately, quite consciously, set out to avoid becoming stereotyped because most people who pay any attention to public entertainments at all will know that it's all too easy for actors to fall into playing a certain "line" of parts. That's why, of course, when I first started to work in the U.S. of A. in New York and in Hollywood, I made it a rule — if I could — to avoid playing English parts. That's what led to this great distinction I'm very proud of, of my becoming the only British actor ever to have played a leading role in an American television series as an American with an American accent. It's never been done before or since. That, of course, was the great series *The Fugitive*. [Barry's record stood for more than forty years, until British actor Hugh Laurie appeared in the U.S. television series *House,* playing an American, beginning in 2005.]

Which was your favorite episode from *The Fugitive*?

It's hard to guess, really, because not many people realize that my character "Lt. Philip Gerard" did not appear in every episode. He did appear in the "teaser," the little introductory passage at the beginning of each episode, which made it clear that David Janssen's character "Dr. Kimble" was being pursued by my character. Beyond that, Gerard didn't appear fully in every episode. It was an enormous advantage from my point of view in that it enabled me in the time I had free from actually shooting *The Fugitive* to do all sort of other things. Among them, the famous event in the theatre where I was able to help launch the full scale professional theatre festival — based on George Bernard Shaw — at Niagara-on-the-Lake in Ontario, Canada. I did actually direct one of the episodes towards the end, but I played in a whole range of different stories. I don't remember them sufficiently in detail to be able to distinguish any particular show which I thought particularly noteworthy. But the general quality of the writing, overall, was the secret or the main credit, which led to the distinction of the show as a whole. The concept and the development of characters were so good and so strong.

How did your family handle your work within the entertainment industry?

Sydney and I worked together until the babies came along and then she put her career on the back burner. When the children were grown up, she went back to acting a certain amount again and was wonderfully good in all sorts of different parts. Both of my children became actors and Hayward, my son, has become quite well-known both for his work on the stage and as a voice artist for a great many recorded books.

Not everybody might know that my own family had no connection with show business at all. My parents had been servants and the occasion which led to their meeting and eventual marriage was when they were working — my father as porter and my mother as a maid — at a hospital just outside London in Richmond. It was outside London in those days, the beginning of the 20th century, but now is an outer suburb of London. They married in 1913. Not long after, my father was called up to fight in the First World War because he had initially, as a volunteer, fought in the Boer War when he was only sixteen. But my parents had never been to any type of legitimate theatre! They'd been to the music halls a bit, which were popular entertainments of the day, amongst working people. They'd never seen a professional production of a play or anything like that. So my blundering into the theatrical world was really a series of flukes and coincidences.

In those days, it was rare for people to venture far from their own district. As an example, my Mother had never set foot in the central fashionable part of London until I was playing in the West End — on Shaftsbury Avenue, as it happened. Sydney and I wanted my Mother to come and see this play in which I was starring with my name above the title. We arranged one matinee day to bring my Mother up to the West End. Sydney went and picked her up and we got seats for them right in the front stalls. She sat through this play, and we took her out for tea afterwards, then back down to Shoreditch. Afterwards I said to Sydney, "Well, what was it like? What did she make of it?" And Sydney said, "Oh, it was extraordinary. She was so excited and thrilled; just trembling with excitement. Sitting in this theatre where she'd seen your name on the posters over the title. She sat there and lapped it all up with great excitement — but you could tell all the time she was half afraid a hand might fall on her shoulder and someone would say to her, "Here! What are you doing 'ere? *Piss off out of it!*' She didn't feel entitled to *be* in the West End." There was the feeling among working class people that they weren't entitled to be in this other part of London. That they needed some sort of permit or passport to be there.

It's just been recently announced that seven years from now the 2012 Olympic Games will be held in London. I understand that you have a story involving the last Olympics that were held there.

Yes, that's right. Because of my brother Len's excellence as an athlete, I'd always been very much interested in what is generally known as track and field events. I was quite a fair runner myself, but Len and I as Boy Scouts always did very well in the Boy Scouts athletic championships. Indeed, there was one year that I won all the junior events and Len won all the senior events! It was coming up to 1948 and I knew that the Olympic Games would be held for the second time in London; the first time was in 1908. I longed for the chance to be able to see as many of the track and field events as I could, but that, of course, was quite an expensive prospect, because it was being held at Wembley Stadium on the northwest side of London.

In 1948 I was in a play called *Written for a Lady* by Leo Marks at the Garrick Theatre in the West End. Playing opposite me was a lovely and gifted actress by the name of Margaretta Scott. Understudying me, I remember, and also playing a small part, was a young lad who became one of our closest friends — Eric Bretherton. Anyway, in this part I was required to make a number of very quick changes in costume, so the management hired a dresser to take care of me. He turned out to be an elderly, ex-jockey. This fellow was always being pestered by people for tips with regard to racing and race horses; but he was very reluctant to give people these tips. But he became quite fond of me, and I of him. When our play was closing, he said to me, "Well, there you are, I never gave you anything in the way of a tip — I don't give out tips carelessly. But if ever I hear of anything which might be 'a good thing' I'll let you know." This was in the spring of 1948 and only a few weeks later, I got a line from this chap. It said:

> "Dear Mr. Morse,
> Next Thursday, Newbury Racecourse
> 3:30 P.M. — <u>Neuralia.</u>
> *A good thing.*

I thought that was an extraordinarily kind thing for him to do, to take the trouble to write me and give me this tip. It also indicated that he was pretty confident it was going to do well! Since I was so anxious to get some money to buy tickets for the Olympic Games, I took my jockey friend's advice and put *ten pounds* — a lot of money to us at that time — on this horse Neuralia. Well, lo and behold; it worked and it won! It won at twelve and a half to one earning me one hundred twenty-five pounds, which was enough to buy moderately-priced seats for all of the track and field events at the Olympic Games. I bought a pair of tickets for each of the days that they were running these various events and I would take Len, my brother, on one day; then another day Sydney; and so on. There were a total of, I think, twelve days of track and field events. Of course, betting on a horse was something that I had never done before — and have never done since. But I have very fond memories of those Games. I hope I last long enough to be able to go again to the upcoming Olympics in 2012.

A few years later, in Canada, you worked with some very interesting performers in radio, including John Colicos, Douglas Rain, and John Drainie. What do you remember of them?

John was a very skilled actor. He was one of the actors living and working in Toronto, Canada, largely for CBC when Sydney, the children, and I first went there. He was a young man — much younger than me — and had a certain amount of theatrical training, but had become very skilled because in addition to his talent he had a very fine voice. He had become quite popular in radio and of course in those days, the early 1950s, there were so few professional and professionally experienced actors in Canada that we automatically formed ourselves into what you might almost call a radio repertory company. It wasn't officially known in that way, but it was a group of ten or twelve actors and actresses whom the producers at the CBC knew had knowledge and experience both in the theatre and also on radio. I'd done literally hundreds of radio shows before I left England, so in my case they knew right from the word go that they had somebody who knew their way around radio technique. Among this company there were a number of actors including the young Donald Herron, James Doohan, and the great John Drainie who was considered the "senior" radio actor in Canada in those days. John Drainie had become crippled through a boyhood accident and walked with a stick and a limp and made a great career in radio. Now, Dougie Rain has had a great career in Canadian television and theatre. But well before that, he worked with us in radio and was one of the youngest in that group of "repertory" actors. He went on to become quite famous as one of the leading actors in the Shakespeare Company at Stratford, Ontario and also played at the Shaw Festival in Niagara in more recent years.

What authors, philosophers and thinkers speak most strongly to you?

Now there's a leading question! One of the authors — aside, of course, from William Shakespeare — who has probably had the most effect on me in general way both professionally and personally, is

George Bernard Shaw. I think he's a wonderful example of someone quite literally who worked his way into becoming the world's greatest living dramatist, having started out with virtually no encouragement or natural instincts towards being a dramatist. You might say he almost talked himself into becoming the world's greatest dramatist. He realized that the creation of great drama has nothing to do with words on paper. It was he who was always stressing — which I always stress — that ninety-five percent of the audiences who crammed into the Globe Theatre to see the original productions of Shakespeare's plays were illiterate, they couldn't read or write.

Earlier in his life when Shaw first began to try and speak publicly — and he was aflame with new ideas — he tried to get up to speak at some debating society's meeting. He only got out three or four words before he was overcome with shyness and had to sit back down, having more or less made a fool of himself. Shaw describes how his personal shyness was such that when he was invited to visit some people who were friends of his family from Dublin, who were now living in London and whom he knew well and were old friends, he walked up and down in the rain for the best part of half an hour before he could summon up enough courage to quench his shyness and ring their bell to go in and visit. He turned his whole perspective of life around and became one of the foremost authors and speakers of his day. That's why one of my favorite proverbial quotes of Shaw is, "So long as I can conceive something better than myself, I cannot be easy unless I am striving to bring it into existence or clearing the way for it; that is the law of my life."

Among other writers one of my favorites is John Bunyan. His *Pilgrim's Progress*, although not really written as a drama, *is* one of the world's great dramas. When you get to the end of the story of Mr. Valiant-for-Truth, the leading character, the whole thing winds up with, "…and so he passed over and all the trumpets sounded for him on the other side." Well, that's great drama, isn't it? It wasn't written as drama but Bunyan could have been, and would have been if he'd been encouraged in the right directions, a great dramatist. Whereas so many other writers who have great reputations: Keats, Shelley, Byron, Tennyson, Henry James — all immensely respected writers — all tried to write plays and not worth a damn, any one of them! It's because they weren't instinctive actors. All the great plays written in every country on Earth throughout the whole of human history have been written by people who were of histrionic disposition.

You've had a very active career in film, theatre and television. What would you say is your greatest achievement?

Parenting two lovely children and all those grandchildren and great-grandchildren; there's no question. It's the simplest answer in the world! All that stuff that you do professionally doesn't add up to *that*, does it?

What can you tell us about your upcoming memoir?

It's thrilling to have had the good luck to encounter two such lads such as you and Robert Wood who have encouraged me to the extent of starting to believe that having such a book was both possible and worthwhile. I don't think, aside from the kind of "dreamland" that you induce in yourself once in awhile, that I ever seriously considered being part of making a book. But I realize now that it is a book concerning someone who didn't necessarily achieve world significance in the sense of Clark Gable, Spencer Tracy, or Charlie Chaplin, but who nonetheless because of the sheer volume and variety of work has had a career if not necessarily richer, at least wider and more varied than most people in our profession have ever had. That's what it comes down to. Recently someone asked me why I wasn't thinking of retiring and I said in response, "Well, so long as you can say the lines in the right order and not fall over the furniture, you don't want to retire!" I invite all of you to read much more about my memories of working on *Space: 1999* and many other events, all stretching over now more than eight decades!

Thank you for your kind comments, Barry. It's been fun to conduct this interview here in your London flat.

Well, It's been wonderful to reminisce with you about the old *Space: 1999* series and to talk about my life. There's nothing better, is there, than to sit and talk about one self — it's an egomaniac's paradise!

My co-author, the aforementioned Robert Wood, and I traveled in 2007 to visit Barry Morse in London to celebrate the release of his theatrical memoir, *Remember with Advantages*. Barry had just passed his 89th birthday and although we recognized he had physically slowed since our last meeting, he was still as mentally energetic and as interested and engaged with life as ever. He insisted on keeping an appointment to attend a public event to sign copies of the new book, telling us, "The fans are expecting me to be there and I don't want to disappoint them." Indeed, when we arrived — Robert pushing the wheelchair Barry was using for this occasion — he became visibly animated and excited to speak with every person waiting in line to see him.

Following this successful and happy visit, it came as a crushing blow to both of us when we received the news of Barry's passing on February 2, 2008, just a few months after spending those amazing

The memorial bench in honor of actor and director Barry Morse, St. James's Place, London. Friends, family, and fans raised the funds for its purchase and installation. PHOTO COURTESY OF ROBERT E. WOOD.

days in London, in what had turned out to be our last visit with an old friend. Barry had touched our lives so deeply, for so many years; the loss of our friend was almost unbearable. Something that made the pain a bit easier to take was the knowledge that so much of his work in television, radio, and film survives on. Another was the realization that Barry's life and friendship had meant so much to a great many people around the planet.

Barry often said that he "wants to stick around to see how it all turns out." He wasn't able to "stick around" long enough to attend the Olympic Games of 2012 in London for his beloved track and field events; but his delightful story about how he was able to attend the 1948 Games appears here in print for the very first time anywhere.

Robert and I returned to London in 2011 to give a lecture to The Shaw Society of England on the immensely expansive subject of Barry Morse and Bernard Shaw. While we were there, Barry's son Hayward Morse invited us to accompany him on a special journey to the park in St. James's Square, just around the corner from 41 Pall Mall, where Barry and his wife Sydney Sturgess had maintained happy residence for nearly 40 years. As the sun set, we were honored to help sprinkle Barry's ashes among the flowers, shrubbery, and trees surrounding the two memorial benches that stand in recognition of Barry and Sydney. His ashes joined those of his late wife and are nourishing the lovely park, which Barry and Sydney so enjoyed when they were alive.

Barry gave Robert and me an incredible gift for which we are very grateful. He trusted us — two guys having limited professional writing credentials and experience — with crafting his compelling life story and experience into his memoir. That project and that trust grew into a broader working relationship and friendship between us. While Barry is now physically gone, an important part of our continuing work is to perpetuate and cement his theatrical legacy. Robert and I have brought out several other Barry Morse-related books in addition to *Remember with Advantages*, including: *Merely Players — The Scripts, Stories of the Theatre*, and most recently, *Valiant for Truth: Barry Morse and his Lifelong Dedication to Bernard Shaw*, based on the lectures Robert and I presented in Canada and the UK.

Our work has also included the establishment of a repository of papers, scripts, video, audio, memorabilia, theatre programs, and many other items in the "Barry Morse Collection" of the L.W. Conolly Theatre Archive, located at the University of Guelph, in Ontario, Canada. There is still more to do; so we will continue our work to maintain, document, and enhance recognition of Barry Morse's many contributions to the entertainment industry through publicity of his varied work on stage and screen as actor, director, and writer.

Index

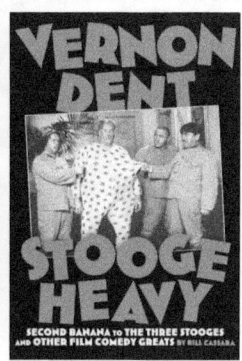

www.ingramcontent.com/pod-product-compliance
Lightning Source LLC
Chambersburg PA
CBHW070222030726
47505CB00006B/1775